TREASURES
OF THE
HEART

*Also by Jacquelin Thomas
in Large Print:*

The Prodigal Husband

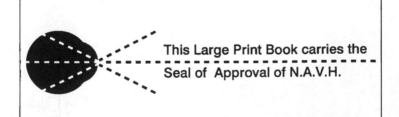

This Large Print Book carries the
Seal of Approval of N.A.V.H.

TREASURES

OF THE

HEART

JACQUELIN

THOMAS

Thorndike Press • Waterville, Maine

Published in 2004 by arrangement with
Kensington, an imprint of Kensington Publishing Corp.

Thorndike Press® Large Print African-American.

The tree indicium is a trademark of Thorndike Press.

The text of this Large Print edition is unabridged.
Other aspects of the book may vary from the original edition.

Set in 16 pt. Plantin.

Printed in the United States on permanent paper.

Library of Congress Cataloging-in-Publication Data

Thomas, Jacquelin.
    Treasures of the heart / Jacquelin Thomas.
      p. cm.
    ISBN 0-7862-6760-7 (lg. print : hc : alk. paper)
    1. African American women — Fiction. 2. African
American clergy — Fiction. 3. Murder victims' families
— Fiction. 4. Diamond industry and trade — Fiction.
5. Witnesses — Fiction. 6. Large type books. I. Title.
PS3570.H5637T74 2004
  813'.54—dc22
                               2004051796

To my sister, CARMEN.

You are not only my family,
but a treasure as well.

As the Founder/CEO of NAVH, the only national health agency solely devoted to those who, although not totally blind, have an eye disease which could lead to serious visual impairment, I am pleased to recognize Thorndike Press* as one of the leading publishers in the large print field.

Founded in 1954 in San Francisco to prepare large print textbooks for partially seeing children, NAVH became the pioneer and standard setting agency in the preparation of large type.

Today, those publishers who meet our standards carry the prestigious "Seal of Approval" indicating high quality large print. We are delighted that Thorndike Press is one of the publishers whose titles meet these standards. We are also pleased to recognize the significant contribution Thorndike Press is making in this important and growing field.

Lorraine H. Marchi, L.H.D.
Founder/CEO
NAVH

* Thorndike Press encompasses the following imprints: Thorndike, Wheeler, Walker and Large Print Press.

PROLOGUE

Eight-year-old Kemba Rufaro turned to Minnie, her stuffed teddy bear, and asked, "Would you like some sugar in your tea?" Her father, Molefi, had slipped into the den and was standing near the door. "Hi, Papa," she greeted. "Want to play with me?"

"Sure. I think I have a few minutes for a cup of tea."

Kemba observed his commanding presence through rich chocolate brown eyes as he strolled toward her and sank down on the floor beside her. She recalled the last time her father attempted to sit in one of her chairs. It had broken from the strain of his weight.

She giggled at the memory as she pretended to pour him a cup. "It's so nice of you to join us, Papa. Minnie was just saying that we don't see enough of you."

Molefi laughed. "Oh really? Minnie said that, did she?"

Kemba nodded.

He reached over to stroke her cheek. "My beautiful daughter, you are wise beyond

7

your years. It is true that I am often away from home, but I promise that one day soon I will be able to spend more time with you and your mother."

"And Minnie?"

Laughing, Molefi nodded. "And Minnie." He pretended to drink his cup of tea. "This is very good tea, Kemba."

"Thank you, Papa."

Molefi rose to his feet and continued to watch his daughter play. He crossed the room in determined strides and took a seat on the sofa. Calling to Kemba, he said, "Come here, daughter. Come sit with me." Molefi motioned to a vacant spot beside him on the overstuffed couch. "What I have to say is important. There are things you should know about your family . . . your history."

"Yes, Papa." Sighing softly, Kemba joined him on the sofa. She started to swing her legs, kicking the chair with the heel of her sneaker-clad foot as she traced the cabbage rose pattern on the sofa with her fingers.

Taking her small chestnut-colored hand in his, he asked, "Did I ever tell you that one of your ancestors was an *induna*, a great chief in Shaka's army? His name was Nyandoro and it was said that he was an evil man with a vicious temper. Before the Zulu King died, he expelled Nyandoro from what is now Northern South Africa after it was said that he murdered his own brother to become chief. Vowing revenge, Nyandoro led his people north over the Limpopo River and found Matabeleland (in Rhodesia) where he became King."

Kemba's round face, dark and delicate, rose to attention. "Did he really do that?"

Making a small gesture with his hand, Molefi replied, "I do not know for sure. His brother died mysteriously and the people believed he had been poisoned."

Kemba's head shook in disbelief, causing her long ebony braids to swirl around her head like a merry-go-round. "I don't think he could've hurt his own brother, Papa. Nobody would do that to their own family."

Molefi was silent.

"Papa?" she prompted. Kemba scratched her head, baffled. "He couldn't have done it, could he?"

"We will never really know what happened. Have I ever told you about your ancestor Dumisani, our last king?"

"Yes, Papa." Kemba knew the story by heart. He'd told her about her family many times before.

"Dumisani was a very peaceful man, unlike his father, Nyandoro, who was said to be possessed by an evil spirit. When Nyandoro was killed in battle, Dumisani, being his only son, became the new king. On the day of Dumisani's installation as king, the soldiers standing all around him numbered about seven thousand. Dumisani had a long staff in his right hand. He wore a cape of black ostrich feathers and a bandeau of yellow otter skins. The great mass of people presented themselves with black-and-white, red-and-white, and other colored shields in their left hands, singing their songs of praise to our illustrious ancestors, the former kings."

"Wow, I bet that was really something."

"I am sure it was, daughter." Molefi pulled Kemba onto his lap. "You come from a long line of kings." His coarse hands caressed her smooth, soft ones as he continued to speak. "Royal blood flows in your veins. You should be proud."

"I am."

Molefi held her close to his heart. Kemba could hear it beating a continuous rhythm.

"You must never forget your history. Do you remember what I have told you of the diamond mines in South Africa?"

She nodded politely. Kemba had heard about all of this before. She listened as he told her of the white men who had come to look for gold and diamonds.

". . . Some of our ancestors worked for the diggers and they used to smuggle diamonds out of the mines and give them to King Dumisani. Dumisani owned several large huts that were used to house his treasures. He stored the smuggled gold and diamonds in two large rusty biscuit tins. According to history, no white man was ever permitted to see his treasure. The king was a selfish man, but he allowed his favorite son, and most loyal *induna*, your great-great-grandfather, to keep one of the diamonds. And before King Dumisani died, he gave him another very special gift."

"He did?" Kemba's bright eyes were round with childish curiosity. "What was it?"

"The Dumisani Diamond has since been passed down in our family, always given to the eldest son."

Again the tale commanded Kemba's full attention. "Who has the diamond now, Papa?"

"I do," Molefi said proudly. "I am my

father's eldest son. I am the Keeper of Tradition. That is what my name means." Pulling a glittering object from out of his pocket, he placed it in her hand. "Since you are my only child, this is your legacy, daughter. One day this and more will be yours."

"*Ohhhh my.* This is a diamond?" Kemba ran her fingers across the smooth facets of the stone. "It's beautiful."

"Yes, this is the Dumisani Diamond. When we came to America, it did not look this way. It was not yet polished or cut. I had it cut just a few years ago. It is worth thousands and thousands of dollars, but it must never be sold. It *must* remain in our family always. A piece of the past." His voice suddenly became so low, Kemba had to strain to hear him.

"When it is in your possession, you will have to be very careful — there are people who want the stone and they must never find it. I keep it hidden in a place no one will ever think of looking." He made a sweeping gesture with his hands. "This house and everything here will be yours one day. Your legacy. Raise your children in this house. Like the Dumisani Diamond, I want this house to pass from generation to generation."

Kemba gazed at the sparkling stone in her hand. Looking up at her father in awe, she said, "We're rich, Papa."

"No, honey. We are not rich. But when the time is right, we will be."

"But —"

"Listen to me, daughter. This is very important. There is a much greater treasure. A treasure estimated to be worth more than five million dollars. Remember, I said Dumisani gave his *induna* a very special gift?"

Kemba nodded.

"Well, Dumisani knew he hadn't much longer to live, so he ordered his royal *kraal,* his house, to be burned to the ground. He had a small group of loyal soldiers load his treasures on a big wagon and they headed to the banks of the Zambezi River. There he found a cave, and ten of his most loyal men were ordered to store his possessions in there and make the entrance inaccessible. They rolled a great rock in front of its small opening. After that, he had them executed one by one.

"The only people left who knew about the hidden treasure were Dumisani and your great-great-grandfather. After that, Dumisani died. He was buried sitting in his favorite chair near his father somewhere in the mountains near the Zambezi River. To this day no one has been able to find his grave." Molefi placed a kiss on Kemba's forehead.

"King Dumisani's final resting place and his treasure passed into legend like the story of King Solomon's mines. Hundreds of men, black and white, have searched all over Rhodesia for over a hundred years, but the treasure has never been found." Molefi pointed to himself. "The map had been lost to our family for years, but I found it right before we came to America. I have the map. That is the real treasure and *it is ours.*"

"Papa." Kemba stopped short. She was staring toward the doorway.

Molefi glanced up to find his wife standing there. "Sarah . . ."

"*Molefi.* I hope you aren't in here filling her head with those tales, are you?" Kemba's mother strolled into the room. Standing before her husband with her back straight and her arms folded across her ample breasts, she said flatly, "I asked you not to do this."

Even though Sarah tried to keep her voice low, Kemba knew she was angry. "Mama?"

"Go to your room, Kemba. I need to talk to your father."

Kemba wasn't sure if Sarah's anger was directed at her or her father. Confused, she crawled off her father's lap and ran out of the room, but not before hearing Sarah telling Molefi that she didn't want Kemba to turn out like his brother. *His brother?* Kemba had no idea that she had an uncle. She wanted to know more about this relative, but glancing back once more at her mother's angry stance, Kemba decided now was not the time. She rushed into her bedroom and climbed onto the window seat, fighting back tears.

Her parents found Kemba a few minutes later. Sarah apologized profusely and assured her they were not angry at each other or her. Her parents spent the rest of the afternoon in Kemba's bedroom, talking about Africa and how they met. Neither one of them mentioned the Dumisani Diamond.

That evening as Kemba climbed into bed, she could still recall how the stone felt in the palm of her hand. Her last thought as she drifted off to sleep was of the day she would own the diamond and the rest of King Dumisani's treasure.

Molefi carried Kemba in his arms as Sarah followed them into the dimly lit house.

"Papa, I really liked the fireworks. I wish we could have stayed much longer," Kemba murmured sleepily.

"It's already past your bedtime, young lady. You've had a long day today," Sarah announced before planting a kiss on her daughter's cheek.

"But it's the Fourth of July, Mama. It's a special day."

Sarah laughed. "If it were up to you, every day would be a special day."

"They are," Kemba said. " 'Cause I have you two for parents."

Molefi smiled. "Now, what can you say to that, Sarah?"

"That's a very sweet thing to say, but you still have to go upstairs to bed, baby." Sarah stretched and yawned. "I'm going straight to bed myself."

Just as they neared the library, Molefi heard the unmistakable sound of glass breaking. It sounded like it was coming from the kitchen.

Sarah turned to Molefi, a terrified expression on her face. "Did you hear that?" she whispered. "It sounds like —"

Holding on to Sarah, Molefi whispered, "Take Kemba with you into the library and take the passageway to the room downstairs. I want you to stay down there until I

16

come for you. If I am not there in fifteen minutes, leave and go to Claire's house and call the police. Do not stay here."

"Molefi, come with us," Sarah begged. "Please come with us."

"I'll be fine. Now do as I say. Take Kemba downstairs and stay there," he ordered. Molefi kissed them both before handing a frightened Kemba to Sarah. "When it's safe, I'll come to you."

With one last pleading look, Sarah opened the door to the library, walking briskly toward a wall covered with books. She quickly pressed a button hidden behind the oak bookcase and waited. The panel of books began to move languidly.

When Molefi knew they were safe, he headed upstairs and into the master bedroom. In the dark, he sank down on a pale blue chaise and waited.

Over the loud thumping of his heart, Molefi could hear the faintest sound of footsteps. Even in the shadows of the room, he could see the doorknob turn ever so gently. Swallowing, Molefi gathered his courage and said, "Come on in. I've been expecting you."

"Mama, what's taking Papa so long? I thought he was coming to get us?" Kemba asked for the third time in fifteen minutes.

Sarah bit her lip to keep it from trembling. Wrapping her arms around her waist, she said, "He'll be here soon, dear." Trying to appear calm, Sarah smiled. "Why don't you lie down and go to sleep? Papa will be here before you know it."

She paced back and forth across the room with nervous energy. *Molefi, please hurry up,* she wished. *I need to know that you're safe.*

Kemba curled up in a ball and drifted off to sleep. Sarah eased into the bed to lie beside her. *Everything will be all right.* She had to believe that. Just as Sarah closed her eyes, she heard a loud noise. Jumping up, she realized it sounded like gunfire. A thread of fear spread through her body as Sarah slowly comprehended what it meant.

CHAPTER 1

Twenty years later

Hiding in the shadows outside of the Wilshire Business Center, he glanced down at his watch and decided to wait another ten minutes before leaving. His contact must have gotten delayed for whatever reason.

A dark-skinned man of average height, looking around nervously, walked out of the building. Spying him, he rushed over. "I'm sorry I'm late. My boss needed a report pulled at the last minute."

"I understand." He wanted to get right to the point. "Are you sure this is the Dumisani Diamond?"

"I am positive. I took the call from Dr. Avery myself. From his description, it can only be the Dumisani Diamond."

"Does anybody else know about this?"

The man shook his head. "No, I've purged all information regarding the diamond out of the system."

Pulling a wad of hundred-dollar bills out of his pocket, he handed them to the nervous young man. "I will never forget this."

"Thank you." The man glanced around. "I'd better be getting back to my desk."

He nodded and disappeared in the shadows.

Kemba was in deep thought. She had to find a way to get the diamond back.

"Kim, are you all right?" Dr. Malcolm Avery asked as he strolled into the room. "You look troubled."

She tried to smile. "I'm fine. Did you need something?"

"I want to go over the selections for the guest bedroom with you, but I need to make a phone call first."

She nodded. "Okay, I'll be right here." Kemba waited until she heard him enter the library before getting up to follow him. She tiptoed down the empty hallway. Kemba released a breath at finding the door slightly ajar.

Malcolm was on the phone discussing the diamond. What she heard made her heart pound faster. Kemba knew what she would have to do. It would have to be done tonight. She stealthily made her way back to the sunroom.

When Malcolm returned, he stated that

he had an emergency and had to leave immediately. Kemba waited until he drove away before telling the housekeeper that she needed to take some final measurements in the library.

She cautiously entered the room surrounded by floor-to-ceiling shelves containing books of all types and sizes.

Alone, she searched quickly throughout the room. There was a safe hidden from view behind a huge oil painting. Now all she needed was the combination. She was sure Malcolm had placed the diamond there for safekeeping.

A thorough inspection of Malcolm's desk rewarded her with what she'd been looking for. The combination to the safe. Kemba smiled. Tonight Malcolm would be taking his daughter to the theater and the housekeeper would be gone. No one would be in the house.

The night air offered no relief from the August heat. Biting her lip, Kemba pulled her shirt away from her back, letting the air touch her skin for brief comfort. She once more surveyed the expansive grounds of the Brentwood estate before easing inside a door, weathered with age and hidden from plain sight by climbing plants and a clump of flowers. Once inside the secret room, she turned on a flashlight before laying her left hand over her wildly beating heart. Kemba fought the nausea that threatened to consume her as fear creeped through her soul. "Oh God, I hate having to do this," she muttered to herself. *How could I betray Malcolm's trust like this?*

With slow, deliberate movements, Kemba made her way along the dark passageway, glancing uneasily over her shoulder. She swallowed hard, attempting to pull herself together mentally. She moved quietly up the stairs, her flashlight providing the only source of light. As soon as Kemba made it to the landing, she felt around the wall, searching until she found a tiny button. When she pressed it, a door silently swung open. Kemba stepped from behind what she knew appeared to be a simple bookshelf on the other side.

Standing as still as a statue in the spacious library, Kemba glanced around the room, listening. For what she had no idea. She had never done anything like this in her life, and she was very jumpy. All of her earlier feelings of nervousness slipped back to grip her, knotting her stomach with apprehension.

Forcing the bile from her throat, Kemba thought about her father. *This is for you,*

Papa. I'm going to reclaim our legacy. She ran apprehensive fingers through her short-cropped hair. Wanting to get this over and done with, Kemba walked briskly across the room toward a beautiful painting. Lifting it gently off the wall, she now faced the safe that had been secreted behind the painting. It was exactly where she remembered. Retrieving a piece of paper from her pocket, she quickly keyed in a series of numbers. Kemba opened the safe and removed the contents.

She breathed a sigh of relief as her fingers curled over the perfectly emerald-cut diamond. The stone weighed twenty carats and was beautiful. For a few seconds she stood and savored the warmth of the gem in her hand. Kemba had found what she was looking for, and now it was time to leave. Looking down at the diamond once more, Kemba put it back into the safe. *I can't do this — this is wrong.* Tomorrow she would talk to Malcolm and tell him everything. Glancing around the room once more, she took in the shadows bouncing off the walls. She couldn't wait to get out of there.

Just as Kemba was about to close the safe, an oddly primitive warning rang in her brain. Sounds gushed in from the hallway, battering her. A shadow of alarm touched her face when she heard the unmistakable noise of voices coming from the other side of the library door. Panic chilling her to the bone, Kemba glanced frantically around the room. *Nobody is supposed to be home.* She knew the housekeeper went home every night, and Malcolm and Crystal were supposed to be out. Frozen to the spot and wearied by indecision, Kemba tried to still her trembling body.

The voices grew louder. Oh no. They were right outside the library door. Just as she turned to leave, Kemba heard the deep booming voice of a man.

"What are you doing in my home? What in hell do you want?"

CHAPTER 2

Before Kemba could turn around, a heavily accented voice responded. "I believe you know why I'm here, Dr. Avery. I want the stone. I do not want to hurt you —" She could hear the alarm in Malcolm's voice as he said, "You can have it and anything else you want. Just let my daughter go."

"Your generosity is astounding, but I seek only the diamond."

"It's in the library in a safe. You can have it. But please let my daughter go."

"I'm sorry, I cannot do that. When the diamond is safe in my hands, I'll let her go."

"Daddy —"

"Now, Crystal, *run*."

Kemba heard what sounded like people fighting.

She gasped, realizing a shiver of panic. *Oh God, I can't let him steal my legacy.* Reaching into the still-open safe, Kemba hastily removed the diamond and placed it into the security of her pocket. Wanting to put some distance between herself and the events taking place, Kemba willed her legs to move. Just as she took a step to leave, she heard gunfire, followed by a terrifying scream. It was Crystal. Then she heard the intruder's voice yelling for her to shut up, his accent more prominent now. Kemba felt a sudden prickle of recognition. *He's African.*

Panic rioting within her, Kemba came to an abrupt stop instead of heading to the hidden passageway. Her heart thumping loudly in her chest, she moved toward the door. She had to help Crystal. Her body tensed when she heard a large crash and the intruder's curse. A cold knot formed in her stomach when the door suddenly opened and Crystal ran inside, locking the door behind her. She turned and, upon spying Kemba, started to scream again.

How did I get myself in such a mess? Kemba wondered as she rushed to place a hand over the little girl's mouth. "It's me, Crystal," she whispered. "It's Kemba. I'm going to get you out of here. I know a way we can get out of here. But you have to promise to be very quiet, okay?"

Standing in the middle of the room, the frightened girl stared deep into Kemba's eyes and finally nodded.

"Come on, let's get out of here." Kemba

grabbed Crystal by the hand and headed toward the bookshelf.

Crystal stopped suddenly. "We can't get out that way, Kemba."

She stopped, and her fear of being discovered in the house by the intruder caused her to become impatient. "Look, we don't have much time. I know what I'm doing. Now, are you going to trust me or would you rather I leave you here with whoever is on the other side of the door?"

Before Crystal could respond, they heard the intruder trying to force open the locked door.

"Open this door. You cannot get away from me."

Kemba quickly pressed the tiny button hidden behind the bookshelf. She took a deep breath and tried to relax as the hidden panel sluggishly swung open.

Crystal's mouth dropped open as she stared at Kemba in amazement. "How did you do that?"

Pulling her by the hand, Kemba gently ordered, "Come on, Crystal. I'll tell you all about it in the car."

Just as the door closed shut, they heard gunfire on the other side. Kemba quickly covered Crystal's mouth. "Honey, don't scream. You can't let him know where we are. Let's just get out of here," she whispered in a low voice.

Crystal tried to pull her hand out of Kemba's firm grasp. "M-my d-dad. I can't leave my dad. That bad man shot my dad."

"*Honey, we've got to get out of here.* We'll call someone to come help your dad. I promise. As soon as we get to my car, we'll use my cell phone. I'll call the police and they'll check on your father. Okay? Right now, let's go."

"Is my dad going to die? He was shot."

"I don't know. But if we hurry, we might be able to help him. I'll call for an ambulance, okay?"

Crystal nodded, tears spilling down her cheeks.

Kemba felt ashamed for being so short-tempered. After all, she'd been at the house for the same reason as the other intruder. Brushing away the little girl's tears, Kemba told her, "Honey, I'm sorry we can't go back inside. This is the only way we can help your dad."

Running as fast as their legs could carry them, Kemba and Crystal made their way across the grounds to her car. She quickly drove off, leaving the Brentwood area as quickly as possible. As promised, Kemba called the police and reported the break-in.

"The police and the ambulance are on their way," she announced.

Crystal sat with her hands folded neatly across her lap. Peering up at Kemba, her doe-shaped eyes bright with tears, she mumbled, "Kemba, can I ask you somethin'?"

"Sure, what is it?"

"What were you doing . . . in our house? I mean, were you working? And how did you know about the secret room?"

Apprehension crept over Kemba as she struggled to think of a plausible reason to satisfy Crystal's curiosity. "Yes. Sometimes I have to work late. It's better for me. As far as the hidden passageway, I found it by accident," she lied.

"Did you know that man was in the house?"

"No, I had no idea." That much was true. Kemba thought she'd been alone. She trembled at the thought of what would have happened if the intruder had discovered her before Malcolm and Crystal returned home.

Listening to Crystal's soft whimpers, Kemba tried to sound as reassuring as possible. "I'm so sorry about what happened back at your house."

"I just want my dad to be okay."

Nervously Kemba bit her lip as she drove. "Honey, is there somewhere I can take you?"

"Can't we go back to the house?"

Kemba shook her head. "Crystal, I don't think that's a good idea. The person that shot your father knows you saw everything. He may still be out there somewhere watching, and he may try to hurt you. I don't want to take that chance." Kemba spared a brief glance her way. "Do you understand?"

Crystal nodded. "Can you take me to my uncle Eric's house? He's my dad's brother."

"Sure. Do you know how to get there?"

She nodded once more. "He lives in Baldwin Hills."

Kemba followed Crystal's directions as she drove. She stopped in front of a home with the porch light on. "There doesn't seem to be anyone home," she observed.

"Can we wait here for a few minutes? If he doesn't show up, I have some cousins who don't live too far from here. I can go there."

"We'll wait here for a short while."

"Kemba . . ."

"What is it, sweetie?"

"I'm glad you were working late tonight.

I'm glad you were at the house."

"I'm glad I was there too." Kemba tried to assuage her guilt by telling herself that she'd been in the right place at the right time, but even she had trouble believing that.

The hot weather swirled around Eric Avery as he carried a stack of hymnals into the church. He was about to head back out to his car when he encountered a young woman. She was a sultry five-seven and walked in grace and confidence, back straight, one foot in front of the other.

Jennifer Whittaker ran a French-manicured hand down her pink-and-yellow floral sundress, smiling prettily. "Hello, Pastor Avery."

"Hello, Jennifer. What are you doing here this evening?"

"I was just driving by the church and I saw your car. I thought I'd come by to see if you needed any help."

"That's very kind of you, but I have everything under control. I came by to drop off the new hymn books, that's all."

"Oh, okay. Just thought I could be of some help."

Eric heard the disappointment in her voice. "I appreciate it, Jennifer. As a matter

31

of fact, I was just about to lock up and leave. I'll walk you out to your car."

Jennifer paused for a moment. "On Sunday I'd like for you to come have dinner with me and Ma. She's cooking her famous collard greens. For dessert I'm making a peach cobbler." Grinning, she added, "I know how much you love peach cobbler and homemade ice cream."

"Sounds good. It would be my pleasure to have dinner with you and your mother."

After locking up, Eric walked Jennifer to her car. When she drove away, he followed her in his own car out of the parking lot, heading home. Pulling into his driveway, Eric was surprised to find a strange car parked in front of his house. He sat in his car for a few minutes, trying to discern who his visitor might be. Curiosity getting the better of him, Eric got out of his car and headed toward the black Camry. Recognizing the cherubic face of his niece, he walked faster.

Crystal jumped out of the car and ran to her uncle. "Uncle Eric, a bad man shot Daddy. *He shot Daddy.*"

"Whoa, princess. Hold on. Now, what happened?" Eric glanced over at the woman sitting in the car.

"A bad man broke into the house. He

and Daddy got into a fight. He shot him."

"Where is your dad now?"

"I don't know. Kemba said we ha—"

"Kemba?" He pointed toward the car. "Is that Kemba?"

"Yeah."

Eric walked over to the car. He regarded Kemba quizzically for a moment, his gaze sliding over her short, gleaming ebony curls, the golden creaminess of her smooth chestnut-tinted skin and her sparkling chocolate brown eyes. He estimated her age to be around twenty-five or so.

"Hello, I'm Eric Avery, Crystal's uncle. I understand someone broke into my brother's house. The intruder shot Malcolm?"

Kemba nodded woodenly.

"Where is Malcolm now?"

"I called the paramedics on the way here, so I'm hoping he's at the hospital by now. With everything that happened, all I could think about was getting Crystal out of the house. I didn't know where else to take her."

"You did the right thing by bringing her here." He lowered his voice. "Do you have any idea if my brother is still alive?"

Kemba looked away. "No, I don't. I'm sorry."

Eric rubbed his hands over his face. He studied her once more, trying to read her. He felt in his spirit that something was going on with her, but he wasn't sure what. Thinking quickly, he asked, "Would you mind coming in? I want to find out exactly what happened back at Malcolm's house."

"I really should —"

"Please. I have to know what happened to my brother."

Eric noted the way Kemba looked around tentatively as if she wanted to be sure of the situation before she made a move to get out of the car. Finally she nodded and got out.

He watched Kemba closely as she locked her car and walked toward him. At least five-nine, she was tall and slender. Eric waited until they were in the house before responding. "Please sit down," he said, pointing to the black leather couch sitting in the middle of the living room. After calling a relative to come over, he turned to Kemba, saying, "Why don't you start by telling me how you came to be at my brother's house."

The room seemed to swell with tension. Kemba looked pensively around the room, and Eric could tell she was taking time to think of an appropriate answer. He wondered why.

Crystal spoke up quickly. "Uncle Eric, Kemba saved me. She kept the bad man from shooting me."

His smile was indulgent. "I know, honey, but I'm curious about the reason she was there in the first place."

"She's a friend of Daddy's. He hired her to decorate our whole house. She's been there a lot of times. Kemba likes to work late."

Eric's eyes narrowed, but all he said was "I see."

Kemba cleared her throat. "I *am* an interior decorator, and I *do* have a signed agreement between your brother and my company," she replied curtly. "It's in my briefcase. Out in my car."

This time Eric studied her openly for a moment, noting the signs of tension in her face and hands. There was something more to her being in the house. He was sure of it.

"I called the police from my cell phone. I didn't call from the house because" — she glanced over at Crystal — "the person was still there."

Eric indicated by a slight movement of his head that he understood.

"Do you think Daddy is okay?" Crystal asked in a frightened voice.

"I don't know, sweetie. I have to go over there so that I can find out."

Large, round tears pooled in Crystal's eyes as she climbed onto his lap. "What if he's dead?"

"Sweetheart, let's not jump to conclusions, okay?"

Crystal slumped against him, sobbing loudly. "I — I s-shouldn't have left h-him."

Gathering her to him, Eric wrapped strong arms around her. "Baby, there was nothing you could do. We don't know anything right now, but we have to be strong. You can do that, can't you?" Holding her close, Eric felt her hot, wet tears on his neck. Pulling Crystal closer to him, Eric murmured as he stroked her back, "Go ahead, honey. Cry it out. . . ."

Kemba fought the tears that threatened to spill. She hadn't been much older than Crystal when her father had been killed, and the agony over losing him was still seared on her soul. The raw ache in her heart would remain there forever. Her father had loved her and Sarah so much; he'd left his beloved Africa to start a new life in America. Sarah, an American, had longed to return to the United States, and Molefi wanted to make her happy. In the end it had cost her father his life.

Not only had Kemba lost her father, but also her beloved home. Years later, she'd lost Carl, her fiancé. Now Malcolm could be dead. Kemba sighed heavily, too tired to go through it again. She fingered the necklace she wore to ease the thread of tension running through her body.

She looked up to find Eric's eyes on her, his expression unreadable. Kemba shuddered from the cold brown of his watchful eyes. Trembling slightly, she said, "I hope you will believe that I had nothing to do with your brother's . . . shooting your brother."

Before Eric could respond, the doorbell rang. He stood up slowly. "This should be Jillian. She's going to stay here with Crystal. I need to leave, but I'd like to talk to you when I return. I really need some answers. So will the police. After all, from what you've said so far, you are a potential *witness.*"

Kemba stood up too. Tonight was to be quick and simple, and now . . .

A slender, light-skinned woman entered the house, saying, "Have you found out anything more, Eric? Ray is on his way over there to the house."

"Thank you for coming on such short notice, Jillian. This is Kemba — she was doing some work for Malcolm. . . ."

Jillian smiled. "I'm so glad you were able to save little Crystal."

"I am too. I wish I could have done more." Kemba opened her purse, took out a business card and a pen. Writing as fast as her shaky fingers allowed, she said, "Here is my address and phone number if you need to contact me." Kemba handed the card to Eric. Without glancing back, she rushed out of the house. She could hear him calling her name, but Kemba kept walking. She was glad to be away from Eric Avery and his deep, probing eyes.

When Kemba drove off, Eric turned his attention back to his niece. Hugging her tightly, he said, "Crystal, why don't you go lie down in the guest room? I'll be back as soon as I can. In the meanwhile, pray for your father, okay, sweetheart?" Eric led his niece over to where Jillian was standing. "Jillian is going to stay here with you."

"Hello, sweetie."

"Where's Leah?" Crystal asked.

"She's at home studying, but she wanted me to be sure and give you a big hug for her." Jillian embraced her small frame.

Crystal peered up at her uncle. "Tell Daddy that I love him."

"I will."

Tiny shoulders slumped, Crystal walked down the hallway to the guest room. As soon as Eric heard the bedroom door close, he turned his six-foot frame to Jillian. "Thank you for staying here with her. I really appreciate it."

Walking him to the door, she replied, "It's no problem, cuz. Just go on and see what you can find out. Crystal is going to be fine. Call me as soon as you can. Or have Ray give me a call."

"Don't call Aunt Amanda yet. Not until I find out something definite. I don't want to upset her."

Jillian nodded in agreement.

Inside his car Eric prayed for both of their sakes that he would have good news when he returned.

He muttered a curse under his breath. Everything had gone wrong tonight. His body and head still ached from his scuffle with Malcolm Avery and from being hit in the head with a brass figurine. Something puzzled him. . . . How had the little girl and the mystery person been able to escape? It was as if they had walked through the walls. By the time he had gotten into the library, they were gone and so was the diamond. In their haste, the safe had been left wide open.

From the library window and stunned beyond belief, he watched them as they ran across the grounds to a car hidden from view. There had to be a secret entrance, but he didn't take time to search for it. He wanted to be long gone before the police arrived.

He could tell from the gait that the mystery guest was indeed a woman, but who? And what was she doing here? She clearly wasn't an invited guest because she'd chosen to hide her car, instead of parking it in the driveway. And the way she was dressed — wearing all black, from head to toe. She was dressed very similar to him. Like someone wanting to cloak herself in the dark night.

His white teeth gleamed as a smile spread across his dark chocolate face. *Could it be?* Was she there for the same reason as he? She had to be, but somehow it didn't make sense. Would Avery's daughter have gone willingly with her, otherwise? Clapping his hands together, Mapfumo knew one thing for sure — the woman had the diamond in her possession. Now all he had to do was find her. And find her he would. Malcolm Avery's daughter would lead him to her.

CHAPTER 3

When Kemba was safe within the confines of her own home, her jumbled thoughts strayed to Eric Avery. His searching saddle brown eyes sparkled with a deep brilliance as she beheld the handsome outline of his clean-shaven face, narrow, straight nose and full lips. A tiny scar trailed through his right brow, breaking their otherwise breathtaking symmetry.

"What would happen if Malcolm was dead? Would Eric try to blame me for what happened?" she wondered aloud. Kemba was scared — really scared.

Kemba knew one thing for sure. She just couldn't sit around and wait, doing nothing. She reached for her keys and purse, then headed out the door. She was going back over to Eric's house.

When Kemba arrived twenty minutes later, Jillian's face registered surprise. "Kemba, what are you doing back here? Did you forget something?"

Shaking her head no, Kemba brushed past Jillian into the house. "I need to speak with Mr. Avery."

"He's not back yet." She followed Kemba into the living room. "Are you okay? I've just made some tea. Would you like some?"

"Yes, if you don't mind." Kemba's voice wavered. "Malcolm and I were friends. I really hope he's okay."

Jillian nodded. "So do I."

Kemba sank down on the sofa, twisting her hands nervously. "Whatever happens to him is my fault. If only I hadn't just left him there. But I was so scared."

"You did the right thing, Kemba," Jillian assured her. "Don't blame yourself for whatever the outcome will be." She moved toward the kitchen. "I'll be back shortly with your tea. How do you take it?"

"Sugar and cream." Kemba glanced around the room, really seeing it for the first time. It was beautifully decorated, from the polished black lacquer tables to the brass and ebony figurines. There were cushioned seats beneath the large picture window.

In the dining area a huge black lacquer table with matching chairs dominated the room. Wide planked hardwood floors gleamed to perfection, reflecting hues of burned orange and rust found in the throw pillows and rugs that decorated the black leather furniture in the living room. Ornate gold-framed abstracts in colors of cherry red, orange, black and rust complemented the cream-colored walls along the hallway, leading to the bedrooms.

Kemba stood up and went to join Jillian in the kitchen. Black-and-white coordinated accessories adorned the gray marble Formica counters. Leaning against the counter, she sipped the hot tea, savoring the spiced-apple flavor. "This is good."

Nodding, Jillian agreed. "This is one of my favorites. Eric's too."

Kemba watched the clock as she sipped her tea. Maybe Malcolm had been taken to the hospital. Maybe that's what was taking so long and why they hadn't heard from Eric. She fervently prayed that Malcolm was alive.

"Thank you," Kemba murmured.

"For what?"

"For not questioning me right now."

"Eric told me what he knew."

"I just hope Malcolm is okay."

"So do I."

Back in the living room, Kemba peered at the various photographs on the entertainment unit; she stopped to pick up a gold frame containing a picture of Eric and Malcolm. Her gaze traveled over Eric's face and searched his eyes. They were deep and probing, even in the photograph. Although the two men were very handsome, Kemba did not want to tear her attention away from Eric.

Reluctantly she returned the photo to its proper place, accidentally knocking over another photograph that had been partially hidden from view. Picking it up, Kemba noticed it was a wedding photo. She examined it closer. Malcolm was the groom. She'd seen a similar photo in Malcolm's library.

"She died about two years ago." Jillian's voice came from the doorway.

"How sad for him." Kemba returned the photo to its place and then straightened out the rest of the pictures. She headed over to the love seat.

Jillian settled back on the couch, remote control in hand, preparing to watch television. She nearly jumped when a scream rent the air. Jumping up, Jillian ran the short distance to the room where Crystal was sleeping, with Kemba following on her heels.

When they rushed in, they found Crystal sitting up and trembling terribly. Jillian ran over and gathered the little girl in her arms. "It's okay, honey. It's okay. Nobody is going to hurt you."

"Daddy . . ."

"Your uncle's gone to check on him," Kemba offered. "He'll be back soon."

"Kemba's right, sweetie. Eric should be back shortly. Why don't you lay back down and try to get some rest."

"I'm scared, Jillian. I'm so scared."

"I won't let anything bother you."

"I won't either," Kemba stated as she joined them on the bed. "Remember? I'm your protector."

Crystal smiled. "Will you both stay here with me?"

She looked to Jillian, who nodded her approval.

The little girl climbed off Jillian's lap onto the bed. She moved over to the far side, making room for Kemba.

"Now I want you to close your eyes and get some sleep," Jillian ordered. "You've been through a terrible ordeal."

Silently Kemba sent up another prayer for Malcolm.

Eric closed the door gently and glanced around. When he didn't see Jillian in the living room, he headed to the guest room, where Crystal was sleeping and where he found Jillian asleep in the rocking chair and Kemba sleeping next to his niece on the bed. He eyed Kemba a moment, noting the look of pure innocence on her face. Innocent? He really had to wonder. When he saw her car parked in front of his house upon his return, Eric had been surprised to find that Kemba had returned to his house. He figured this would be the last place she'd want to be.

My brother is dead. Eric felt tears prickling the back of his eyes. He and Malcolm had been very close. No two people were closer. He heard Kemba moan and glanced in her direction. He nodded when she opened her eyes.

She sat up and got out of bed. Stifling a yawn, Kemba crossed the room to stand beside him. "I'm sorry," she whispered. "I must have fallen asleep." Kemba glanced at her watch before continuing. "Jillian and I heard Crystal scream. When we came to check on her, Crystal asked us to stay in here with her. I only meant to stay until she fell asleep. I hope you don't mind."

Eric wiped his red-rimmed eyes. "Why did you come back?"

Ignoring his question, she asked, "H-how is Malcolm?"

Eric motioned for her to follow him to the living room. He gently woke up Jillian, who got up and followed them out of the room.

In the living room he announced to them both, "Malcolm was shot through the heart. He died instantly."

Kemba collapsed to the floor as her knees buckled from the news. *"Noooo . . ."* She couldn't believe it. "I — I am so s-sorry."

Jillian dropped down beside her, covering one of her hands with her own. "Please don't cry. I — I . . ." She burst into tears.

When Eric could no longer control his own grief, he strode to the window and stared out, tears falling from his eyes.

Behind him Kemba was saying, "I s-should have tried to d-do something. Maybe . . . maybe I should have tried to save h-him." Suddenly she jumped up and ran toward the bathroom.

Eric could hear the sounds of her retching. A part of him wanted to help Kemba, but he wasn't sure how she would react.

He was vaguely aware of Jillian touching his shoulder. "She'll be all right, Eric. She's just overcome right now."

Finally, when he heard the water running in the sink, Eric relaxed a little.

Kemba walked out of the bathroom a

short while later and sat down on a nearby recliner. "I'm sorry. I don't know what happened."

"You have nothing to be sorry for. You've been through a lot tonight," Jillian stated softly. "Thank God you were able to get Crystal out of the house safely."

Kemba chewed on her lower lip and stole a look at Eric. "I wish there was something I could've done. Malcolm was a good man. He didn't deserve to die."

"What were you really doing there?" Eric questioned. "And before you answer, I must warn you that I just lost my only brother . . . a brother I was very close to, so I'm really not in the mood for lies. I know you're hiding something. I can feel it."

Kemba ignored Jillian's gasp of surprise. "I told you. I was there to work."

Eric lifted his head alertly. "Did you know someone else was in the house?"

Kemba shook her head. "No, I didn't."

Eric pulled Jillian to the side. Kemba tried to hear what he was saying to her, but she couldn't.

Jillian turned to face her and said, "It was nice to meet you, Kemba. I'm glad you and Crystal are safe." Grabbing her purse and keys, she made her way to the front door.

While he walked Jillian to her car, Kemba struggled to control her emotions.

Eric soon joined her once more in the living room. After easing back onto the sofa, he gave her a glinting glance. "Malcolm wasn't home either. Was he? If no one was home, how did you get in? Did you have a key?" He was quiet for a moment before asking, "Were you and Malcolm lovers?"

Kemba was stunned. "That's none of your business, but no, we weren't lovers. Why are you asking me all these questions? Do you think I had something to do with Malcolm's murder?"

"I'm simply trying to make sense of what happened tonight."

"I didn't break in. Malcolm didn't give me a key to the house, but I didn't break in." She paused for a second. "I didn't have to because I had a key — not to the front door, but to a hidden door."

Eric sat up straight. "*A hidden door?* What hidden door?"

"On the left side of the house, there's a door. It's pretty much hidden by plant growth. You'd really have to be looking for it to know it's there."

"How did you know about it?"

"If I tell you everything, will you

promise to keep it between us?"

"I don't know if I can make such a promise without hearing you out," Eric stated truthfully. "Does this have something to do with my brother's death?"

"It might. I don't know for sure —"

His gaze narrowed. "Then you *are* involved?"

"Not in the way you think," Kemba answered quickly. "Please, hear me out."

Eric nodded. "I'm listening." His tone was noncommittal.

"I didn't just find the hidden door by accident. I knew about the passageway."

He stared, complete surprise on his face. "How?"

"Please just let me finish. The house has a secret passageway leading to a hidden room in the basement. I know about it because I grew up in that house."

Eric opened his mouth to speak but closed it. "Go on."

"I lived in that house until my father was killed twenty years ago."

"What does this have to do with Malcolm?"

"The man who killed Malcolm had an African accent."

"*And?*"

"And my father was African. I know this

50

is going to sound strange, but I really think the two deaths are connected."

Eric's eyes widened in astonishment and he leaned forward, his arms resting on his thighs. "What makes you think the two deaths are related? None of this is making sense."

"Maybe this will change your mind." Kemba reached into her pocket and pulled out the diamond. She placed it on the coffee table.

"Where did you get this? I thought Malcolm had already . . ." Comprehension dawned on him. "This is what the intruder was after. How did you get it? I know my brother wouldn't have left something like this lying around. *Not Malcolm.*"

"He didn't," Kemba confirmed. "I took it from the safe."

"I see."

Kemba could tell Eric clearly didn't believe her story. "Did Malcolm ever tell you how it came to be in his possession?"

His eyes came up to study Kemba's face before nodding.

"Then you know he found it in the house, so it really didn't belong to him. It belonged to my family."

"Can you prove it? Malcolm said the person he bought the house from was some actor who is living in Europe now. He never mentioned anyone else."

"The Dumisani Diamond belonged to my family. It's easy to verify that my family originally owned that house."

"Is that why you stole it?"

"I didn't steal it," she said quietly. "I originally thought about taking it, but when I got there, I knew I couldn't go through with it. I'd already decided to talk to Malcolm tomorrow — that's when all hell broke loose."

"Why didn't you discuss this with Malcolm in the first place? You said you two were friends."

"I didn't think Malcolm would just hand it over to me. It's been lost to us for years. When it recently turned up again, I'd planned to ask him for it, but then I overheard him on the phone earlier. He was arranging to have it picked up tomorrow, and I panicked."

"You want me to believe this rock belongs to your family?" Eric examined it closely. "This is worth a fortune."

Kemba was clearly insulted. "*It does belong to us.* When my father died, I looked everywhere for it. My mother figured the diamond had been stolen the night my father was murdered."

"And clearly you didn't agree?"

"No, my father told me he kept it hidden in a place it would never be found."

"Did he tell you where?"

"No," Kemba admitted. "He never had a chance. I take it you know where Malcolm found it?"

"Is that why you became Malcolm's decorator? And his *friend?* To gain entrance into the house so that you could steal the diamond?"

Kemba winced at his words but answered nonetheless. "Yes and no. Yes, I wanted to return to the house and look for the diamond. Unfortunately, Malcolm found it before I could. As for being Malcolm's friend — I really liked him. He was a very sweet man. That's why I decided not to just take the stone. But then I heard the intruder and I changed my mind. I didn't want to lose it again."

Their eyes clashed as Kemba said, "Look, the fact remains that someone else found out that the diamond resurfaced and that person killed your brother. Two people have died because of it."

Eric met her gaze with a lifted brow. "You're positive you don't know who the other intruder was?"

"I don't know who he is. No matter what

you may think of me, I'm not a killer, Mr. Avery. I didn't have anything to do with that man."

He leaned forward in his chair. "Did he know about you? That you were there?"

"I don't think so. Crystal was very brave. She hit him with a lamp or something, then ran into the library. I was about to leave through the secret passageway when I heard all the commotion and the gunshot."

"Where is this secret passageway?"

"It's in the library. There's a little button hidden behind the bookcase on the right. My father had it built shortly after we moved into the house. He said if there was ever some type of disaster, we would have an escape route. We had to use it — the night my father was killed."

Eric moved to stand in front of the brick fireplace. He stuck both hands in his pants pockets as he watched her. "That person is still out there. As long as he is, Crystal is in danger. Maybe you heard something that will aid the police in his capture. You need to talk to them. I want the person responsible to get the punishment he deserves."

Kemba peered into his dark eyes. "What are you going to do? Crystal can't stay here."

Eric shook his head. "I don't know. I'll

have to give it some thought."

"If there is anything I can do —"

He cut her off by saying, "I think you've done enough."

Kemba wasn't sure what he meant by that, but it hurt her deeply to have Eric think she was capable of murder. "I didn't have anything to do with killing your brother. I'm telling you the truth."

"I don't know why, but I do believe you," Eric admitted finally. He had been mulling over everything she'd told him, and in a weird sort of way — it all made sense. "For now. I do have one more question, though. How did you get into the safe?"

"When I was with Malcolm doing a walk-through earlier today, I came up with the idea to take the diamond," she answered, turning her face away from him. "He left me alone — that's when I went through his desk and found the combination."

"I see."

Kemba stared down at her black sneakers. "I'm not really a bad person."

"I can see that."

"Tell me something, please. Where did Malcolm find the diamond?"

"He found it in the bottom of an old fish tank. It was down in the basement."

"My fish tank . . ." Kemba gazed at Eric. "I used to have a huge fish tank with lots of marbles in the bottom. I didn't get much use out of it because my fish never lived that long. . . ."

"Malcolm was cleaning it out for Crystal. That's when he found the diamond."

"It never would've been found. Papa was right about that." Standing up, Kemba said, "Thank you for being so kind, Eric." She paused for a second before adding, "I'm not feeling so well. I think I should go home."

Eric stood up also. He moved around the coffee table to block her exit. "The police will want to talk with you. You know that, don't you?"

"I don't have a problem with talking to the police. It's just that I don't want to tell them about my part in taking the diamond," she admitted.

"Why not?"

"If you were in my shoes, would you?" Kemba inquired as she grabbed her purse. "I've got to get out of here."

As soon as she reached the door, the doorbell sounded. Eric peeked out before opening the door. A black female, dressed in a pair of navy blue pants and a white button-down shirt, moved forward. She identified herself as Detective Janet Williams. She introduced her partner, a white male, as Detective Bob Hawkins.

Backing away from the door, Kemba couldn't control the spasmodic trembling within her. She was going to jail — she just knew it.

Eric opened the door wider to let the detectives in. "Come on in."

"We'd like to speak with your niece, Mr. Avery."

"She's asleep. I would rather you wait until morning."

"I think it's best if we speak to her now. While the events are still very fresh in her mind," Detective Williams stated.

Kemba touched Eric lightly on the arm. "I'll go wake her," she offered, wanting to escape the scrutiny of the two homicide detectives.

Kemba headed down the hallway, stopping just outside the room Crystal was in. Her heart almost broke listening to the little girl cry. Knocking softly, she entered the room slowly. "Hi, Crystal. May I come in?"

Wiping her face with the back of her hand, Crystal tried to smile. "I — I t-thought you l-left."

"No. I was talking to your uncle. We didn't want to wake you, so we went into the living room."

Crystal was looking past her. "I heard the doorbell. Who's at the door?"

"The police."

"Where's Uncle Eric?"

"He's out there with the detectives."

"Where's my daddy? Is he out there too?"

At a loss for words, Kemba looked up to find Eric standing there watching them silently by the door. Crystal followed her eyes.

"*Uncle Eric.* You scared us. Where's Daddy? Is he talking to the police?"

"I'm sorry, honey. Your father isn't here."

"Do you want me to leave?" Kemba asked.

"No, please stay."

"Where's Daddy?" Crystal asked a second time.

"Honey —" Eric began.

"He's dead, isn't he?"

Eric nodded. "Y-yes, he's gone. I'm so sorry."

Crystal curled into a ball, sobbing.

Kemba stirred uneasily on the bed. She fought her own tears as she caught sight of

Eric's. Rubbing Crystal's back, she murmured her condolences.

Eric came into the room and sat beside Kemba. Pulling his niece into his arms, he said, "I know this is hard for you, but the detectives want to talk to you. Are you up to it, sweetheart?"

Crystal clung to him tightly. "Uh-huh."

Seeing the two of them, Kemba wished for the floor to open up and swallow her. She averted her eyes to shield her anxieties. "If you'd like, I can comb Crystal's hair and help her get dressed."

Eric stood up. "Thanks. I brought some clothes over from the house. They're over there. On the rocking chair."

Just as she and Crystal headed to the bathroom, Eric pulled Kemba to the side. "I didn't tell them about your having the diamond."

"Thank —"

Eric interrupted her. "I think you should tell them yourself."

Hope died. "I see."

"It will work out, Kemba. You only have to tell the truth."

"*Right.* That is what's going to land me in jail," she muttered under her breath.

Eric bit back a smile. Turning on his heel, he strode to the door.

Kemba helped Crystal dress and touched up her hair. Embracing her, Kemba said, "Don't be afraid, sweetheart. Your uncle and I will be right beside you. Just remember to tell the detectives everything you can remember." Grabbing the small girl by the hand, she asked, "Are you ready?"

Crystal nodded.

The two detectives stood up when they entered the living room.

Crystal sat next to Eric on the love seat, tears in her eyes. Kemba sat alone on the leather couch, praying for this day to end.

"Crystal, I'm Detective Janet Williams and this is Detective Bob Hawkins."

"Hullo."

"How old are you, Crystal?" Bob Hawkins asked.

"Six."

"Six, that's a nice age. You're a big girl."

"I know why you're here."

Janet Williams smiled. "Yes, I'm sure you do. Do you want to tell us what happened earlier tonight?"

"My dad took me to see *Snow White*. When we came home, a man was in the house. Daddy got shot by the bad man. *He killed my daddy.*"

Detective Hawkins knelt down. "Did

you get a good look at the person who shot your father?"

Crystal shook her head. "He wore a mask, but I remember that he talked funny."

"He talked funny?" Detective Hawkins glanced over at his partner. "How?"

"I don't know. He just talked real funny."

Kemba spoke up. "She means that he spoke with an accent."

"You're Kemba Jennings." It was a statement.

Terrified, she nodded.

The doorbell sounded, sparing her from further questioning. Kemba stood there trembling while Eric answered the door.

"Ray, come in. The police just arrived to question Crystal. I'm glad you're here."

Eric made the introduction. "This is my cousin Ray Ransom. He's a U.S. marshal."

Kemba felt her whole world crumbling away.

CHAPTER 4

"You were there?" Detective Hawkins moved to stand in front of her. His eyes scrutinized her from head to toe, no doubt making note of her dark clothes — clothes that someone with something to hide would wear.

Kemba nodded and exhaled her breath when he sat down beside her. Janet Williams continued to question Crystal. Out of the corner of her eye, she could see Eric and Ray watching them.

"Where were you when the intruder confronted Crystal and her father?" Detective Hawkins questioned.

"I was in the library. He didn't know I was there. The intruder, I mean."

"He?" Detective Hawkins wrote hastily. "How do you know it was a man?"

"I could hear him talking. It was a man and he had an African accent."

"How can you be so sure?"

"My father was from Africa."

Detective Hawkins glanced up from his notes. "Where is your father now?"

"He's dead. He died twenty years ago."

"Did you happen to get a look at the man?"

"No." Kemba paused. "I'm sorry I can't tell you more. I never got a look at him. I just heard him."

"He had no idea you were there?" As the detective scratched his balding head, he asked, "You're sure?"

Kemba nodded. "I'm pretty sure he didn't."

"What were you doing at the house?"

"Malcolm and I were friends. He hired me to decorate his entire house. I often worked late in the evenings." Kemba was trying hard not to lie. *I'm innocent,* she wanted to scream.

"So, you were working?"

Kemba nodded.

"Where?"

"In the library."

The two detectives eyed one another. Detective Williams said to Eric, "Do either of you have any idea what the intruder could have been after? We found an open safe in the library, but nothing in it — just papers." Detective Hawkins watched her closely as he spoke. "Do you know anything about that, Ms. Jennings?"

Taking a deep breath, she said, "I think

he — no, I *know* what he was after. It was a twenty-carat emerald-cut diamond."

"How do you know this?" Detective Hawkins asked.

"Because I took the diamond out of the safe and brought it to Eric."

Bob Hawkins appeared to be going over his notes. "How did you know about the diamond, Ms. Jennings?"

Crystal spoke up then. "I told her about it. And that's what that bad man wanted. Daddy told him he could have it — just let me go, but he wouldn't. He was mean."

"Was the safe open?"

"No, I opened it. The combination was in Malcolm's drawer. The one on the left."

"So where is the diamond?" Janet Williams inquired.

Eric held out his hand. "Right here."

Detective Williams cleared her throat. "I see. Well, I think we can safely assume the intruder was looking for the diamond."

Eric nodded. "Look, my brother was murdered earlier tonight. We have the diamond, so can we concentrate on finding the killer?"

Kemba inclined her head in a small gesture of thanks. Her heart thumped so loudly, she was sure everyone could hear it.

"By the way, Mr. Avery, where were you around eight o'clock last night?" Detective Hawkins asked.

"I was at First Christian Church. There were several people that will say they saw me there. I delivered the new hymnals."

"Is that it?" Kemba asked. "Or do you have more questions for me?"

Bob Hawkins spoke without looking up from his notes. "That will be all for now, Ms. Jennings."

Kemba wandered from the living room to take a seat at the dining table to watch the group. Listening dazedly as their questioning flowed back and forth, she tried to ignore the pounding pain in her head and behind her eyes. Within minutes she saw Eric advance from across the room. The detectives wanted to talk to Crystal once more.

"You look a little thoughtful," he said, drawing a chair beside her. "Have you remembered something else?"

"No, not really. . . ."

"Then what's wrong?"

She shrugged, but his interest was undeniable. "I've . . . I'm just tired, that's all."

He wasn't convinced. "You're afraid —"

"Yes, but not so much for me." She looked over at Crystal. "I'm scared for her, now she's lost her father."

"You saved Crystal's life." Eric savored the long, curling lashes falling over her cheeks and her bowed head as she struggled to maintain her composure. When she finally looked up again, her eyes were steady.

"Thank you for believing me, Eric." She cast her eyes over to where the detectives were sitting. "But I'm not so sure they believe me."

"Everything will be fine, Kemba."

"Well, I guess I'd better leave before they decide they want to question me further," Kemba said, standing up and reaching for her purse.

The two detectives approached them. "I'm sorry about your loss," Detective Williams stated.

Eric looked at her then. "Thank you. My brother was a good man. He didn't deserve to die like this."

"Ms. Jennings, where can you be reached if we need to talk to you again?" Detective Williams asked.

She handed her a business card. "You'll find me there. I wrote my home address on the back."

"Thank you again, Ms. Jennings," Detective Hawkins said.

She nodded. Turning to Eric, she said, "I'd better get home."

Kemba was aware of Ray's perusal as she made her way to the door. Willing herself not to look back, Kemba left quickly.

"You want to tell me what's really going on?" Ray inquired.

Eric gave him a quick rundown of what Kemba had told him.

"So, you believe her?"

Nodding, Eric answered, "Yeah. I do."

"What do you know about her? Anything?"

"Nothing really. But like Kemba said, it's easy to verify her story."

Ray nodded in agreement. "I hate that Malcolm got caught up in this mess. It cost him his life."

Eric picked up the diamond. "All because of this little gem."

"It's not that little, I guess." Ray shook his head. "I don't think I've ever seen a diamond that size. Well, almost . . ."

"What are you talking about?"

"You should have seen the diamond Brennen bought Elle when they first got engaged. She didn't want it, though. You know your cousin. She wanted something a little smaller."

Eric smiled. "That sounds like something Elle would do. Malcolm was like that too. He wanted to find the rightful owner. He thought it might have been the actor he bought the house from."

"I'm going to check out Kemba Jennings, Eric. I have to know if she's credible."

He nodded in understanding.

Ray rose to his feet. "I'll be back tomorrow. Carrie's probably worried and I'd better get home."

"Thank you for coming out. I really appreciate it."

"That's what family is for." Ray embraced him. "We're all going to miss Malcolm."

Eric walked his cousin to the door. "Give Carrie and the kids my best."

Ray nodded. "I'll see you tomorrow."

After Ray drove off, Eric went to check on Crystal. Satisfied that she was fine, he went to his room. He lay in bed staring up at the ceiling. Eric wanted to pray — he needed God's unfailing strength to carry him through this period of his life, but he just didn't feel like it. He wasn't angry with God. Eric was disappointed. Malcolm was his older brother — his only brother, and now he was gone.

Kemba did not allow herself to fully relax until she was safely encased in her car and driving along the freeway, heading home to Culver City.

Within the safe confines of her own condo, Kemba quickly prepared for bed and tried to fall asleep but couldn't. The night sounds around her seemed incredibly loud. Even her own heart was high-stepping a skittish rhythm and was in danger of bolting.

Each time she closed her eyes, Kemba visualized the fear she saw in Crystal's eyes. Her father had been murdered right in front of her. She wondered if Crystal would ever be able to live a normal life.

Two hours later, and still unable to fall asleep, Kemba got out of bed. On her knees she prayed for Crystal and Eric. Pausing slightly, she added, *Please forgive me for trying to steal the diamond. Even though it belongs to my mother and me, I never should have gone about getting it the way I did. I'm so sorry. Amen.*

It wasn't until hours later that she finally slept.

CHAPTER 5

Deciding to work at home, Kemba tried to concentrate on a project to keep her mind off what happened the night before. She mechanically went through the motions of selecting upholstery fabric from several swatches. Kemba couldn't shake the feeling of self-contempt flowing through her body. *I am no better than a thief.* Eric was right, she should have just gone to Malcolm, but would it have changed what happened? Or would she be the one dead? The question froze in the air, chilling her to the bone.

Pushing the sample books aside, Kemba gave up on the idea of working. She couldn't concentrate because her mind kept replaying the events leading up to Malcolm's death. Kemba decided a long, hot bath was what she needed and got up from her desk. She headed upstairs to her room, hoping the water would ease her mind as well as her body.

Submerged in the heated, bubbly liquid, Kemba lay back and closed her eyes, wishing she were on a secluded tropical island somewhere. Anywhere but here. The murderer was still out there, and he wanted the diamond.

She wouldn't feel safe until he was caught, Kemba admitted silently. She hoped the detectives found him quickly. Thinking about Detectives Hawkins and Williams, she wondered if they believed her story. Or was she their number-one suspect?

Trembling slightly, Kemba stepped out of the now-lukewarm water. Wrapping a peach-colored body sheet around her, she dried off slowly. The early morning wore on, and Kemba's nerves grew taut. Fear of being arrested consumed her. She couldn't go to jail. Her mother *needed* her.

Eric spent the morning watching Crystal sleep. Tears of grief slipped down his face as he mourned for his brother and the little girl whom Malcolm left behind. Eric wished he could shield Crystal from all of this madness, but he couldn't. She was a witness to her father's murder.

Would Crystal be safe until the killer was caught? He had already called his sister, Tina, to tell her about Malcolm. They agreed that it would be best if Crystal went to live with her after the funeral. His

71

parents were too old to care for an active six-year-old. Although Eric would miss Crystal, he knew it was best to get her out of Los Angeles.

The doorbell rang, scaring Crystal. She woke up screaming.

He quickly plopped on the bed beside Crystal, gathering her into his arms. "It's okay, honey. It's Uncle Eric. It's just the doorbell. Calm down, you're safe. Now I have to answer the door." He kissed her on the forehead. "I'll be right back, okay?"

"Okay." Crystal fought back tears.

Eric opened the door, expecting to see the detectives. His eyes widened in surprise. "Kemba, I didn't expect to see you back here."

"May I come in?" Her voice drifted in a hushed whisper.

"Sure, come on in. I apologize for my lack of manners."

She took a seat on the couch. "I guess you thought I'd be long gone by now."

"Yeah, I did," he admitted honestly. Eric knew she was scared.

"Believe me, I thought about it," Kemba stated. "But I didn't leave town because I'm not a criminal and I have a mother who needs me. I also have a job that I love, Mr. Avery."

Eric sat on the arm of his couch with his arms folded across his chest. "Why did you come back here to see me?"

"I . . . I don't know really. I guess I wanted to check on Crystal and . . ." She paused a second before adding, "I wanted to see how you were doing."

Eric stared into her large eyes. He could see fear in them. Finally he spoke. "I miss my brother. Crystal misses her father. We're both trying to cope."

"But do you think the police suspect me?" Kemba asked after a moment of silence.

"I don't know. I just hope they find the person responsible."

"I do too. For all of our sakes."

"Maybe you should tell them about your relationship to this stone before they find out for themselves. You can prove your claim, can't you?"

"What do you mean?"

"I'm sure you must have something. Like insurance papers. This stone is worth a lot of money. Your father must have insured it."

"I'm sure my mother would know. She would have the papers. I'll have to ask her."

"Kemba, what does your mother think happened to the diamond?"

"She thinks it was stolen the night my father was murdered. Why?"

"I'm wondering if the insurance company paid her."

Kemba shrugged. "I really don't know. Please don't say anything until we know for sure. I don't want her getting into any trouble."

"Why don't you go and talk to her," he suggested. "Find out what you can."

Kemba nodded in agreement. "I'd better do that right now." Looking up at him, she said, "Thank you, Eric. Would you tell Crystal that I stopped by? If I can, I'll try to come back to see how she's doing. If you don't mind, that is."

"You're welcome to stop by anytime."

After leaving Eric's house, Kemba drove the short distance to see her mother, stopping briefly to buy a dozen roses. She knew how much Sarah loved flowers — especially red and white roses. Combined, she'd always told Kemba, they meant unity.

She parked her car right behind her mother's gray Volvo. Using her key, Kemba let herself into the neat, three-bedroom town house. It was a nice place but a far cry from the luxury estate home in Brentwood. First she checked the modern kitchen, then navigated upstairs to Sarah's room. Inside, Kemba pulled ivory-colored drapes back to let the sunlight peek in. Her soft singing while arranging the roses in a crystal vase brought about the desired effect of rousing her mother.

Stifling a yawn, Sarah smiled. "Oh, Kemba. I didn't hear you come in."

"I know. I was beginning to wonder if you were going to sleep the whole day through. How are you feeling today?" Grimacing, Sarah sat up gingerly against the goose-down pillows, a Mother's Day gift from Kemba, and yawned. "Those roses are beautiful," she said, her thickly lashed eyes moving to the arrangement. "I feel fine today. How about you? You look tired — like you barely got sleep." Sarah patted the multicolored scarf on her head. She had a honey-colored complexion, and when she smiled, it lightened the hard contours of her round face.

"I'm fine, Mama. Enough about me. Have you eaten today?"

Sarah made a face. "Don't you start on me now. I haven't eaten because I'm not hungry yet."

"Mama, you know you have to eat," she admonished. "With all the medicine you're taking —"

Sarah waved her off. "I'll eat when I'm hungry."

"But —"

"No more, Kemba," Sarah said tersely.

She gave an impatient shrug. "Fine, Mama. I'm just worried about you. Eating properly is part of managing diabetes."

"I feel fine. I do." She patted a vacant area on the bed. "Come here, sit next to me, child."

Kemba sank down beside Sarah. "I don't mean to upset you, but I love you, Mama, and I don't want anything to happen to you." She laid her head on Sarah's shoulder.

Reaching to pat her daughter's hand, she said, "I know, baby. I love you too. Quit your worrying about me. God's will be done where I'm concerned. I've put myself in His hands."

Kemba raised her head to look at her mother. "When do you go back to the doctor?" Lately Sarah had been complaining of being tired all the time and a tingling in her hands and feet. Just yesterday she was saying her headaches were becoming more frequent. Kemba was worried that it could be a sign that her mother had high blood pressure.

"I'm supposed to go this Friday. Are you going to have time to go with me?"

"Of course. You know I'm not going to let you go through this alone." She nodded toward the flowers. "We're a united front, remember."

"I know, dear. But I also realize you've got to work too. I could get Claire to take me —"

"That's nonsense," Kemba interrupted. "I'm going to take you; while you're there, I thought I'd go see Dr. Kedrick."

"What for? Are you sick?"

Kemba shook her head. "No, Mama. I'm just going in for a physical. It's been a while."

"Make sure they check everything," Sarah warned.

"I will." Kemba knew her mother worried about her having diabetes. Her grandmother had had diabetes also. Her doctor had informed Kemba that she was more likely to develop the disease than someone without a family history of diabetes.

"I really appreciate all the things you do for me, Kemba. I know how busy you are. I just wish you'd spend some time doing the things you like to do."

"Mama, I would do anything for you." Kemba leaned back and fit her fingers together, placing them beneath her head. As casually as she could, she asked, "Mama, did you watch the news last night or this morning?"

Sarah shook her head no. "Why?"

"The man who bought our old house . . . was killed last night. Someone broke into the place."

Sarah pressed a hand to her breast. "Oh no. That's horrible. I don't know what this world is coming to."

"Mama . . ."

"Do they have any idea who could have done it?"

"They know he was African." She watched Sarah's face carefully.

"African?" Sarah's wide eyes opened even wider. "Are you sure about this? Did they say this on the news?"

Kemba shook her head in denial.

"Tell me, Kemba. How do you know so much about this?"

"Because I was there." Kemba felt Sarah's body stiffen in shock.

"*What?*"

"I was there." Kemba managed to say this as casually as she could. "I heard everything. The intruder's voice and . . . the gunfire. I saved Malcolm's little girl."

Sarah's dark brown eyes widened in astonishment. "How?"

"I was in the library. The little girl came in. We left through the passageway." Kemba eased off the bed and went to peer out the window.

"You had no business being there, Kemba," Sarah practically shouted. "You could somehow be implicated in that man's death. What were you doing there in the first place? Oh, dear God. No, Kemba —"

"Mama, Dr. Malcom Avery was my client. I was decorating the house."

"You were looking for that diamond," Sarah accused. "You don't fool me for a minute. I told you to forget about that stone."

Kemba's temper flared. *"The diamond belongs to our family.* Why do you want to settle for this place when you could live in a mansion? We used to live in Brentwood, Mama. Now you're in this town house."

"When your father died, I was glad to be rid of that house. Then when your stepfather died, I decided I didn't need the worry of a big house. You have your own place, so I bought this for me."

Turning to face her mother, Kemba shifted indignantly from foot to foot. "Papa never wanted us to sell the house in the first place."

Sarah glanced around her home. "This place isn't so bad. I've lived here in peace. I feel safe here. First time in a long time."

"You deserve better. And the diamond —"

"No, Kemba, *no.* I want nothing to do

79

with the Dumisani Diamond. It only causes death and destruction."

Kemba noticed the pensive shimmer in the shadow of her mother's dark eyes. "Mama, why do you keep saying this? Why does it seem to scare you so much?"

Sarah waved her hand to halt Kemba. "I don't want to talk of this anymore."

"The Dumisani Diamond is our legacy, Mama. You thought it had been stolen all these years, but it wasn't — doesn't that tell you something?"

Sarah's eyebrows rose inquiringly. "Where is it? Did you bring it here?"

"Malcolm's brother has it. His name is Eric."

"Then let him keep it, Kemba. Please forget about the Dumisani Diamond."

"Mama, did you ever report the diamond stolen?"

"Why do you ask?"

"Did Papa have insurance on it?"

"Why are you asking all these questions?"

Kemba didn't miss the way her mother's hands twisted nervously. "I need to know."

"Yes, your father had the diamond insured, and no, I never reported it stolen."

Confused, Kemba questioned, "But why?"

"Because your father died because of it
— I just hoped it was gone and we could
go on with our lives. No one would bother
to look for us."

"Who, Mama?" She regarded Sarah with
intense curiosity. "Who would be looking
for us?"

"What? Oh, never mind me, I'm just an
old woman. I worry too much."

"Why would you worry about someone
looking for us? Who would be looking for
us anyway? And what does it have to do
with the diamond?" Kemba thought about
the intruder and his accent. "What is it
that you're not telling me? Do you know
who killed Papa?"

Sarah closed her eyes, and Kemba knew
she pretended to be asleep to avoid answering
the questions. "Mama?"

Sarah did not respond.

Sighing in frustration, Kemba stood up
and grabbed her purse. "I guess I'll see
you later."

Still no response.

Closing the door to Sarah's room,
Kemba headed to the spacious living
room. Sinking down on a green-and-white-
striped couch, she picked up the telephone
to check her messages. After returning a
couple of calls, she left.

Eric greeted Elle with a kiss and shook Brennen's hand. "Thank you for coming over."

"I wouldn't be anywhere else. Mama's coming with Jillian. She came down last night."

"How is Aunt Amanda handling all this?" Eric wanted to know. His father's sister adored Malcolm.

"She sounded fine when I spoke with her." Elle's eyes grew wet. "I could still hear the grief in her voice, though." Shaking her head, she added, "I still can't believe Malcolm's gone."

Gesturing to her protruding belly, Eric asked, "How have you been feeling?"

"Fine. The baby's very active. I think more than the twins ever were."

They were joined by more of the Ransom family. Allura and her family entered the house, followed by Ray and his wife, Carrie, with their three children.

Eric was grateful to be surrounded by family and believed it would do Crystal some good.

"Where's Crystal?" Carrie asked.

"She's in her room. She really loved her father. She was only four when her mother died and now she's lost Malcolm. When I spoke with Tina, she suggested that Crystal see a grief counselor. I think it's a good idea."

Carrie agreed. She and Eric spoke for a few minutes more before she announced, "I'm going to check on her. Make sure she's okay."

Eric nodded. "Thanks."

Ray joined him. "The house was originally owned by a man named Molefi Rufaro. Didn't Kemba say her last name is Jennings?"

"She could be married," Eric stated, although he hated the thought for some reason.

"Is she?"

Eric shrugged. "I don't know. Her marital status never came up."

"Your instincts have always been good, Eric. I have to know something. Do you really believe everything she's told you?"

"I do," he confirmed. "I can't explain it, Ray. I just know in here." Eric pressed a hand to his chest. "She's telling the truth."

Their conversation came to a sudden halt when Amanda Ransom arrived with Jillian and her family.

"Eric, I'm so sorry," Amanda murmured. "Sweetheart, if you need anything, just let me know."

"I do need something. What I need right now is a cup of your special strawberry lemonade."

Amanda smiled. "I'll make some now." She wrapped her arms around him. "You and Malcolm mean as much to me as my own children. Don't you ever forget that."

"Thank you, Aunt Amanda."

"How is that brother of mine?"

"Dad's fine. He and Mom will be arriving in a couple of hours."

"I'll pick them up from the airport," Jillian offered.

"You're sure?" Eric questioned. "I can do it."

Placing a hand on his arm, she confirmed, "Sweetie, I'll do it. You need to stay here and talk to Garrick about the funeral arrangements. That's a chore in itself."

"Thanks, Jillian."

She stole a peek outdoors. "Is my brother here yet? I don't see his car anywhere."

"Garrick had some car trouble. He rented a car. He should be here shortly." After giving Jillian the flight information, Eric escorted his aunt to the kitchen. He gave Amanda a brief tour before leaving her alone and strode back to the living room to greet more family and friends as they arrived.

Kaitlin and her husband, Matt, entered the house just as he reached the front door.

Matt offered his condolences and Kaitlin gave her cousin a hug. Eric placed a kiss on their daughter's forehead.

"Where's Crystal?" Kaitlin asked.

Eric gave her the same answer he'd given Carrie earlier. "Your mom is in the kitchen."

"She's making her famous strawberry lemonade?"

Breaking into a grin, Eric nodded.

Looping her arm through his, Kaitlin said, "We'd better get in there. If we hurry, we can get to the lemons before everyone else."

When they were children, Eric and Kaitlin would hang around the kitchen wanting to suck the juice out of leftover lemons. It didn't take long for the other family members to catch on.

On the way to the kitchen, Allura stopped them.

"It's too late. The lemons were given to the grandchildren."

Kaitlin groaned. "I told Mama that lemons weren't good for the children," she complained.

Eric laughed. He was thankful to have so

many of his relatives around during a time like this. His cousin Garrick arrived with another man and the trio headed to Eric's office. Garrick owned a funeral home, and his assistant would be handling Malcolm's funeral arrangements.

Two hours later, Eric's parents had arrived. Eric spent time talking to them while Jillian helped her mother and Carrie in the kitchen. Kaitlin and Elle were in the family room with the children. Amanda glanced up and smiled. "Dinner is almost ready," she announced.

A couple of people from the church had dropped off cakes and pies along with some fried chicken and a pot of collard greens. Amanda had whipped up some potato salad and corn bread. Carrie made corn on the cob and a pot of rice. Jillian was removing a dish of baked chicken from the oven.

"Everything smells delicious, ladies. Thank you."

"We're family, Eric." Jillian took the foil off the pan. "We have to support one another during times like this. You don't need to thank us."

He went around the kitchen giving each of the women a hug.

Amanda asked him, "Dear, could you

tell everyone that the food's ready?"

"Sure." Eric left and did as he was told.

"Have you heard anymore from Kemba?" Jillian inquired as they sat around the dinner table and ate. Eric and Ray had brought in two card tables and set them up in the kitchen and in the formal dining room.

"Who's Kemba?" Allura asked.

"She's the woman who saved Crystal last night."

"What was she doing in the house?" Ivy asked. "Were she and Malcolm seeing each other or something?"

"Or something," Eric responded. "Kemba is the interior decorator Malcolm hired."

"I don't know why Malcolm needed an interior decorator," Ivy grumbled. "Jillian and I offered to help him for free. We could have really hooked up the house."

"Malcolm had an eye for beautiful women, and Kemba is stunning." Picking up her glass, Jillian eyed Eric. "Don't you think so, cuz?"

"Eric's not thinking about a woman," Ivy replied. "Eric has his mind on the Lord, don't you? That poor Jennifer Whittaker at church — she's been after him for a long time."

"I'm glad my son is a man of God, but even so — he still needs a wife," Lorene Avery announced. "I don't know what he's waiting on. I guess he's planning on God sending her straight from heaven."

Eric and Ray exchanged amused looks.

"When Eric is ready to settle down, *he'll* make that decision," Elle pointed out. "Not you, Ivy."

"*I know that.* You need to tell Jillian," Ivy countered. "She's the one trying to do the matchmaking."

"All I said was that Kemba is a very nice-looking woman," Jillian interjected. "I was just curious as to whether Eric — who by the way is not only a preacher but also a single man . . ." She stopped for effect. "I just wondered if he noticed. No harm in that."

"Can you believe Jillian is matchmaking?" Allura broke into a short laugh. "I never thought I'd see the day."

"Eric doesn't have to marry the woman," Jillian argued.

Laughing, Eric listened to his cousins banter back and forth. This wasn't unusual for the Ransom siblings. He and Malcolm had always enjoyed spending time with them and lived for the Sundays their parents would take them to Riverside for the delicious family dinners. Since their retirement, his parents had moved to Florida, but Malcolm and Eric had still managed to attend some of the dinners.

Now that Eric was senior pastor at First Christian Church, he wasn't able to get out to Riverside as often as he'd liked, but he usually made it for the holiday dinners. Every now and then he would meet up with the male Ransoms and play basketball.

Laine Ransom and his family arrived shortly after dessert. They gathered in the family room, kitchen and breakfast nook to watch old family videos. Even Crystal seemed to cheer up some upon seeing her father on the screen.

CHAPTER 6

For two hours Kemba's fingers flew over the sketchpad as she put to paper the vision in her mind. Picture completed, she scanned it critically. She sighed dispiritedly. "What is wrong with you, girl?" Kemba asked herself aloud. After leaving her mother's house, she had come home and tried to work.

Slumping down in her chair, Kemba frowned. Crystal was alive because of her. But the diamond was still out of her reach. Dejectedly Kemba shook her head. Her father would be so disappointed. *No point in thinking about that now. Especially since I've already given it to Eric Avery.* "How stupid is that?" she muttered angrily.

The phone started ringing. Kemba answered on the second ring. "Hello."

"Hi, honey. It's your mother."

"Hi, Mama." Kemba became instantly concerned. "What's wrong? Do you need anything?"

"No, baby. I'm just fine. I called to tell you something I should've said earlier today when you were here."

She didn't want to argue with her mother anymore. "Mama . . ."

"Now listen to me. I'm proud of what you did. It was a very brave thing to do, especially since you weren't supposed to be there in the first place. But I'm glad you were able to save that little girl."

"Thank you for saying that, Mama, but I have to tell you something. I've been thinking of asking Eric for the diamond back. I made a promise to Papa."

"Kemba, *no.*"

She pressed her lips together in frustration. "Then tell me why."

"I've told you the reason. Two men have died because of that cursed diamond."

Rolling her eyes, Kemba said, "Mama, we have to be realistic."

"Child, I am being very realistic." Sarah huffed. "I want nothing to do with that blood stone."

"I know, Mama, but all I'm trying to say is that you've been through so much already. Papa's death and then losing Dad. Lately you haven't been feeling well. . . ."

"Baby, I know you have good intentions, but you don't understand. Neither did your father and look what happened to him."

"Mama —"

She interrupted her daughter. "Kemba, I hope one day you'll understand that money and wealth —"

"Mama, I hate to cut you off, but my dinner's burning. I'll call you tomorrow. Okay?" Kemba lied about cooking, but the last thing she wanted was to listen to a lecture.

"I love you, Kemba." Sarah clicked off.

Kemba hung up the phone. The tale of the hidden treasure came to mind — a treasure of diamonds and gold hidden long ago by King Dumisani himself. "Whatever happened to the map?" she whispered.

The more Kemba thought about it, the more she became genuinely interested in finding it. Sarah didn't want her to bother Eric about returning the diamond to them. But she never said anything about not trying to find the map and the treasure.

Kemba hoped to convince Eric to let her into the Brentwood house so that she could search for it. She needed a few days to formulate a plan of action.

After Sunday services Eric stood at the entrance of the church, speaking to his parishioners. He was soon joined by Jennifer and her mother, Ida Whittaker.

Ida patted her black pillbox hat with the

bright red feather. "Hi, Pastor Avery. Good sermon today. I really enjoyed it."

"Thank you, Mrs. Whittaker. I'm glad to hear that."

Jennifer was determined she would not be ignored. She moved to stand as close to him as humanly possible. "Oh yes, Pastor. Today's sermon was a good one," she cooed, her gaze sweeping over him like a cat eyeing its next meal. "Now, are we still on for dinner today? I made a peach cobbler especially for you. You're welcome to bring your parents."

Eric smiled politely. "I think Crystal and I will just go on home. My parents are still adjusting to this time zone."

Ida Whittaker nodded accordingly. "I'm so sorry about what happened to your brother. It's such a shame. Of course I understand."

Jennifer placed her hand gently on his arm. "I hope they find the person who's responsible. I don't know what this world is coming to."

"Have you decided when you're having the funeral, Pastor?" Ida inquired.

"Yes, the funeral will be on Tuesday."

"Uncle Eric." Crystal ran over to him. "I want to go home."

He bent to pick her up. "We'll leave shortly, okay?"

"Can I go help Ivy put away the crayons and stuff until you're ready to go?"

He smiled indulgently. "Yeah, you sure can." Putting her down, his eyes filled with pride as he watched Crystal run off. Turning to Mrs. Whittaker and her daughter, he said, "I need to take care of some matters in my office."

"We'll see you next Sunday, Pastor. Perhaps you'll feel up to having dinner with us then?" Jennifer suggested.

Eric pretended not to notice the warning glare Mrs. Whittaker sent her daughter.

Kemba read over the announcement of Malcolm Avery's funeral in the *Los Angeles Times*. She bit her lip as she struggled with deciding whether or not she should attend. He was going to be buried tomorrow at noon.

She still hadn't made up her mind by the time she finished her breakfast. Kemba hurriedly dressed, then headed to her shop on Melrose Avenue.

Antoinette, her best friend and business partner, arrived just moments after she did. Her light brown curls were windblown, her wispy bangs falling across her forehead. Lifting her sweeping lashes, she looked surprised to see Kemba. "Hey, girlfriend, I thought you were going to work at home this morning." She immediately set out to make coffee. "I planned to give you a call this morning, so it's good you're here."

Kemba headed straight to her office. "I was, but I changed my mind. I didn't want to stay a moment longer at home." She stopped just inside her office and called out, "Did the conservatory bench from Sutherland Teak Collection ever arrive?"

"Hold on a minute, I'll be right there," Antoinette called from her office. She entered with a portfolio under her arm and two cups of steaming black coffee, one of which she handed to Kemba. "Not yet. Let's give it a couple more days. Oh yeah, Rubio —"

"Who?"

"Rubio, that new singer everybody's going nuts over. He signed the contract and wants us to order the entire thirteen-piece collection of Portico."

Kemba's mouth dropped open. "*What?* Are you serious?"

"Yeah, and get this. He wants it all upholstered in silk."

Kemba raised her eyebrows. "Really?" When Antoinette nodded, Kemba added, "Well, it's his money."

"It's for his music room and I think it'll work. Look at this." She held up a fabric swatch. "This is what he wants to use. This is a picture of the room. Now try to visualize the Portico chairs covered in this fabric. . . ."

Kemba studied the photo and the swatch. "You know, you're right. This would work. Actually, it'll look fantastic. It'll give the room kind of an Egyptian feel."

"Exactly. That's what Rubio wants. Between you and me, he may not be able to carry a tune, but he definitely knows how to pull a room together. He has some great ideas for his new house."

They exchanged a subtle look of amusement.

"Maybe he missed his calling. He should be an interior decorator instead of trying to sing," Kemba said with a frown. "I hate his voice."

"Well, you and I may not like his music, but women all over the world love Rubio. They love all that pleading and begging he does."

Kemba gave a forced smile and a tense nod of consent. She took a sip of her coffee.

"What's wrong, Kim?"

Antoinette and her clients were the only

people who called her Kim. "There's nothing wrong," Kemba responded.

Antoinette gave her partner a quick once-over. "You don't look like yourself. Did you have a bad night?"

Kemba shook her head. "No. Did you watch the news last night or this morning by any chance?"

Antoinette grinned as she settled into an armchair that faced Kemba's desk. "Naw, I had a *hot* date last night. Girl, we did things that —"

"One of our new clients was murdered," Kemba interrupted.

Antoinette's mouth dropped open. *"What?"*

"Malcolm Avery. He was killed by an intruder last week. They did a big story on him last night." She took another sip from the huge coffee cup. "Don't you ever watch the news?"

Antoinette shook her head. "Naw. It's too depressing."

"Someone broke into his home to rob him. He tried to fight the intruder and was killed."

"It's just not safe out there anymore."

Kemba leaned back into her chair and closed her eyes.

Antoinette placed a comforting hand

over Kemba's. "I can tell you're very upset about this. Why don't you go home? I'm planning to call an employment agency today and have them send over some applicants." She sat down on Kemba's desk and picked up a contract. "I think it's time we hired a receptionist."

"You're right; we do need one. I think I'll stay here and help with the interviews. I just don't want to go back home. I need to keep busy."

Antoinette glanced up from the contract she was reading. "This is really bothering you, isn't it? You and Malcolm were good friends, weren't you?"

"He was a very sweet man. He didn't deserve what happened."

"The world is getting worse and worse every day."

Kemba ran her fingers through her short curls. "Why don't we change the subject?"

"No problem."

Forcing a smile, she asked, "So who did you have that *hot* date with?"

Antoinette's eyes twinkled. "His name is Michael and, girl, he is so *fine*. He's every bit of tall, dark and handsome. Michael's six-nine and black — jet black, with the prettiest white teeth you've ever seen. He's bald and sexy. Very, very sexy."

Kemba fanned herself. "Have mercy."

A mischievous look came into Antoinette's eyes. "After last night *and* this morning, he can ring my bell anytime."

"How did you two meet? When did you two meet?"

"We met at a club in Long Beach, and we've been dating for three weeks now."

"That long, huh?" Kemba grew serious. "You'd better watch out, Antoinette. I hope you're using protection," she warned.

"Girl, I'm not crazy. I *keep* a supply of condoms on hand."

"That's fine and all, but this is the third guy in three months you've slept with. Why not find one nice man and settle down?"

"That's who I'm looking for. I think Michael is him."

Kemba could only shake her head. "That's what you said about the last one."

"I know, but it just didn't work out. He started asking for money right off the bat. Now, you know, I don't give no man my hard-earned money or my trust fund."

Kemba laughed into her hands. "I don't know about you, girl."

"What? Would you give some guy money that you barely knew?"

"No, but neither would I give him my body."

Antoinette raised a hand. "Don't start lecturing me, Kim. Men screw around all the time and it's accepted. Let a woman get her sex on, and the whole world wants to call her a whore."

"I *never* called you a whore. Honey, I love you like a sister. You know that. I worry about you, that's all. You're a very special person and I just think you shouldn't share so much of yourself. Especially with people who don't deserve to know your name — much less your body."

Antoinette sighed. "You're probably right. It's just —"

"You don't owe me any explanations. You're a grown woman and I know you can take care of yourself."

"Kim, I want to ask you something."

"What is it?"

"How come you haven't started dating again? It's been what? A couple of years now."

She gave this some thought. "I don't know," she admitted honestly. "I guess I've been so busy, I haven't given it much —"

"Aren't you lonely?" Antoinette interrupted. "Don't you miss . . . you know, *being with a man?*"

Kemba shrugged. "Not really. I just haven't thought about it. Maybe it's because

Mama has been through so much in the past two years."

"I know that's bothering you too. I . . . I worry about you, Kim. Since Carl's death, you don't seem happy anymore."

She laughed nervously. "That's ridiculous."

"No, I'm being honest. You're not like you used to be."

Kemba stood up and stretched. "But enough about me." She pointed a finger at her friend. "I don't want to see you get hurt. You deserve much better."

"Thanks for caring, Kim. I'm glad somebody cares about me."

"Make sure *you* care about you. We'd better get started if we're going to be interviewing applicants later this afternoon."

"I've got an appointment with a David Weinberg this morning. He's with that new show coming out this fall. I can't remember the name right now. Anyway, he's interested in having us design the set."

"Really?" Kemba stood up, heading toward the door. She peeked out into the reception area. Finding they were still alone, she drew back into the room and leaned against the wall.

"Yeah. He's a close friend of John Goldman's, the guy I used to work for. You remember him? From the set of *Malibu*

Breeze? He was the producer."

"Oh, that's right. He was sort of a jerk, wasn't he?"

Antoinette's laugher was a full-hearted sound. "He could be at times, but most of the time, John was all right. With me anyway. Besides, I was only the set designer."

"That's enough. *I* haven't been that close to Hollywood."

"You're a nutcase, you are," Antoinette teased.

"Well, good luck with the appointment. We need it," Kemba said lightly.

"Girlfriend, I know it. But don't worry, we're moving in the right direction. Even if we don't get this job, there will be others. I did a few sketches. Want to see them?"

Nodding, Kemba answered, "Sure."

Antoinette laid a sheet of paper on Kemba's desk. "Here's one with French and English antiques, lots of crisp white fabrics. I added touches of blue and gold for effect. I thought this was better than using terra-cotta, like I used over here." She laid down another sketch. "On this one I used Navajo rugs, Native American baskets, Spanish artifacts and some primitive-looking wooden crosses. I thought it would give off a more Southwestern feel."

Kemba nodded approvingly. "These are very nice, Antoinette. I'm sure Mr. Weinberg will be pleased. At least I hope so. We need the money."

"Like I said before, even if he doesn't, we'll be fine, Kim. Something bigger and better will come our way."

"That's easy for you to say. You have money coming out of your ears."

Antoinette shook her head. "Naw. My parents have money coming out of their ears. My dad's the big-time actor. Remember? Only he's so big time — he forgets he has a wife and children."

"And it really bothers you, doesn't it?"

Antoinette shook her head. "Naw, not really. I'm used to not having a father around. You know, most people think that what they see on TV is real. My dad plays such a loving and attentive father on television, but that's not him at all. I used to wish I was one of the kids on the show." Shrugging, she continued, "Oh well . . . I'm going to my office now. I'll see you in a bit."

She wanted to give comfort to her hurting friend, but she knew Antoinette well enough to know she just needed someone to listen.

"See you when I see you." Kemba

worked diligently, but Eric and Malcolm kept creeping into her mind. Gnawing on the end of her pencil, she closed her eyes for a moment. *What should I do? Should I attend the funeral? Malcolm was my friend, but would Eric want me there?* For reasons she didn't want to consider now, Eric's impression of her really mattered.

By the end of the day, Kemba had decided what she was going to do.

CHAPTER 7

Kemba felt Eric's eyes on her as he walked behind his parents toward the front of the church. He walked with Crystal and a tall, full-figured woman who had to be his sister. They resembled each other greatly. She must be Tina, and the two little girls who followed were her daughters, Kemba surmised.

Malcolm lay in a steel blue coffin, among scores and scores of flowers. Remorse spread through her body, almost choking her with its grip. *I'm so sorry, Malcolm,* she whispered with her heart.

Hot tears welled up and slid down her cheeks. She had been there and had done nothing to help him. Kemba wondered if she would ever be able to live with the guilt. Right now it was eating her up inside. Hearing Crystal's sobs only served to make her feel even worse.

The choir stood up to sing. It was a sad, mournful song, and Kemba closed her eyes, hoping to shut out the grief she saw in people's faces. It didn't help — instead their expressions of grief burned in her memory.

Eric remained stoic throughout the service. She admired his tall, slender form as he stood to say a few words about his brother. But it was his touching final goodbye that ripped through her like a knife. The memory of him tearfully kissing Malcolm farewell would forever be engraved in her mind.

Never having had any siblings, Kemba could not quite understand how it felt to lose a brother, but she knew firsthand what it felt like to lose someone you loved dearly. First her father and then her stepfather.

She had pushed her father's death to the back of her mind for so long, but Malcolm's funeral forced her to deal with it. Kemba admitted she was angry — angry with Molefi for dying. In reality, she knew it wasn't his fault, but the feelings were there. She didn't like to think of the night her father died — it was just too painful.

Her gaze wavered and drifted to Eric. His head was bent, and an arm was around Crystal. He appeared to be comforting her. A part of her wanted to run up the aisle — just to give him the same comfort he was giving his niece. She hated seeing him suffer like this.

He sat in the back of the church, his eyes missing nothing. He had a feeling that his mystery lady was there. He could feel it in his bones. Today he would find the one person who would lead him to the Dumisani Diamond. It belonged to his family and he wanted it back. It never should have left Africa in the first place. But it wasn't just the stone he sought. He wanted to find the treasure too. And the only person who could tell him where to find it was dead. But then there was the man's wife. But she'd disappeared years ago. He vowed one day to find her.

After the services they journeyed slowly to Forest Lawn, where Malcolm would be laid to rest. He laid his eyes on a slender, dark-skinned woman of tall stature; her jet-black hair was short and curly. Her strong facial features declared her to be of African descent. Very beautiful, he thought. He watched with interest as she made her way to Crystal, Malcolm's daughter. A thin smile played across his full lips. *It is her.* He had found his mystery woman.

"Thank you for coming today, Kemba.

107

I'm sure it made Crystal happy." Eric openly admired the tasteful two-piece black dress she wore. "I know Malcolm would be pleased."

"How about you?" Kemba asked. "I wasn't sure I'd be welcome here. After all that's happened . . . I kind of expected your family to throw me out."

Eric watched her intently. Inclining his head, he asked, "Why is that? I hope you're not still beating yourself up."

Kemba averted her eyes. "I guess I am. Eric, I still feel so guilty about everything."

"But why?" Eric asked.

"Because I couldn't do more . . . to save him."

"You came forward . . . in spite of everything. I appreciate it." Eric watched her. Kemba was trying so hard to be brave, but he could see the tremors of distress shivering along her strong frame. She stared solemnly into the open grave, but dampness had begun to bead along her lower lashes. She looked as miserable and alone as he felt at that moment. So Eric opened his arm to her and patted her shoulder with his other hand. Kemba settled in without a word. He told himself he was doing it because she understood and shared the pain he felt. And because he felt sorry for all she'd been through. Or because he was just a decent human being. But the truth touched on none of those reasons. The truth was he needed her as much as she needed him. At least for the moment.

Eric's touch caused unnameable sensations to run through her, sending currents like none she had ever felt before. Kemba pulled away from him slowly. "Take care of yourself . . . and Crystal. She really adores you."

"And I her." He paused for a minute. "She's leaving this evening . . . with Tina."

Kemba's eyes widened in surprise. "She's going to stay with your sister?"

Eric nodded. "I think she'll be safe there."

She bobbed her head up and down. "I agree. I know you're going to miss her."

"Yeah, I am."

Kemba wrenched herself away from her ridiculous preoccupation with his handsome face. "Well, I guess I'd better leave. I need to check on my mother. She's not eating like she should."

"Thank you for coming, Kemba."

"Take care." With long, purposeful strides, she walked down the grassy hill.

Watching Kemba's retreating form intently, Eric wasn't aware that he was no longer alone. The minister cleared his throat, indicating his presence. Eric turned to look at his companion.

"Thank you, Pastor Stevens," he began. "I appreciate your giving the eulogy today. I just couldn't." He held out an out-stretched hand.

Pastor Stevens shook his hand firmly. "Eric, my condolences are with you. I understand. Believe me, I do."

"I've seen more funerals than most, but it's never easy." Eric shook his head. "I hurt for my niece. . . ."

"She still has you and the rest of your family. I was just talking to your father. I didn't realize he was still an associate pastor at a church in Florida."

"Yeah. He couldn't completely retire. He loves it too much."

"Well, I'd better be going. . . ." The portly pastor slapped a chubby hand on Eric's back. "If you need to talk . . ." He left the statement open.

Nodding, Eric replied, "I will. Thank you." The two men shook hands again. He was so tired of saying the same thing over and over as he murmured more thank-yous to well-wishers.

Finally everyone had gone and Eric

stood alone by Malcolm's grave, tears in his eyes. "I still can't believe you're gone." He peered down into the opening of the grave. "I feel as if a huge chunk of me is in there with you, big brother. I'm going to really miss you."

He turned to find Ray waiting nearby. Eric left the grave and walked toward his cousin.

CHAPTER 8

He watched the tall, dark-skinned woman depart for her car. He headed to his. From a safe distance he followed her as she drove toward Pomona. *Who is she and what is her connection to the diamond?* Maybe she was Malcolm Avery's girlfriend. Or probably just another gold digger. *America certainly has its share of those,* he thought bitterly.

He had been in love with an American woman once. It was many years ago. He had loved her with all of his young heart, but she betrayed him. Betrayed him with his own brother. Feelings of hatred rose in his throat, causing him to roll down the window and spit. Abhorrence for his brother filled his soul.

He was so consumed with his memories that he almost missed seeing her exit off the freeway. He quickly got into the correct lane, causing the driver in the next car to slam on his brakes before honking and shaking his fist at him. His only reaction was laughter. *People in this country don't know how to drive,* he mused.

He hated being in the United States any longer than he had to be. The last time he had been here was twenty years ago. He wouldn't have come back if he hadn't received a call from a trusted friend informing him of the diamond resurfacing.

The Dumisani Diamond never should have left Africa. This time, however, he would not leave until he had everything he had come for. When he returned to Zimbabwe with the diamond and the map to the treasure, he would be hailed a hero. His family would welcome him back with open arms. They were blood descendants from royalty and would live as such, he vowed silently. Dumisani had been the last king in their family. His three sons had all been born before his accession, and only a son born after the accession could be installed as the new king.

The black Camry led him to Montclair Mall. Muttering a curse, he debated whether or not to follow her inside. He decided to wait until she returned. He didn't have long because she suddenly turned around and headed back to her car. He followed her back on the 10-Freeway west into Los Angeles.

Forty-five minutes later, she parked in front of a small shop. He surmised that she worked there, since she used a key to gain entrance. His stomach chose that time to rumble. He hadn't eaten all day. Guessing that she would be there awhile, he felt comfortable leaving to seek out food.

However, when he returned, he found the Camry gone. He was not upset, though. He knew where she worked. He could find her anytime he wanted. But first he would go back to the brother's house.

Relieved to be at home, Kemba practically tore the buttons off her top in an effort to rid her body of the sticky black silk material. Next she pulled off the flared skirt with the elastic waist. Garbed in only her bra and panties, she sighed in relief. She was looking forward to the winter months. Kemba couldn't remember a summer being as hot as this one. The heat drained her, making her feel tired beyond belief. She hadn't felt like shopping or working, so she'd just come home to relax.

She headed to the kitchen in search of a cool, refreshing drink. After pouring a glass of cranberry juice, Kemba sank down on a nearby bar stool. With glass in hand, she placed it to her temple. "I've got to get the air-conditioning fixed." Her small fan did nothing but blow hot air. Kemba leaped off the seat to open a window. Feeling the cool air drift in, she smiled. "Yes, this feels much better," she murmured.

Suddenly a little girl stuck her face to the burglar bars. "Hello, Miss Kemba." She had a heart-shaped chocolate face, large eyes and a pixielike smile. Shiny black twisted braids fell to her shoulders.

Hiding in the folds of her curtains, she called out, "Hi, Mila. How are you?"

"Fine. Miss Kemba, are you going down to the pool today?" Her voice was loud and friendly.

"Hmmmm, I hadn't thought about it, why?"

" 'Cause if you were, I wanted to go with you."

Mila wore such a hopeful expression Kemba couldn't refuse. "You know what? I think I will. It's such a hot day."

"Will you ask my mom if I can go with you? *Pleeze*."

Kemba's eyes twinkled with amusement. She laughed. "I sure will. I'll call Tanya right now."

"Thanks, Miss Kemba."

"Thank you, Mila, for the idea. I was just trying to find a way to cool off."

"See you in a few minutes then. I'll tell Mommy you gonna call her, okay?" She started to walk away but turned back to face Kemba's window. Pressing her pug nose to the bars once more, she said, "Now don't forget. You sure you gonna remember?"

Smiling, Kemba said, "I'll call her right after I change clothes. I promise I won't forget."

"I'll tell her that you gonna call. See you, Miss Kemba."

"I'll see you in a few minutes." Kemba left the window to run into her bathroom. Just as she turned on the shower, the bedroom phone rang. "Hello."

"Hi, Kim. This is Joyce. I just got back from lunch and I saw your note. Antoinette left for the day. She had a doctor's appointment. Do you want me to handle this?"

Kemba was pleased. The new receptionist was a sweetheart. Joyce attended college in the evenings for interior design. "No, it's not anything that's urgent, but thank you for offering."

"Oh, no problem. Do you want me to forward your calls to your home or just take messages?"

"Hmmmm." She thought about it for a minute. "Just take messages."

"Will do. I'll see you tomorrow then."

"Bye, Joyce." Kemba clicked off, then called Tanya. She arranged to meet Mila in fifteen minutes and then hurried to change.

Mila was at the door knocking by the time Kemba was dressed in a solid red swimsuit and matching floral print sarong in sheer fabric.

Opening the door, Kemba smiled. "Perfect timing, Mila. I take it you're all set then. Towel, goggles . . ."

The little girl held up a hot pink tote bag made of plastic with yellow-colored fish printed across the bottom. "I have everything. I'm ready."

Mila's pudgy little body was encased in a neon pink swimsuit that seemed almost too small for her. She made a mental note to buy her a larger one for her upcoming birthday. Kemba picked up her keys, her towel and her sunglasses. She was ready for a cool swim in the pool. "Well, let's go." She grabbed the little girl by the hand and headed downstairs.

Two hours later, the wet duo climbed the stairs, returning to their respective homes. Kemba jumped in the shower to wash her hair. With conditioner-saturated hair enclosed in a plastic cap, and dressed in a loose cotton romper, she headed to the kitchen to make a sandwich. Just as she opened the mayonnaise, there was a loud knock at the door.

As she made her way to see who it could be, Kemba caught sight of herself in a mirror. *Oh God. I look like a Martian.* She stopped and debated whether or not she would answer.

"Kemba? It's me, Eric. I — I . . ."

She could hear the sadness in his voice. "Hold on, please," Kemba called out. "I'll be right there." Opening the door, she held her head down to hide her embarrassment. "Come on in, Eric. Please excuse my appearance."

"Hello, Kemba. I guess I caught you at a bad time. I'm sorry, I'll leave." He turned to leave.

Kemba caught him by the arm. "No, you don't have to go. I just washed my hair, that's all. Come on in."

"Are you sure?"

She nodded. Kemba sidestepped to let him pass into her house. "Why don't you take a seat?" She motioned to the ivory club chair. "Let me go wash out the conditioner and I'll be right back."

She returned wearing a scarf tied around her head. Rearranging large overstuffed pillows in purple and ivory, Kemba settled back into a plaid-patterned love seat, crossing her legs. "This is quite a surprise. You're the last person I expected to be at my door."

"Kemba, the reason I came by . . ." Eric gave an embarrassed laugh. "I'm not sure why I'm here. I just felt like seeing you, I guess." An easy smile played at the corners of his mouth.

"It's all right." She found it impossible not to return his disarming smile. "To tell you the truth, I could use some company right now."

They threw one another a quick glimpse.

Kemba clasped her slender hands together. "I thought the service for Malcolm was nice, didn't you?"

"It was very nice." Eric hesitated a moment, then said, "Crystal left with Tina. I just dropped them off at the airport." A look of tired sadness passed over his features.

She observed his bowed head and the way his body seemed to slump in despair. "You miss her, don't you?"

"Yeah, I do," he said heavily. "I wish I could have kept her with me."

"Maybe after all this is over, you can," she offered.

He was quiet for so long, she thought

maybe he hadn't heard her. "Yeah, you're probably right." He glanced around her condo. "This is a nice place. You've done a lot with it. Purple and cream. I never would've thought of putting the two colors together. Especially in the living room."

She took a quick breath, astonished by his observations. "You like to decorate?"

"Well, yes, I do." He scanned her face as if expecting her to ridicule him. "It's not just a woman's job, you know," he added defensively.

"I know that. Personally, I think it's great. Most men I know couldn't tell the difference between Louis the Eighth and neoclassic furnishings. They just think I'm a glorified personal shopper for the filthy rich. They don't understand that what I do is an art." She looked down at her hands. "I'm sorry, I didn't mean to get on my soapbox."

"It's okay. I understand. Really."

Kemba looked him in the eyes. "Yes, I believe you do." She glanced around the room nervously.

"You miss him a lot, don't you? I've been through it too — losing my father." Kemba looked down at her hands, clamped tightly together. "I don't know if I ever will accept his dying."

"That explains the sadness I see in your eyes. I've wondered who or what put it there."

"What?"

"There's sadness in your face," Eric stated. "I noticed it the first time we met."

His scrutiny made her uncomfortable. It was as if Eric could see through to her very soul. She fingered the gold necklace she wore. Looking down at her gold sandals, she murmured, "I've been through a lot. I guess it's wearing on me." She looked at him, a smile on her face. "You're really sweet, you know that? Here you are, sitting here willing to listen to my problems, and you've just buried your brother."

"It's part of my job. Malcolm is gone, but life goes on. People go on."

She nodded. "Yes, we do." Kemba got up. "There were times after my father's death when I thought I wouldn't make it. And with Mama sick . . ."

"It's not been easy for you. Losing your father like that."

She shrugged in resignation. "Dad too."

"Dad?"

"He was my stepfather. We grew to be very close, but then he died five years ago." She paused. "Mama took his death hard. Almost as hard as my father's." Kemba

121

sighed. "But she always says that we were never promised a rose garden without thorns."

Eric laughed. "She's right, you know, although I never thought of it in those terms. She sounds like a wise woman."

"Oh, she is. Give her a Bible and the Seven Hundred Club and she's a very happy woman. She's very brave too. Never complains."

"How is she? You mentioned her being sick."

"She has . . . She has diabetes." Kemba held her head down. "Lately she seems to be getting worse. It scares me to think that I may lose her too."

"I'm sorry."

"It's okay. She's doing fine." Kemba stood up. "I'm starved. How about you?" she asked, clearly wanting to change the subject.

"Actually, I am. They had a lot of food at the church, but I needed to get away from . . . the people. I know they mean well, but I had to get out of there. I couldn't stand another person telling me what they thought I needed to hear. It was getting on my nerves."

Kemba headed to the kitchen, returning a few minutes later with a plate of turkey sandwiches, potato chips and a pitcher of iced tea. She placed them on a brass-and-glass serving cart, then returned to the kitchen to get glasses and plates.

Kemba fixed a plate for Eric and handed it to him. "Here you are."

He gave her a smile that sent her pulses racing.

"Thanks." Eric waited until she fixed a plate for herself, and he sent up a short prayer of thanks. "I didn't realize I was so hungry." He bit into his sandwich. "This is good."

"Thank you, but it's only two pieces of bread, mayo, lettuce and some meat. You're probably saying that because you haven't eaten all day. I do that sometimes. Food always seem to taste better when you're starving."

Eric gave her a warm smile. He glanced over at a nearby photograph of a little girl sitting on the lap of a man. "Is this you and your father?"

"Yes. We took this picture a couple days before he died."

"You were very close to him?"

Kemba nodded. "He used to join me in my play tea parties. No matter how busy he was — he was never too busy for my mother and me. Papa never failed to make us feel we were the most important people in his life. He used to say we were his treasure." She reached for her glass and took a long sip of iced tea.

√The vague memory of the last tea party with her father came to mind. Kemba struggled to recall her father's deep voice and the way his face lit up whenever he talked about the Dumisani Diamond. As the images and the words became clearer, Kemba remembered something. All those years ago, her father had mentioned something about a map. He had been about to show her something — could it have been the map? She wondered.

Kemba bit into her sandwich, chewing thoughtfully. She had to find out if there really was a map. Glancing over at Eric, she said, "Eric, I need to ask you something. Do you think it's possible for me to go back to the house in Brentwood?"

"May I ask why? Or do I even want to know?"

"There is a map that my father used to tell me about. I need to find it."

"A map? What does it look like?" His soothing voice probed further.

"I'm not sure. I've never seen it, but I know it exists."

"What is it a map of?"

"It's a map of a hidden treasure."

Eric almost choked on his iced tea. "W-what did you say?"

"I know you think I'm not making any sense. But I have —" She stopped short.

"What?" His eyes came up to study her face.

Kemba knew he was searching to see if she'd lost her mind. "I know this sounds crazy, but I need to find the map."

"How did your family get the diamond in the first place? What did you call it?"

"The Dumisani Diamond. It's been in our family for years."

"But where did it come from?"

The ringing telephone interrupted them.

"Please excuse me." Her expression changed to one of concern when she heard her mother's voice on the other end. Kemba wiped her mouth with a napkin, causing her voice to sound muffled. "Mama, hi. Are you okay?"

"Honey, I'm fine. What were you doing?"

"I just finished eating. What about you?" She glanced over at Eric. He smiled and her heart did a flip-flop.

"I just wondered if you could pick me up some soup. I'm all out."

"Have you eaten today?"

"I was going to, but I'm out of soup. That's all I feel like eating right now. I would go myself, but I just don't feel up to it. I'm feeling poorly today."

"No problem, Mama. I'll be there shortly." She hung up and smiled apologetically. "My mother needs me to go to the store for her."

Eric nodded. "I understand. I need to be going anyway." He stood up slowly.

Kemba was disappointed over having to end their visit so soon, but her mother needed her now. And she hadn't been ready to answer his questions. But Kemba hoped he would come again. "Thanks for coming by. I was worried about you, but I didn't want to intrude."

"You wouldn't have been intruding. Not at all. Thanks for letting me interrupt your quiet time." Eric pointed to his empty plate. "And for lunch, Kemba."

She walked him to the door. "Anytime. Come by anytime."

He smiled. "Take care."

"You too." Kemba admired his strong, slender body. *What a nice butt,* she mused silently as Eric made his way down the stairs. He was a very sexy man. Suddenly another thought formed in her mind. She had no idea what he did for a living.

126

The following Sunday, Eric drove out to Riverside to spend time with his family.

Elle greeted him at the door. "I'm glad you could make it, cuz."

"Me too." Eric nodded a greeting to other members of the family as he strode toward the back of the house where everyone usually gathered.

"Hello, Eric," Jillian called out. "Good to see you."

Before he could respond, Ivy entered the room, saying, "I didn't know you were coming out here. I thought you were having dinner with Jennifer."

"Why would you think that?" Eric questioned.

"Only because she told me that she'd invited you over."

Eric searched his memory. "I don't recall making any plans with Jennifer."

"She's going to be upset with you," Ivy warned.

Jillian strolled past and said, "She'll get over it."

Ivy and Eric shared a laugh.

While the women helped Amanda in the kitchen, Eric and the other men hung out in the backyard, setting up card tables near the picnic tables. It was a clear day, so they all decided to eat out on the patio.

"You know, Mom is always in the kitchen," Laine announced. "We really should do something for her. And for our wives and sisters. We should cook a real nice dinner for them for a change. They shouldn't always be the ones cooking."

Matt laughed. "What you mean is that Eric and I should cook. The rest of you all . . ." His voice died as he shook his head.

"Okay," Laine agreed. "Then it's a plan. Matt was kind enough to volunteer him and Eric. We'll bring flowers and . . ."

"Candles," Garrick threw in. "Daisi loves candles. So do Carrie and Allura."

"What do you want me to do?" Brennen asked. "I made Elle a promise that I'd become more involved with the family. I don't want to let her down."

"You must be in the doghouse," Laine stated with a laugh. "Nothing worse than making a pregnant woman mad."

The other men started to tease Brennen. He took it all in stride, joining in the laughter every now and then.

Handing Eric a soda, Garrick said, "I know what you can do. We'll let you be in charge of buying gifts. You know . . . a token of our appreciation. We can make it a special day for the women."

"What kind of gift?"

"What about perfume?" Laine suggested. "They all love perfume."

"I can handle that," Brennen stated.

"So when are we doing this?" Nyle asked. "I'm kind of in the doghouse with Brennen. Chandra just started talking to me this morning. Even then it's only short sentences."

Wrapping an arm around his baby brother, Laine said, "I feel for you, man. I just got out of the doghouse three weeks ago. Regis is talking to me, but she's still kind of cool at times."

Laughing, Ray shook his head. "Carrie and I are great. In fact, things couldn't be better," he bragged.

"Ray, did you pay Mikey's and Brigette's tuition last week?" Carrie asked from behind him. "I asked you to do it on Monday."

He turned, with a sheepish expression, to face her. "I forgot, honey. With everyth—" Ray began.

"Ray . . ." Carrie sighed and rolled her eyes heavenward. Folding her arms across her chest, she stated tersely, "*You're* paying the late fee." She turned on her heel and went back into the house without another word to him. However, they could hear her complaining to the other women.

Ray heard Carrie say something about his only remembering to play basketball. . . .

Turning back to the men, Ray asked, "How soon can we do this? I don't think next Sunday is soon enough." Shaking his head, he muttered a curse under his breath.

Eric patted him on the shoulder. "God be with you, man."

"Guess you won't be joining us on the court Saturday," Matt teased.

"You won't be there either," Kaitlin threw in. "You promised to take me to see the Dance Theater of Harlem ballet."

"Why don't you take one of your sisters?" he suggested.

"Because I want to go with you. We've already discussed this and I'm not going to let you back out now." Kaitlin sent him a look that brooked no argument.

Daisi stepped out onto the patio, prompting Garrick to say, "I guess I won't be playing ball either." He asked his wife, "Okay, what did I do?"

She stared at him in confusion. "Honey, what are you talking about? I just came out to let y'all know that everything is ready."

Eric burst into laughter.

CHAPTER 9

Eric left Riverside around six in the evening, heading home. When he arrived, he settled back into his favorite chair to relax. Spying a nearby photo album, he leaned forward to pick it up.

Turning the pages slowly, he stared like a zombie at the photos nestled on his lap. Family photographs, lots of them, that had been taken over the years. Malcolm's prom picture. Eric laughed. "Man, you thought you were so cool that night." Tracing the edge of the photo with his finger, he observed, "Look at you in that powder blue pimp suit. And check out that Afro. You worked so hard on that thing." He laughed so hard that tears formed in his eyes. "I've got to save this one for Crystal."

There was another. The day Malcolm graduated from Morehouse College in Atlanta, Georgia. Then another one. Here Malcolm stood, surrounded by their parents, Tina, Eric, and Angela, Malcolm's fiancée at the time. In this one he'd graduated from Howard University College of

Medicine. He and Angela were married a year later.

The next page was Malcolm and Angela's wedding. They were an attractive couple. Crystal had inherited the best qualities from both her parents.

As Eric peered through teary eyes at the photographs, he thanked God for the happiness they'd all shared throughout the years.

Malcolm lost Angela to cancer two years ago. After that, Eric persuaded Malcolm to sell his San Francisco medical practice and move to Los Angeles. He was a very successful plastic surgeon and had a beautiful office in Beverly Hills.

Eric let his tears flow. How he missed Malcolm and Angela. Losing them, he was minus a huge part of himself. Eric knew that it was only through God that he would manage to survive.

Now there was Kemba. Somehow she'd crept into his life. From the moment he'd laid eyes on her, Eric knew she was destined to fill some void in him. She may have been trying to steal a diamond, but she'd stolen something far richer: his heart.

Although Eric didn't believe in love at first sight, he had to admit that he and

Kemba shared a special connection. A bond that wouldn't be broken. Eric knew she felt it too. Each time they saw each other, an invisible thread bound them closer and closer together. They were in and of each other. But why? A contemplative frown furrowed Eric's brow. He hadn't felt this way in a long time. Not since Cheryl. He'd loved her beyond reason, but she was not his soul mate.

Although he was lonely at times, Eric did not actively pursue relationships with the opposite sex. He firmly believed that God would send his wife to him. However, there was no explaining that to Ida and Jennifer Whittaker.

Eric stretched out on his sofa, his mind still on Kemba. She'd made him realize that now he wanted to love again.

After Cheryl's betrayal, though most of his friends and family had encouraged him to start dating again, he hadn't felt any need to do so. Whether that was because of his own selectiveness or God's leading, he didn't know. Either way, as year followed year, as opportunity rose only to be ignored, Eric felt himself always holding back. He was thirty-eight, and up until the day he met Kemba, he had almost decided he would remain a bachelor.

Kemba Jennings intrigued him to the extreme. Something about her had called out across the years to that part of him long dormant and he had found himself at last willing to pursue a relationship. He admired her wit, her vulnerability and her determination.

Kemba woke up with beads of moisture covering her body, causing her thin nightgown to stick to her body. Chills ran through her body, causing her to shiver. Why on earth had she been dreaming about her father and the last time he'd sat her down to tell her about the diamond and her legacy? Her mother had come into the room interrupting them. Kemba recalled how angry she'd been.

A brother. Her father had a brother. Kemba remembered asking her mother about her African relatives when her father died. She wanted to know if they would be attending her father's funeral.

Sarah told her firmly that her father had no living relatives. None would be coming to bid farewell to her father. Once Kemba had overheard her father stating his wishes to be buried in his country. When she questioned Sarah about this, her mother grew very angry. Her maternal grandmother assured her that Sarah was upset because of her father's death. She admonished Kemba, saying she had to respect her mother's wishes. She wanted Molefi buried here in America. When Sarah died, she wished to be buried beside him.

Kemba attributed her inability to sleep to the events of the day: Malcolm's funeral and Eric's unexpected visit. She'd spent other sleepless nights thinking about everything that had transpired since Malcolm's death, not understanding any of it.

Nonetheless, she was convinced that the same person who had killed her father had also killed Malcolm. The intruder being African was her first clue. Deep down in her gut, she knew there was more to this, but what? Maybe the answer lay in Zimbabwe. Assuring herself that she would find out the truth, Kemba turned to her left side and tried to go back to sleep.

With sleep still eluding her, Kemba turned her thoughts to Sarah. In a few days her mother would have her first round of dialysis.

Memories of the day Dr. Wilson gave them the news that Sarah's condition had progressed to end-stage renal disease rushed to the forefront. Sarah had sat there calmly, saying nothing. Her mother seemed to just accept what they'd been told as if she'd been offered a cup of coffee. Kemba couldn't believe it. She half expected Sarah to break down once they were back in the familiar confines of Kemba's car, but she didn't.

Earlier tonight, she'd tried to get her mother to open up, but she wouldn't. Sarah said she was too tired and just wanted to go straight to bed. Kemba had cleaned the kitchen and then went home.

Half an hour later, she still tossed about, longing for sleep. Kemba had an early day tomorrow and wanted to be rested. When she closed her eyes, Eric Avery drifted to mind.

No one had piqued her interest since Carl. Once again she wondered what he did for a living. He didn't seem the lawyer or doctor type. Engineer? Hmmmm.

She fell asleep trying to guess Eric's occupation. Her last thought was that it was probably something she hadn't even considered.

Sipping a hot cup of coffee, Kemba sank down on the hospital bed. Running a nervous hand down her leg, she sighed impatiently. *I wish they would hurry up and bring you back, Mama.* September 8. Kemba was scared, but tried to hide it. She didn't want to upset her mother. She looked up just in time to get a glimpse of Eric as he passed by the room.

Hastily setting the cup down on the bedside table, Kemba rushed down the hall to catch up with him.

"Hi, Eric." She stuck her hands in her pockets to hide their trembling. "What are you doing here?" She couldn't imagine why he'd be at the Dialysis Treatment Center, of all places.

He initially seemed just as surprised to see her, but then his dark brown eyes softened. "Hello, Kemba. I'm here to pick up a church member." Two deep lines of worry appeared between his eyes. "What about you?"

"My mother is here. I think I told you that she has diabetes, didn't I?" When he nodded, she continued. "She's here for dialysis. Her kidneys are failing her." Just thinking about what her mother had to undergo made her shudder.

"I can tell this scares you, but we have to believe she'll be fine. I'll keep her in my prayers. As a matter of fact . . ."

It was then Kemba noticed the Bible he carried in his hand and the navy blue suit he wore. *Dressed like that,* Kemba thought, *he looks like a . . .*

"Hello, Pastor Avery," someone called out.

"Hello, Rose."

"P-pastor? *You're a minister?*" Kemba was shocked to the core. *He's a minister.* She leaned for support against the wall, feeling as if she would faint.

"Yes." Eric placed a steady hand on her arm. "You seem shocked by this. I thought you knew."

She shook her head. "I had no idea. You never mentioned it."

Eric seemed confused. "I thought . . ."

"No, I certainly would've remembered." She stood straighter, having finally regained her composure. "With everything that has happened, I guess we just never talked about what you did for a living. I meant to ask the day Malcolm died."

"I . . . Maybe you're right. We both had a lot on our minds."

Eyes darkened with emotion, Kemba's gaze fell to the floor. She couldn't let him see how upset she was over the revelation.

"I was about to say I'd like to stop by your mother's room to pray for her."

"She'll like that, Eric . . . er, Pastor."

He studied her, his gaze tracing the length of her face. "You can call me Eric. I don't mind."

"I-it doesn't seem right somehow. I'd better get back to my mother's room. She's probably back by now. She had to have some tests done."

"Which room is she in?"

"Room 5213B."

"I'll see you in a few minutes."

Not if I can help it, she thought to herself. *Oh, my God. I've been lusting after a minister. I'm hell-bound for sure,* she thought sadly. When Kemba entered the room, she found Sarah settling into the bed with the aid of a nurse. She looked up when Kemba entered the room.

"Honey, what's wrong?"

Shaking her head, Kemba answered, "Nothing. Why do you ask?"

"You look like you've just lost your best friend," Sarah observed.

She placed a hand over Kemba's. "Don't you worry 'bout me, child. I told you, I'm in the Lord's hands now. It's up to Him. What happens from now on."

Kemba's voice was shakier than she would've liked. "I don't want to lose you, Mama. You're all I have."

"What's come over you, child?"

"Nothing, Mama," she responded.

Sarah studied Kemba's face for the truth. "You sure?"

"Mama, Eric, I mean Pastor Avery, is going to stop by to pray with you. I told him it was okay, that you'd like that."

"Pastor Avery? Isn't he the one whose brother just recently died?"

Kemba cast her eyes downward. "He's the one."

Sarah's eyes sparkled. "I see. You never mentioned him being a minister."

"That's because I just found out a few minutes ago," she responded dryly.

"I see. Are you disappointed?"

Kemba's head snapped up. "Disappointed? Why should I be disappointed?"

"I have a feeling you're sweet on him."

Sweet on him. Kemba frowned in disagreement, her delicate brows furrowing. "Mama, where in the world did you come up with that phrase? It sounds so old-fashioned."

"Well, are you?" Sarah persisted.

"No, Mama, I'm not *sweet on him*. Now just lay back and rest for a while. They are going to start your treatment soon." Kemba paced the room impatiently. She wanted to get out before Eric arrived. Taking her cell phone out of her purse, Kemba stated, "Mama, I need to make a couple of phone calls. I'll be right back, okay?"

"Take your time, baby. I'm not sure how

long this is going to take."

"I won't be long," Kemba promised. *Just long enough to avoid Pastor Eric Avery,* she added silently.

Eric knocked on the hospital door before entering. Coming fully into the room, he quickly scanned the midsize cubicle for Kemba. Finding a thin woman alone in the room, he introduced himself. "Hello, Mrs. Jennings. I'm Eric Avery."

Sarah sat up, propped against a couple of pillows. She fingered the brightly colored scarf fashionably tied on her head. "Ah, you must be Pastor Avery. Come on in. My daughter told me you'd be stopping by. It's real nice to meet you. Kemba's told me quite a lot about you."

His eyebrows sprang up in surprise. "Where is Kemba? I thought she'd still be here."

"She needed to make a few calls. Please, Pastor, have a seat. You won't grow no taller by standing up."

Eric chuckled lightheartedly, but Sarah could read his disappointment. It showed in his eyes. Sitting in the visitor's chair beside her bed, he said, "Well, the main reason I came by is to see you."

"That's wonderful."

Placing her hand gently in his, heads bowed, they prayed together.

Sarah smiled when he was done. "Thank you for coming by to see me and praying for me. I enjoyed meeting you. If you have a few minutes, I'd like to talk to you. It's about my daughter."

"Sure, I have nothing pressing right now." He wanted to learn more about Kemba.

"I want you to know something. Kemba had nothing to do with your brother's death. She's headstrong —"

Eric held up a hand. "Mrs. Jennings, I don't believe she did. But the fact of the matter is, Kemba did break into my brother's house. She should have tried talking to Malcolm. He wasn't an unreasonable man. However, I doubt if it would've changed the outcome."

Sarah sighed. "She knows she was wrong. She's got it in her head that that diamond is going to make us rich, that it's ours, but it's not. That stone will only bring us grief. Look what happened to her father and your poor brother."

Eric tilted his head in curiosity. "Why is this diamond so important, besides the fact that it's worth a lot of money? Somehow I get the feeling it's not just about money."

Sarah's fingers fumbled with the satin ribbons on her robe. "The stone is called the Dumisani Diamond — Dumisani means 'Herald of the Future.'" Sarah snorted. "*Some future.* It's been in the Rufaro family for generations, passed down to the eldest son. Molefi, Kemba's father, is the firstborn to Hondo Rufaro. Hondo's other sons, except for Bekitemba, were enraged when Molefi was given the stone. When he decided to come to America with me, they accused him of turning his back on the family. What they wanted was for him to return the stone to the family."

"So, you think his own brothers are responsible for his murder?"

She nodded. "This stone has been dipped in blood. Molefi and your brother's blood. It is a blood stone all right."

"Has there since been any contact with his family?"

Sarah was quiet for a moment. "No . . . they never liked me. Always considered me a *vatorwa,* it means a 'foreigner.' After Molefi died, I saw no reason to maintain a relationship with them. He and I originally decided when we came to America to tell Kemba that he had no living relatives. She knows nothing of them. When Molefi died,

I sold everything and moved to Phoenix, Arizona. Shortly after that, I married the first man who asked me and had him adopt Kemba. I wanted to disappear so they would never find us. That man was George Jennings and he died three years ago."

Sensing her sadness, Eric said, "I'm sorry."

Sarah peered at Eric through tear-bright eyes. "I miss George. He was a good man, Pastor. He loved me. Loved me, even though he knew I still loved and mourned Molefi. He and Molefi were good friends, you know."

"How much of this does Kemba know?"

"None of it. She wouldn't even have known of that cursed diamond if Molefi had listened to me. I wanted him to leave it in Africa — just give it back to his brothers. If he had, Molefi probably still would be alive." Tears spilled from her eyes. Sarah put trembling hands to her face to hide her crying.

"Mrs. Jennings . . ." Eric took a handkerchief out of his pocket and handed it to her.

She wiped her face. "I'm fine now, thank you." Gesturing with the cotton handkerchief, she said, "I'll have Kemba

144

return this to you . . . after we clean it. I shouldn't have gone on so. I'm sorry."

"It's all right. I sensed you needed someone to talk to."

"It's been . . . a heavy burden. I just wish Kemba wouldn't wish so much for wealth. Being rich doesn't make one happy. True treasure is of the heart. To love and be loved. Now, that's worth more than all the money in the world."

"I think your daughter will have to come to that conclusion on her own."

Sarah sighed. "You're probably right, Pastor Avery."

He stood up. "It's been very nice to meet you, Mrs. Jennings." Eric handed her a business card.

"Call me Sarah. And thank you so much for stopping by."

Eric made his way slowly to the door. "I'll keep you in my prayers. I'll stop by tomorrow if you're up for visitors."

"I look forward to seeing you again, Pastor." Sarah studied his handsome face. Obviously pleased with what she found there, she nodded. "My daughter is a good girl, Pastor. She never meant for anyone to get hurt. It's important that you understand why she did what she did. Her father made her promise to keep the Dumisani Diamond and the house in our family for generation after generation. She was a small child — he shouldn't have done that."

"I guess I can make some sense out of her determination." He came to a halt near the door. Turning back around, Eric pointed his Bible toward her. "You have my card, Mrs. Jennings. Call me if you ever need to talk."

Eric was about to leave the room when Kemba appeared in the doorway.

"You're leaving?" she asked.

He nodded. "I'm glad to see you, though. There's something I'd like to ask you."

Kemba couldn't hide her curiosity. "What is it?"

"I'd like to take you with me to Riverside. Ray and his family have these great Sunday dinners and I'd like you to join me. Besides, Jillian really wants to get to know you."

"You're sure about this?"

"Yes, I am," Eric replied. "I would really like for you to get to know them."

She looked past him to her mother, who was grinning from ear to ear. Kemba smiled, then said, "I'd love to go. Thank you for asking me."

After making arrangements for the coming Sunday, Eric took his leave.

CHAPTER 10

"You can stop grinning, Mama. It's not what you're thinking."

"Since when is a date not a date?"

Kemba stared out of Sarah's hospital window. She didn't have an answer for her mother.

Kemba muttered curses all the way to her office. *He's a man of God.* She had to ask herself: What in the world could she be thinking? What did she expect to gain from this man? Kemba had a strong feeling that Eric was interested in her, but how far would he go with his pursuit? Would it be a hidden passion? If he happened to fall in love with her, would it remain unspoken? He was a man of honor, a man who taught and lived by the Bible. He wouldn't break the Ten Commandments to be with someone like her. Kemba could not allow herself to be involved emotionally with Eric Avery. She would have to deny her attraction to the man. She could not afford another heartbreak.

She pulled into the parking lot, tires

screeching loudly. Kemba rushed into her office, just missing a phone call by seconds. "Darn it."

"Slow down, girlfriend. Whoever it is will call back, I assure you," Antoinette stated while strolling out of her office, to the coffee station. In her hand she carried what looked like a contract. "I couldn't get it because I was on another line."

Kemba swallowed the scream that formed in her throat. *"Antoinette.* You scared the daylights out of me. I didn't know you were here."

"I've been here since seven-thirty this morning."

She waited for her heartbeat to return to normal before speaking. "Why so early?"

"I had a dinner meeting with the president of Chadwick Enterprises last night." She held up what looked like a contract. "We've been commissioned to decorate his offices. *All six of them.*"

Kemba's mouth dropped wide open. "Are you serious? He gave us the contract?"

Antoinette nodded, her hazel eyes bright with merriment. "He sure did. Distinctive Interior Design is on the map. We're moving right on up, girlfriend."

Kemba placed her hand on her chest. *"I can't believe it."*

"Believe it." She handed Kemba the signed contract. "Why don't we celebrate by going to dinner tonight?"

Kemba looked up from the contract. "Antoinette, honey." She paused a heartbeat before asking, "You didn't have to do anything to get this contract, right?"

"Like what?"

"You didn't sleep with him, did you?"

"No. He wanted me to, but I didn't."

Kemba released the breath she was holding. "That's good to hear." She loved Antoinette dearly, but the woman would sleep with just about any member of the male species. She didn't hide the fact that she was comfortable in her sexuality.

"So, Kim, are we going to dinner? I want to celebrate. This is our biggest contract ever."

"What about Michael? No date tonight?"

Antoinette's long, curly tendrils swung in motion as she shook her head. "Naw, I don't have a date with Michael tonight. Girlfriend, I need a break."

"I imagine you do. You've what? Seen him every night for the last three weeks." She opened the door to her office and walked in, turning on the lights.

Antoinette followed her inside. "What

can I say? He's a great guy. I enjoy being with him."

Kemba observed her friend's face and found euphoria written all over it. "I'm very happy for you, Antoinette. I really am."

"So what do you say? Are we on for dinner tonight?"

Shrugging, Kemba agreed. "I guess so. It's not like I have anything else to do." She sank down slowly in her leather chair.

Antoinette sat down on the arm of the green leather couch, crossing her legs. "What's wrong, Kim? You look upset." She ran her hand through her curly locks.

"Nothing," Kemba mumbled as she fingered her necklace.

"Come on, girlfriend. Something's got you down. What is it?"

Kemba drew an invisible pattern on her desk. "I met someone. I like him a lot."

Antoinette's green eyes shot up in surprise. "*Really?* That's great —"

Kemba shook her head sadly. A pain squeezed her heart as she thought of Eric and how nothing could ever come of their mutual attraction.

"That's not great? Why not?"

"I like him a lot but I know we have no future together." The thought brought

Kemba profound sadness.

Antoinette tilted her head in curiosity. "Is he married? Don't tell me he's married." She shook her head in disbelief. "I know you would never fall for a married man."

"He's not married."

"Well, how does he feel about you? Do you have any idea?"

"That's the hard part." Kemba paused and continued in sinking tones. "I think he likes me too."

"Then what's the problem?"

Kemba settled back in her chair. She folded her arms across her chest and said, "He's a minister."

"What's wrong with that? Kim, listen to me. Just take it one day at a time."

"I don't know if I have the energy for all this. Carl's death nearly destroyed me, Antoinette." Kemba's heart constricted with pain. "I don't want to talk about this anymore," Kemba stated. "Let's see those sketches for Chadwick."

"Sure." Antoinette clearly didn't want to drop it but did so reluctantly. "Let me go get them out of my office. I'll be right back."

As soon as her partner left her office, Kemba closed her eyes and visualized Eric. She would allow herself this one fantasy and then she would have to forget about him in that way. Kemba began to question her decision about going to Riverside with Eric. She didn't deserve a man like him. Not after what she'd done.

But even though she felt this way, Kemba didn't want to miss out on spending time with Eric and his family. She rationalized that there would be no harm in being his friend. She could manage that, she told herself. They would simply become good friends — nothing more.

Eric's mind was consumed with the beautiful woman who had suddenly appeared in his life. Kemba Rufaro Jennings. If what her mother had told him was really the truth, then Kemba's life could be in danger too.

But what could he do? Could the Rufaro family be responsible for Malcolm's and Molefi's death as Sarah believed? Eric recalled Crystal saying the man talked funny. *Hmmmm,* he wondered. *Could* . . . Eric let the thought drift. Kemba said the man had an African accent.

He debated whether or not he should tell Kemba what he and Sarah discussed. Even if he did, what good would it do? The man was probably long gone by now. But then he didn't have what he'd killed twice for. Eric wanted to protect Kemba and Crystal; so for now, he decided to keep quiet.

Eric glanced up at a photograph on the wall. It was a picture of him in a military uniform. When he retired from the marines, Eric vowed never to pick up another gun. Unless his life or the life of someone he loved was in danger. He had a feeling they were all in danger.

Eric arrived promptly at two o'clock on Sunday. Kemba was ready and met him at the door. He complimented her as they walked to the car, and Eric made sure to open the door for her. He really wanted to make an impression on Kemba. Noting the flowers in her hands, he questioned, "Are those for me?"

Smiling, Kemba shook her head no. "These are for your aunt. This is my way of saying thanks for allowing me to join you all for dinner."

He was captivated by her smile. Eric forced himself to pay attention to the road. "You are a very caring person."

"I'm glad you think so."

"How is your mother handling dialysis?"

"Okay, I guess," Kemba responded.

"She's never been one to complain. Whenever I ask her if she's okay, she just smiles and says that she's fine."

Eric nodded in understanding. "My grandmother was like that. She never complained of anything. She died when I was in college. It shocked me because I never knew her to be sick. She had breast cancer."

"There are times I wish I were more like my mom." Kemba stared out the car window. "I haven't been to Riverside in a while."

"I've been coming out here a lot more since Malcolm's death. I guess I just need to be around family."

"That makes sense to me."

He glanced her way. "Do I make you nervous?"

Kemba stared at her hands. "Right now I'm very embarrassed."

"Kemba, you shouldn't be. . . ."

"It's not your fault. I just didn't know you were a minister and I feel foolish."

"Why?"

She chuckled. "I'd rather not say," Kemba confessed.

"I see."

Kemba laughed again. This time Eric joined her.

"Does it bother you?"

"Truthfully, I'm not sure how I feel about it. I need some time."

"What I would like is for us to get to know one another. I don't want you having any preconceived notions about me or what I do — in return, I won't do the same."

"Fair enough," Kemba responded.

They pulled up in front of a beautiful two-story house with a broad porch that ran the length of the house. In one corner sat two Philadelphia Windsor armchairs. Two very beautiful Boston ferns adorned both sides of the front door.

Eric opened the car door for Kemba. A car pulled in front of them and parked. He waved and said, "There's Ray and his family."

Kemba stood beside Eric. "His children are beautiful. Oh, Eric, they are a very attractive family." Turning to face him, she asked, "He's the U.S. marshal, right?"

"Yes. I'm glad you came with me because this gives you a chance to talk with him."

"About what?"

"I think it's a good idea for Ray to know everything. He should know about your father, the diamond — everything. Kemba, you could be in serious danger."

"Whoever killed my father and Malcolm doesn't know about me."

"We can't be certain of that."

Eric debated over whether or not he should tell Kemba what Sarah had disclosed to him. That Kemba was in danger from relatives she didn't even know she had. He decided to wait until it was absolutely necessary.

"What if he arrests me, Eric? I can't go to jail. Mama needs me." Kemba couldn't keep the panic out of her voice.

She greeted Ray when he joined them.

"Hello, Ms. Jennings. Good to see you again."

"You too." Kemba glanced up at Eric. He gave her a reassuring smile.

"Why don't we go inside so that I can introduce you to the rest of the family," Eric suggested.

Kemba nodded.

Ray broke into a short laugh. "It's okay, Kemba. We really don't bite."

"I'm okay," she uttered softly.

"Laine and Regis brought the gumbo with them," Ray was saying. "I made it yesterday. Carrie wanted to do a taste test but I wouldn't let her. It should be good because I followed Matt's recipe to the letter."

"That's good. Here is the chicken. I made it this morning."

Kemba looked from one man to the other. "I'm getting the impression that this is not a regular Sunday dinner."

"The men are cooking today," Eric announced.

Kemba stopped walking. "And you decided to bring me out here today of all days?"

"I wanted to impress you."

Ray threw back his head in laughter.

"Is there something I should know?" Kemba asked. She couldn't help grinning.

"Actually, Eric is a good cook. He makes the best barbecued chicken in Los Angeles."

As soon as she walked into the house, Jillian greeted her with a hug. "Kemba, it's good to see you. I'm so glad you came."

"Thank you for having me." Holding out the bouquet of flowers, she inquired, "Where is your mother? I brought these for her."

"I'm right here," said a voice from behind Jillian. Amanda walked to Kemba with the aid of a quad cane. "I'm Amanda Ransom. You must be Kemba. I've been hearing a lot about you."

Kemba stole a peek across her shoulder. "You have?"

"It's wonderful to meet you finally. Please make yourself at home."

"I brought these for you, Mrs. Ransom."

"Thank you, dear." Amanda held the flowers up to her nose. "They smell heavenly."

Jillian took Kemba around the house, introducing her to everyone, while Eric remained downstairs with the men. They were in the kitchen preparing the finishing touches to dinner.

"Do we have everything?" Laine asked.

Matt glanced around the kitchen. "I think so."

"Where's Brennen?" Nyle questioned. "He's supposed to bring the gifts." He checked his watch.

Garrick strolled over to the refrigerator. "He called a few minutes ago. They should be here in about ten minutes. They got caught behind a car accident."

Ray went to the dining room to help his son set the table. Matt and Eric prepared the dinner rolls and set them in the oven to warm. Nyle and Laine filled glasses with iced tea, while Garrick made sure everything was in place for the children. They would be eating on tables set up just for them in the family room and breakfast nook. Jillian's husband went to assist Ray.

Allura's husband gathered the children together and led them to the bathroom to wash up for dinner.

When Eric went to the living room, he found all the women sitting around looking as if they'd been caught with their hands in the cookie jar. Even Kemba couldn't hide her giggles.

"I know you all have been talking about us, but as soon as you eat, you're not going to laugh long. We did well."

Brennen and Elle arrived with the twins. "I'm sorry we're late," they said in unison.

Soon everyone gathered around the dining-room table and the long table that had been added just for dinner. Kemba was seated right next to Eric.

Laine stood up and said, "Ladies, this dinner is dedicated to all of you. This is a token of our affection for you. We want you all to know how much we love each and every one of you."

His wife broke into a smile. "You are so sweet, honey." Regis rose to her feet and gave him a kiss. "I'm sure we're going to love dinner." Turning to face everyone, she added, "Laine has worked so hard to prepare his share of the meal."

"So has Nyle," his wife acknowledged. "I don't remember ever seeing him in the kitchen cooking, until this morning." Grinning, Chandra stated, "I like it."

Brennen walked into the room carrying gifts. Matt followed behind with an arm-load of presents as well.

"What's all this?" Amanda asked.

"A 'get out of the doghouse' dinner," Ivy joked. "You guys are so transparent."

Ray glared at her.

Kemba looked over at Eric and whispered, "Are you in the doghouse too?"

"No, I don't think so. This is my 'get out of the doghouse' card."

Laughing, Kemba reached for her iced tea.

Brennen spoke up. "In honor of my wife and the other women in the house, we had perfumes made especially for you —"

"We did?" Several of the men interrupted.

"We did," Brennen confirmed. "Cunningham Lake Cosmetics created a special scent for each woman. The bottles will all bear your names."

A flutter of excitement erupted into loud squeals of delight as the women opened their gifts.

"Dear heart, this smells wonderful," Ivy stated. "I love it."

Kemba's mouth dropped open in her surprise. "There's one for me?"

Eric nodded.

"Thank you." She tore open the gift with relish. A perfume named after her. She could hardly believe it. Kemba dabbed a little on her arm and sniffed. It wasn't a fruity scent — instead, it reminded her of jasmine and roses with a touch of musk.

"Honey, this smells heavenly," Elle murmured. "You didn't forget how much I love orange blossoms and tangerine scents. It's light . . . not overbearing at all."

The women sat around the table enjoying their perfumes while the men high-fived one another before heading to the kitchen to bring out dinner.

Kemba set her bottle of perfume in front of her.

"You like it?" Eric asked.

"I love it. Thank you so much for bringing me out here and sharing your family with me like this."

"The next time we'll have to bring your mother."

"She would love it."

Conversation died down while everyone concentrated on his or her food. Ivy was the first one to speak. "I have to tell you . . . the food is delicious."

"Yes, it is," Carrie agreed. "The guys did a fabulous job, don't you think, Mother Ransom?"

Amanda nodded. "I'm proud of you all." Picking up her knife, she added, "I expect to see more of this in the future."

"I think the men should cook the Thanksgiving dinner this year," Jillian suggested.

"No," Ray, Matt and Nyle replied in unison.

Kemba and Eric broke into laughter. For dessert there was chocolate cake, carrot cake and sweet potato pie. Kemba and Eric both decided on the carrot cake. Afterward he took her to the patio. Ray joined them a few minutes later.

Eric held out a chair for her and she sank down in it nervously. Ray and Eric seated themselves.

"Kemba, I have some questions, and I apologize if I'm putting you on the spot, but I really would like to be able to make sense of what really happened to Malcolm. Eric tells me there's more to the story."

Eric's gaze met hers. Taking a deep breath, Kemba sat up straight. She took another deep breath. "My full name is Kemba Rufaro Jennings. Molefi Rufaro was my father." She paused to let this sink in. "He was murdered twenty years ago in the house in Brentwood. . . . Ray, I believe the same man murdered my father and Eric's brother."

Ray glanced from one to the other. "And you think it's because of the diamond Malcolm found?"

"The stone is the Dumisani Diamond," Kemba stated quietly.

"The what?"

"The Dumisani Diamond. It's been in my family for years. I've been afraid to tell the police all of this because I thought they'd try to implicate me in Malcolm's murder. I was scared."

"Kemba, you have to tell the detectives everything," Ray stated matter-of-factly. "The police have evidence that someone broke into the house."

"I didn't have to break in. I had a key."

"So you knew all this time that the diamond belonged to your family?"

"Yes," she admitted. "It had been lost to my family for years. It was only after I started working on the house that Malcolm found the diamond. I will confess that I wanted to try to find the diamond myself."

"When Malcolm found the stone, did you go talk to him?"

Kemba shook her head. "I didn't think he would believe me."

"It would have been pretty easy to verify," Ray stated.

"To be honest, I wasn't so sure Malcolm

was honorable. For all I knew, he could have been greedy."

"He wasn't like that," Eric told her.

"But I didn't know that for sure back then. I need you both to understand something. The Dumisani Diamond is my legacy. My father made sure I knew our lineage and our history. He made me promise to keep the diamond and the house in our family. I failed him with the house — I'm not going to fail him again. However, I'm inclined to agree with my mother. Two men have died because of it. Now I want to know what person is responsible and what his connection is to the diamond."

Ray nodded in agreement. "I think that's something we all want to find out."

"I'm going to find out," Kemba promised. "I owe it to Malcolm and my father."

Kemba waved to Eric as he drove away. She had really enjoyed herself with his family. She had fallen in love with the Ransom family. Recalling their teasing and engaging conversations brought a smile to her lips. *I wish I'd been born into a large family like that,* she thought. Kemba hungered to be surrounded by family members. She'd been an only child, and although she knew many of her relatives on her mother's side, she didn't know anyone on her father's.

Wrapping her arms around her waist, Kemba whispered, "I miss you so much, Papa. You too, Dad. I miss you both."

Her eyes filled with tears. "I'm sorry I let you down, Papa. I never wanted to, but it just couldn't be helped. I'm so sorry." Kemba wiped her face with the back of her hand. "I'm going to make this right. It's for you, Papa, and for Malcolm."

CHAPTER 11

The following week, Kemba escorted Sarah into the apartment, saying, "Your bed's all ready, Mama. I'm going to put you in it so you can take it easy. I'm going to stay here with you for a while."

Sarah waved her hand. "Child, you're going to wear yourself down. Claire and I —"

"No," Kemba interrupted. "You're not feeling well, so I'm going to stay here with you. *End of argument.* Antoinette and Joyce can handle everything at the office."

In the bedroom she helped Sarah into bed. Pulling the covers around her mother, she asked, "Are you comfortable?"

Sarah bobbed her head up and down. "I'm fine, dear. Just a little tired."

"You go on and take a nap. I'll be out in the dining room working. Call me if you need something." Kemba pointed to a pitcher and a couple of glasses on a tray nearby. "I've already placed some water in here." She pulled the serving cart closer to the left side of the bed. "If you can't pour

— don't try. Just call me. Okay?"

Sarah smiled. "I guess you thought of everything."

"I hope so. I just want you to get well. I'm going to do whatever I can to help."

"I couldn't be richer. Having such a wonderful girl like you for a daughter. And that nice Pastor Avery praying for me like that. I'm so glad he took you with him to get to know his family. He cares for you, you know. For me too. He's called twice to check on me. Such a nice young man, he is."

Kemba grinned. "Yes, he's very nice." She fluffed Sarah's pillows and made sure she was comfortable. "I still can't believe he had a perfume created for me. He hardly knows me."

Sarah chuckled. "I think that's the point. He wants to get to know you, sweetie."

"I'm not going to get too excited. I'm going to take one day at a time where Eric is concerned. Right now all I want to do is concentrate on you."

"I don't know what I'd do without you, child. You've made me so proud of you all these years."

Kemba leaned down to place a kiss on her mother's forehead. "Thank you for saying that, Mama."

"Well, you are very dear to me. I want you to know that." Sarah yawned. "I guess I'm more tired than I thought. I wear out so easily."

"Just close your eyes and get some rest. I'll be right downstairs in the dining room." She closed the door halfway and navigated to the dining area.

From a box she'd brought over last night, Kemba spread mail, wallpaper samples and catalogs over the table. After separating the mail into three stacks, ranging from important to junk, she set about opening the ones considered a priority.

An hour later, she stretched, raising her hands to the air. She stood up and took the stairs two at a time. Kemba checked on Sarah and found her sleeping peacefully. Satisfied, she crept back downstairs to the dining room. She was about to take a seat when she heard a knock on the door. Peeking out the peephole, Kemba spotted Eric. She opened the door as quietly as she could.

"Hi, Pastor. Come on in," Kemba's dark chocolate brown gaze devoured the sight of him hungrily. It was all she could do to keep from throwing her arms around him and telling him how glad she was to see him.

"How are you?" he asked.

"A little exhausted, but other than that, I'm fine. Mom's really knocked out. How about you? And Crystal?"

"She's doing good. Started a new school and she's made some friends. . . ."

"Pastor?"

"Please call me Eric."

Taking a deep, unsteady breath, she stepped back. "What's wrong?"

"What?"

"I asked what's wrong. You look kind of sad. Is it Crystal?"

He nodded. "She wants to come back to Los Angeles. She wants to live with me."

Kemba looked up at Eric, her eyebrows drawn together quizzically. "But don't you want that too?"

"Yes, I do. I think it'll have to wait for a while, though. She needs a woman in her life."

"So, you want to be married first?"

"Yes."

"It makes sense. Have you someone in mind?" Kemba could have strangled herself. "I'm sorry, it's none of my business."

He laughed. "It's fine. As a matter of fact, I do have someone in mind. For the moment I'll have to see just how far things progress."

"I see." She forced herself to keep her

169

composure. Kemba did not want Eric to see that she was filled with disappointment. Of course, he'd have a girlfriend. She should have figured that out already.

". . . and she played the part of Grumpy," Eric was saying.

"Who?"

"Crystal. She had a part in her school play."

"Grumpy. One of the seven dwarfs."

Eric nodded. "My sister said she was great."

"I'm sure. It sounds like you and Crystal are very close."

He nodded a second time. "We've always been close. Since her mother died. I love her like my own child."

"I can tell. She's very easy to love. But then, I'm crazy about children. Sometimes I wish I'd become a teacher or something."

"I overheard you telling Jillian that you used to teach an art class at the Y. Why did you stop?"

"I stopped so that I could spend more time with my mother. That was around the time I noticed her condition was starting to deteriorate."

"I see. I was thinking about doing something like that at the church. Do you think you'd be interested?"

Kemba broke into a big grin. "It's something I'd definitely give some thought to. What age group are you talking about?"

"Actually, I was thinking about all ages. Splitting them up into various age groups. Preschoolers, kindergarten —"

"Well, I have some ideas on that. Let me think it over and I'll submit a tentative schedule of classes to you."

"Sounds good."

Eric checked his watch. "I guess I'd better go. Would you tell Mrs. Jennings that I came by?"

She escorted him to the door. "I sure will. Thank you for stopping by. I know she would've wanted to see you, but she was so exhausted when we came home."

"I'll give her a call later," Eric promised.

"Well, I'm not going to detain you. I'll be sure to tell her that you dropped by."

Eric reached over, hugging her. "It's good to see you, Kemba."

"You too."

"I know you're not about to leave," Sarah called from the top of the stairs. "I thought I heard your voice."

"*Mama.* What are you doing out of bed?" Kemba ran up the stairs.

Sarah waved her away as she slowly made her way down and over to the sofa.

"Baby, I'm not an invalid. I'm not ready to run the hundred-mile race, but I can walk from my bedroom and downstairs to my living room."

"Mama —"

"Kemba, I'm fine. I'm going to sit right here on the sofa and say a few words to Pastor." She grimaced in pain as she settled back into the chair. "Have time to talk to an old woman?"

He grinned. "I don't know about an old woman, but I'll always have time for you."

"Awww, come on now. You're just fooling with me," Sarah said, blushing.

Eric sank down on the sofa beside her. Kemba listened to the exchange between him and her mother. She was pleased to see how well the two of them got along.

Pushing herself to a standing position, she announced, "I'm going to go start dinner. You two talk. Can I bring either of you something to drink?"

"I'm fine, dear. Pastor?"

"Nothing for me, thank you."

She watched Eric from the kitchen. Each time she saw him, he pulled her more and more into his web. It had been a long time since she'd felt this giddy over a man.

Eric looked up to catch her staring at him. Embarrassed, Kemba smiled. When he smiled in return, she thought she would melt away right then and there. The sly grin Sarah gave her forced her feet to remain on the ground. Taking a deep breath to control her excited nerves, Kemba rejoined them in the living room.

When Eric rose to leave, Kemba wanted to ask him to stay for a few minutes more, but she controlled her urge. She walked him to the door. They embraced once more and he left.

"You're so sweet on him, you can't stand yourself," Sarah announced.

"Mama."

"Well, you are. I can see it. No need to be ashamed of it. I was that way when I met your father. Lord, that man surely swept me off my feet. Yes, he reminds me a lot of Molefi. The right kind of man."

Kemba sat on the floor, hugging her knees to herself. "You miss him a lot, don't you?"

"Honey, every night I go to bed, I thank the Lord for bringing him into my life. Even since he's been gone, I still do. George was good to me, but we were friends. Two lonely friends."

"That's the kind of love I want. Like you and Papa had." Kemba smiled. "Eric is such a sweetheart. I can't wait for you to meet his aunt. You'd really like her."

"I can see you having it with Pastor Eric. My eyes don't ever fail me. You two are falling in love."

"Mama . . . I think that he may have already found someone he's interested in. We're just friends."

Sarah looked surprised. "Did he tell you that?"

"In a way. He didn't really come right out with it — just hinted at it."

"How do you know it's not you?" Sarah questioned.

"Because he didn't say it was."

"Did he tell you who this woman is?"

Kemba shook her head. "Well, no."

"Humph! I don't have no more to say about it."

Kemba laughed. "Come on, Mama, let's get you back into bed."

"No, let me sit out here with you. We can have dinner together in front of the television."

"Well, then, you get comfortable here on the sofa. Dinner should be ready in another thirty minutes. Speaking of which, I'd better go check on the chicken." Kemba rose to her feet.

Forty-five minutes later, they sat in front of the television eating dinner and arguing over what to watch.

"Talk to Kemba lately?" Jillian inquired over lunch.

Eric smiled. "As a matter of fact, I have. I saw her yesterday."

"Really? You seem to be spending quite a bit of time together."

"What of it?"

"You're attracted to her, aren't you? I mean, you brought her to Mom's house and you had Brennen create a perfume for her. Wow."

He gave a slight nod. "It's really the last thing I expected. I didn't want to like her after Malcolm's death, but something draws me to her."

"Are you going to pursue a relationship with Kemba?"

"I don't know," Eric answered honestly. "I think she has a problem with what I do." Frowning, he added, "It reminds me of Cheryl."

"I don't know much about Kemba, but I doubt she's anything like Cheryl. That woman was all about money. If you'd chosen to stay in law school — she would've married you, Eric."

"I know."

"Do you regret it? Not becoming a lawyer, I mean?"

"No," Eric replied. "I think if I hadn't dropped out of law school, I would have regretted becoming a lawyer. The call of God was in my heart too great."

"You are a phenomenal minister, Eric."

"Thanks, cuz. Sometimes it's good to hear it."

"How is Miz Whittaker? Still chasing after you?"

Eric released a slight groan as he reached for his water glass.

"You know you're much too nice. You're going to have to spell it out for her."

"I don't want to hurt her feelings, Jillian. She's a nice woman, but I only think of her as a friend."

Slicing off a piece of her fish, Jillian responded, "Then tell her that. You don't want to mislead her in any way. Especially if you're interested in Kemba. You don't want any drama."

"You're right about that."

"Just be honest with Jennifer."

Eric tasted his chicken. "I will." He took another bite and chewed thoughtfully.

Jillian lapsed into a story about Elle's twins. Soon she and Eric were laughing and discussing the joys of parenting.

"You are going to make a great father, Eric."

"I'm looking forward to it," he confessed. "For a while I was beginning to think that I would never marry. I was actually considering adoption."

Jillian finished her glass of water, then signaled the waiter for more. She asked Eric, "Does this mean you're having second thoughts?"

He nodded.

Grinning, Jillian asked, "Now, this wouldn't have anything to do with a certain young lady by the name of Kemba, would it?"

Eric met her gaze. "What would you say if I told you it did?"

"The preacher and the jewel thief," she murmured with a smile. "It has a certain irony, don't you think?"

"Kemba is not a thief."

"I know that." Jillian reached for her water glass. "I just couldn't resist."

Eric finished off the last of his meat loaf. "Ever since I met her, I've been drawn to her, Jillian. I keep telling myself that I need to proceed with caution."

"Taking it slow is a good thing, Eric. I like this girl, but if she hurts you, I have to confess — I'm going to lose all religion. I'm giving Kemba the benefit of the doubt."

"She's good people."

When Jillian finished her meal, Eric asked for the check.

She waved away his money. "This is my treat, cuz. I invited you out to lunch, remember?"

"Next time is on me," Eric stated.

Jillian and Eric left the restaurant and walked to their cars. She waved from her Explorer as she drove out of the parking lot.

Eric wondered during the drive home if Kemba had any clue of his feelings for her. It was getting harder for him to keep his emotions in check whenever he was around her. He wondered, if he exposed his feelings to her, how would she react to them? Did she feel the same way too? In his heart he believed she did.

He constantly thought of her. Even now he missed talking to her. Eric longed to re-capture the rapport they had shared briefly.

At home Eric headed into his garage to lift weights. He worked out for the next hour, trying to keep his mind off Kemba. Every time he closed his eyes, he could see her wide eyes and kissable lips beckoning to him. After a cold but soothing shower, he settled in front of the television with a can of soda.

Later that evening, Eric made his way to his bed. As he waited for sleep to claim him, visions of the dark beauty with her sparkling brown eyes and full, sensual lips played havoc provocatively through his weary mind. Somehow this woman who had come so unexpectedly into his life had a hold on him, which he could not shake.

Eric punched his pillow, frustrated over not being able to free himself of the erotic pictures in his head. Pictures of Kemba in his bed. Pictures of the two of them together. He squeezed his eyes shut, hoping to block the visions. He admonished himself for fantasizing about Kemba in that way.

"It's been a long time since I've been with a woman," he muttered. "This is normal. I've just never wanted anybody the way I want Kemba." Eric continued to rationalize aloud. "I'm not going to let this get out of control." He was determined to keep a rein on his passions.

Right now he had to concentrate on keeping her safe. He was sure that the person who killed his brother and her father was still around — poised to strike. But he wondered how Kemba would be affected, if indeed it was her relative. In the short time he'd come to know her, he knew family loyalty meant a lot to her.

Kemba read all the information she'd been given on dialysis. She was interested in the home dialysis training and support program. She also read up on kidney transplants. Kemba prayed that her mother wouldn't need one, but deep down she knew the request was in vain. The doctor had said as much.

Eric's face came to her as she settled back for a short nap. He was such a sweet and caring person. Kemba really liked him. She liked him a lot. After Carl's death, Kemba wasn't sure she would ever have deep feelings for anyone again.

The man was a minister, her brain reminded her. However, her heart didn't seem to mind. *What do I do?* she wondered. *I can't even seem to stay away from him.*

Kemba picked up another pamphlet and tried to concentrate on what she was reading. This one was from the American Diabetes Association. She planned to become an expert on diabetes.

CHAPTER 12

Kemba and Antoinette followed the hostess to their table. When they were seated, Kemba said, "Thanks for taking me out to dinner. I wasn't looking forward to cooking. I haven't eaten out in weeks."

Antoinette nodded. "I figured as much. Three weeks is a long time to go without eating out, if you ask me."

"Aren't you sick of eating Mexican food?" Kemba asked as she picked up her menu. "You probably know this menu by memory."

"Naw, believe it or not, I don't. I haven't even tried everything. They keep adding new items." Fixing her with a questioning gaze, Antoinette asked, "Why'd you say that anyway?"

"*Because we always eat here,*" Kemba complained.

Antoinette looked around. "I love this place. It has an authentic feel about it. And you have to admit the food is great."

"I agree, but there are *other* Mexican restaurants in Los Angeles. Maybe we should give them a chance. You never know, there may actually be a better restaurant somewhere out there."

Antoinette laughed. "Okay, next time we'll go somewhere new, but I bet it won't come close to this." She leaned over and added in a hushed voice, "Look at that fine specimen of a man over there."

Kemba followed Antoinette's gaze. Eric was there — with a date! Unable to suppress the shocked gasp that burned in her throat or the stunned expression that twisted her face, Kemba managed to sputter, "That's the guy I was telling you about. He's the minister."

"Maybe we should go over there and say something."

Her eyes opened wide. "We're not going anywhere, Antoinette. Can't you see the man is on a date?" Seeing Eric with a woman sent shock currents through Kemba's body. She felt their electrifying pricks all over.

Antoinette burst into laughter. Noting the look on her friend's face, she then asked, "Kim, you're aren't serious, are you? You're not going to let that woman steal your man."

"He's not my man."

"But you're interested in him, and from

the way he keeps looking over here, I'd say he was just as interested in you."

"He's a minister, Antoinette." Kemba pretended to be engrossed in her food. Now she regretted coming to the restaurant. She should've stayed home instead. She wasn't prepared to see Eric out with another woman.

"Look, girlfriend, being a preacher doesn't make him any less fine. I might start going to church if the preachers look like him. I bet he's something in bed."

Kemba's mouth went slack with shock. "*Antoinette*. I can't believe you said that. If you keep that up, I'm moving to another table."

"Why?"

" 'Cause I don't want to be sitting here with you when God sends a lightning bolt your way."

Antoinette threw her head back, laughing.

"I'm serious. I may not go to church every Sunday, but I don't play when it comes to the Lord. Eric is a man of God and you should respect him as such."

Antoinette stopped laughing. "What has this man done to you?" When Kemba refused to crack a smile, she continued speaking. "You really mean it, don't you?"

"Yes. I can't explain it, but I am a believer."

Antoinette sipped her wine. Placing her glass on the table, she asked, "Well, you were raised up in church?"

"You know how religious my mother is."

"I think my parents are two of the biggest sinners in the world." Antoinette admired her fingernails. "Sunday is just another party day to them. The only time we've ever been in church is for someone's funeral or a wedding. Especially if my father thought the press was going to be there."

Kemba watched as Antoinette flicked an imaginary piece of lint off her sleeve. She knew it was something her friend did when Antoinette talked about something that bothered her.

"You know how my dad loves to perform for the camera."

"I haven't been to church in a long time." She glanced over at Eric and his dinner companion. He looked wonderful. Kemba found it hard to tear her gaze away. It really rankled her to see him with another woman. She had no right to be jealous, but she was. It bothered her to no end.

"How did you meet him?" Antoinette asked softly, her eyes narrowing.

"Who?"

Antoinette inclined her head briefly in Eric's direction. "The preacher man over there. Did you attend his church or something?" She glanced over at the couple sitting not too far from them. "He really is a handsome man."

"Why, are you interested in him?"

Antoinette's eyes widened with false innocence. "Naw. Kim, you know me better than that. I wouldn't do that to you."

"I know," Kemba murmured. "He's Malcolm Avery's brother. I thought I told you that already."

"No, you didn't tell me that. I'm sure I would've remembered. Speaking of Malcolm, I heard that the police found a couple of witnesses. I think it was his daughter and someone else. Did you hear anything about it?"

Kemba almost choked on her water but Antoinette didn't seem to notice. "I really hope they catch the person responsible. Dr. Avery was a real nice man. Actually, your pastor and Malcolm resemble one another."

Kemba followed Antoinette's gaze. She jealously eyed Eric's date. The woman was beautiful with a creamy complexion and long, flowing hair. She reminded Kemba of a sexy siren — until her eyes traveled to the dress she was wearing. It looked all wrong

185

for her. If that's what a wife of a preacher has to wear . . . Kemba shook her head. She definitely wasn't interested in the job.

Antoinette was still watching them. "You know, now that I think about it, they really look more like they're having a meeting. I don't think they're on a date."

Kemba frowned. "Maybe." Inside, she cautioned her emotions. She didn't want to focus on a man right now. She had to concentrate on her mother and the promise she made to her father. Kemba scanned Antoinette's plate. "Hey, you gonna eat that?"

Antoinette placed a hand over her mouth, hiding her laughter as she pushed her plate toward her friend. "No, you can have it."

"I was hoping we would get a chance to spend some quality time together." Jennifer played with her water glass.

Eric cleared his throat nervously. "Jennifer, you and I need to talk. I hope that I haven't misled you in any way. I —"

Jennifer waved off his words. "You don't have to say any more. I already know what you're going to say."

"You are going to make some man a wonderful wife."

"Just not you," Jennifer interjected.

"That is what you're trying to say, right?"

"I'm sorry."

"Don't be." Jennifer shook her head in regret.

It was clear to Eric that she wanted to change the subject. His eyes swept across the room, landing on Kemba. Tonight of all nights, she was here having dinner.

"Would you like to go over and say hello to those women?" Jennifer asked pointedly.

Eric's fork poised in midair. With a surprised expression on his face, he said, "Excuse me?"

"I asked if you wanted to speak to those women over there. They've been eyeing us all evening, and from the way you're looking, well, it's obvious you know them."

He didn't miss the rebuke in her voice. "Maybe later. I'll stop by their table on the way out." He had a feeling Jennifer was waiting for him to say more. When he didn't, she shrugged nonchalantly.

Eric knew Jennifer thought him rude and he had to agree that his actions were not those of a gentleman. "I'm sorry, Jennifer. Kemba and —"

"Kemba?" Jennifer interrupted.

"Kemba and my brother, Malcolm, were friends. I've gotten to know her since his death."

She seemed to relax a little and smiled. "It's okay. I totally understand. I'm sure she must miss him very much."

"We all do," Eric responded.

"They must have been very close."

"They were more like business acquaintances, Jennifer."

Her smile disappeared. "Oh, I thought . . ."

"I know what you thought. Why don't we return our conversation to the matter at hand."

"Sure, Pastor."

Jennifer's demeanor changed from that point on. Eric knew she was upset with him but he decided not to give voice to it. He just wanted to get through the rest of their meeting. He hoped Kemba didn't have the wrong idea about him and Jennifer.

Alone, Kemba stood trembling in front of the rest room mirror, tears glistening in her eyes. Her heart beat so loudly she could hear it reverberating throughout the bathroom. Pulling herself together, she opened the door and walked out, almost colliding with Eric. She quickly averted her eyes.

"Hello, Kemba."

"Hi."

He grabbed her by the shoulders. Noting

her tearstained face, he asked, "Is something wrong?"

She still refused to meet his eyes. "No, I'm just in a hurry. I've got to leave."

"Is it your mother?"

Fighting tears, she shook her head. "It's nice seeing you, but I've really got to go." Pushing past Eric, she strolled to her table.

Antoinette looked up. "Kim, I was about to come check on you. Where were you?"

"I can't explain right now, but I need to leave. I'll see you in the morning," she answered.

Antoinette started to rise.

"Please don't get up. Just stay and have dinner. I have to go."

Grabbing her arm, Antoinette inquired, "Kim, what is it? Tell me."

She slumped down into her chair. Tears spilled down her cheeks. She wiped them away quickly.

"It's him, isn't it? You have the hots for the preacher man."

"Antoinette. I do not have the —"

"Yeah, you do," Antoinette cut in. "Don't be ashamed of it. He's a very handsome man. Seems very nice and he's attracted to you also. I saw the way he kept looking over here at you. Girlfriend, he's interested in you."

"It doesn't matter. I'm not cut out to be a preacher's wife."

"How can you say that? What's wrong with you?"

"Look at me and look at the girl he was with, Antoinette."

"I think he likes you just the way you are."

"It doesn't matter. I'm not the kind of woman he should be involved with."

"Don't cheat yourself, Kim."

"The person he dates has to be nearly perfect."

"If that's the case, all ministers should be single. And what about the ministers themselves? I know there are a few *imperfect* ones."

"I think Eric is very dedicated."

"Eric?" Antoinette grinned slyly. "My, my, my. On a first-name basis, I see. Hmmmm."

"Anoinette, puh-leeze."

"Don't look now, but he's watching you."

Kemba stiffened slightly. "You're kidding, aren't you?"

Antoinette shook her head. "Nope." She lifted her wineglass to her mouth. "I think you've finally found a man you could fall in love with and you're running scared."

Antoinette peered closer at her friend. "I'm right. You *are* scared. You're really beginning to care about him, aren't you?"

"I — I don't know what you're talking about," Kemba lied. "I just thought he was nice. I wouldn't have minded getting to know him. That's all."

"So you say," Antoinette shot back.

CHAPTER 13

Jennifer spoke up as soon as Eric returned to his seat. "Pastor, I'm not feeling well. Would you mind if we rescheduled this dinner meeting?"

"No. No, I don't mind. I'll have the waiter give you a carton."

"That would be marvelous." She pressed a hand to her forehead. "I don't know what happened. I was feeling fine until a few minutes ago."

Eric stood up. "Sure. We can go."

Jennifer nodded her head. "Yes, I'll be fine once I get home."

Eric motioned for the waiter. While Jennifer placed her uneaten food in a foam container, Eric handed the waiter his credit card and watched Kemba and her friend. Something had upset her, but what? He wanted to walk over to her table and confront her, but he decided this was not the time or the place.

She really was a stunning female, all grace and poise. There was no question about her being able to rise above any circumstance — Kemba was a true lady. It was more than her looks, though those were eye-catching enough in that dress of teal blue silk. The dress managed to be both professional and elegant enough for a night out on the town. And the way her thick, neatly cut hair was swept away from her face complemented her Nubian features.

It was more than her beauty. There was a strength of character in her that he greatly admired. Kemba had a certain toughness set against vulnerability that made his pulse quicken.

"Ready, Pastor?" Jennifer asked curtly.

"Yes, I'm ready. How are you feeling?"

Jennifer glanced back over her shoulder to find Kemba and Antoinette watching them. With her teeth clenched, she walked briskly toward the exit.

Two days later, Kemba walked out of her shop on her way to her car. She turned a corner and found Eric coming toward her.

Her steps slowed, then stopped. Her heart thudded once, then settled back to its natural rhythm. "Eric — I mean Pastor Avery. I'm not sure what I should be calling you."

A flicker of disappointment seemed to cross his face, caused no doubt by her wariness. "Eric is my name, Kemba."

"It sounds like I'm being disrespectful." As usual, the warmth in his eyes flustered her and Kemba let her eyes drop, looking everywhere but at him. "What are you doing here?"

"I was coming to see you. And it's not disrespectful to call me by my name. You're my friend."

"Really?" Kemba tried to sound disinterested, but deep inside she was thrilled to the core. Clearing her throat, she pretended not to be affected. She looked up at him then. "Are you thinking of redecorating?"

He laughed, the humor causing his eyes to glimmer. They crinkled at the corners and his smooth cheeks lifted. His sensual mouth curved enticingly, urging her to join in the laughter.

His laughter trailed away, but the smile stayed, both on his lips and in his eyes. Kemba could not tear her gaze from his handsome face.

"No, not thinking about that."

"Well, what is it? What are you doing here?" A thought crossed Kemba's mind. "Is something wrong with Crystal?"

"No."

"Have they found the person respon— ?"

"No. The reason I came by . . ." He gave a small laugh.

"Yes?"

"Are you busy? Do you have to be somewhere?"

Kemba started to lie about having an appointment but changed her mind. "I was just about to grab lunch. Would you like to join me?"

His smile was immediate and its effect on Kemba so devastating that she leaned against the stucco building for support.

"Sure, perfect timing. That's why I came to see you."

"I see. Well, your car or mine?"

"Where are you parked?"

She pointed at the garage across the street. "Over there. Where is your car?"

He pointed to the sleek black Lincoln Town Car parked a few feet away. "Right here."

"I guess we'll take your car then. You ministers really love your big cars, don't you?"

Eric threw his head back, laughing. "Don't start in on my choice of cars."

She joined in the laughter. "I'm sorry, but I just thought you had a different car. A Maxima."

"I do. This car was in the shop the night Malcolm died."

"Oh," she said, wishing she'd kept her mouth shut.

They drove six blocks to a small café. The day was gorgeous; the sky blue, the air clear, the sun warm as a kiss, so they decided to eat outdoors. As soon as their food was served, Eric, with a twinkle in his eye, asked, "Why have you been avoiding me?"

Kemba put down the soda she was sipping. "W-what makes you think I've been avoiding you?"

"Don't bother denying it, Kemba. I suspected it ever since the day you found out I'm a minister. But the other night you confirmed it by the way you acted at the restaurant. What I don't know is why. Do I make you that uncomfortable?"

"No . . . Yes. Oh, I'm not sure why. . . ." She couldn't find the right words.

"Is it because of my profession?"

"Sort of," she admitted. "But I don't mean it in a bad way."

"I didn't take it that way. Look, Kemba, I'm a man. A real flesh-and-blood man." He took her hand and placed it on his arm. "See, I'm just like you. I just happen to preach for a living."

She snatched her arm away. "You're nothing like me. I mean, you're a good person —"

"You are too," he said quietly.

"You wouldn't have done what I did. Breaking into a home and trying to steal the diamond and all. Especially withholding the truth from Malcolm. He trusted me. And then there's all the times you pray —"

"You don't pray at all?" He seemed genuinely surprised by her admission.

"I pray," Kemba quickly clarified. "But not every night. I pray a lot. Mostly when I'm in trouble. I don't read my Bible, though. To tell you the truth, I don't even know where it is."

His eyes sparkled with laughter.

"It's not funny. I never bothered to read it because I didn't really understand it."

"Maybe I can help you understand."

"Why did you become a minister?"

"I guess it was because of my grandmother on my dad's side. She was an amazingly strong woman. Strong in her belief that the Lord was with her every step of the way. We were very close.

"Before she died, she sought desperately for some way to help me, some way to comfort me. In the midst of that desire, she instinctively offered the best strength she had — she directed me toward God. While I mourned her, I developed a close relationship with God."

His impassioned words were nearly Kemba's undoing. The backs of her eyes stung and her lips trembled. "You're amazing. I think most people would be angry and pull away."

"Some do. But my grandmother had already prepared me for her death."

"I pray for my mother." Kemba's mouth pulled into a sad smile. "I don't want to lose her because she's really all I have left."

"You have the Lord . . . and me, Kemba."

She was not sure how to respond, so she offered him a smile.

"My family is throwing a huge barbecue and I wanted to invite you to join us. Would you like to come? You're welcome to bring your mother as well. I'd love for her to meet my aunt."

"Sure, we'd love to come," Kemba replied without hesitation. She just wanted to spend some time with Eric. A part of her wondered why he'd ask her after seeing him with a date just a couple of days ago. "I'm surprised you asked me, but thank you for the invitation."

"Why are you so surprised?"

"After seeing you the other night, I really assumed you were involved with someone."

He smiled his gorgeous smile and said, "I'm not involved with anyone, Kemba."

"I didn't mean to be nosy. I just don't like a whole lot of drama."

Eric's laughter was like music to her ears.

"I don't," she reiterated. "I really prefer a quieter kind of life."

"If you say so."

Over a meal of baby back ribs, baked potatoes and mixed vegetables, Kemba said, "I've been meaning to ask you something. How did you get that scar above your eye?"

"While I was in the marines, I developed a cyst. When the doctor removed it, he said it would leave a tiny scar." He placed his hand to his eye. "I didn't think it was that noticeable."

"It doesn't look bad or anything," Kemba reassured him. "I was just wondering about it."

"Can I take it to mean that you've been thinking about me?"

"Well, ah . . . How is Crystal?"

Grinning, Eric asked, "Are you trying to change the subject on me?"

Kemba smiled. "Yes, I am definitely trying to do that."

"Do you want children of your own?"

"Excuse me?"

"Am I being too personal?" Eric asked.

"No, not at all. Your question just threw me for a minute. Yes, I want children. As many as I can afford." She stared into his deep, penetrating eyes. An undeniable magnetism was building between them. "How about you? Do you want them?"

Eric nodded. "I want children."

"Maybe we should find ourselves a couple of spouses first," Kemba said playfully, glancing at him.

"We could keep it simple and marry each other," he teased.

"Sorry, I'm booked today. Shall we try for tomorrow?"

Eric shook his head. "I'm afraid I'm booked tomorrow. How about the day after?"

"Stop teasing me like that," she said. "I may just take you up on it."

"Then tell me this. Are you interested in dating right now? I know that you and your fiancé broke up two years ago."

"I see you and Mama talk a lot."

Eric chuckled.

"I — I don't know actually." Kemba laughed. "It's been such a long time since someone has asked me out. I really don't have a clue. I doubt if I'd even know what to do on a date anymore."

"I'm like you. It's been a while for me too. I hope I haven't embarrassed myself by coming on too strong."

Kemba grinned. "You did fine. I didn't feel pressured."

"That's good. Things *have* changed quite a bit, you know. Women, I notice, are a lot more aggressive than I remember."

She nodded in agreement. "Well, yes, I'd have to agree with you there, but that's not such a bad thing. If done in the right way."

"What's the right way?"

Kemba shook her head. "Sorry, can't tell you that. *It's a woman thang.*"

Eric laughed. He waited until she finished the last of her grilled chicken and Caesar salad. "Are you ready?"

Gazing steadily into his eyes, she responded, "I'm ready."

When they drove back to her office, Eric asked, "Did you still want to go back to Malcolm's house?"

"Yes, I really need to. You don't mind, do you?"

"No, I don't. The investigators are all done, so just let me know when you're ready."

"Can I come by after work some night?"

Eric answered right away. "Sure, I don't see why not."

"I really appreciate this. Thank you." She paused. "Can I ask you another favor?"

"Sure, what is it?"

"Would you mind very much meeting me there?"

Eric smiled. "I don't mind."

"Good. I'm kind of afraid to be in the house alone."

"I understand."

"Well, thanks for lunch."

"It's been a pleasure." Eric waved good-bye and pulled away.

Kemba watched his retreating car. She felt a lurch of excitement within her as she looked forward to seeing him again.

"Mama, you sure you're up to this?" Kemba asked for the seventh time. "We don't have to go if you're not up to it."

"I'm fine, child. Now stop worrying about me."

"You're going to enjoy talking to Mrs. Ransom."

"So you keep telling me." Sarah laughed. "It's kind of them to include us."

Kemba surveyed herself in the full-length mirror. She wanted to make sure every strand of her hair was in place and her clothes weren't wrinkled. "They are really nice. All of them."

"I bet you're looking forward to spending time with Pastor Eric."

"I am," Kemba admitted. "We have a great time together."

"He's good for you."

"I know that. I just don't know if I'm good for him, Mama."

Sarah looked up in surprise. "Why would you say something like that?"

Kemba didn't want to go into it right now, so she tried to change the subject. "You look really pretty today."

Folding her arms across her chest, Sarah responded with, "Uh-huh . . ."

"Really. You do."

"So do you, sweet pea. That young man is sure going to be smitten."

Shaking her head, Kemba laughed. Her mother was not about to let the matter drop. Sarah was playing matchmaker. Truth of it was, she didn't mind at all.

Eric assisted Sarah out of his car.

"You are such a gentleman," she complimented. Casting a look over her shoulder, she winked at Kemba.

He pretended not to notice.

Ray greeted them at the door. Eric introduced Sarah to everyone and led her to the kitchen, where they found Amanda putting the final touches on a lemon-glazed cake.

She smiled and said, "Hello, Mrs. Jennings. I'm so glad you were able to come."

"Just call me Sarah. It's nice of you to have us. Kemba's told me so much about you and your family."

Amanda washed her hands and dried them quickly. She embraced Sarah before leading her to a chair at a table in the breakfast nook. "You sit here and make yourself comfortable. Would you like something to drink?"

Eric and Kemba stood nearby as Amanda continued to fuss over Sarah.

"Your aunt is such a sweetheart." Kemba gave Eric a nudge. "So are you. I really appreciate all you've done for me and for my mother."

"The pleasure has been mine."

Jillian entered the kitchen and waved. "I didn't know you guys were here. How are you, Kemba?"

"I'm fine." Kemba introduced Jillian to Sarah.

Eric watched in amusement as the three women talked. Despite her health problems, Sarah had a wonderful sense of humor. Kemba . . . Kemba was an intriguing young woman. One he wanted to get to know better.

CHAPTER 14

He entered Distinctive Interior Design and looked about the shop. Although not big, the storefront space was lavishly decorated. In one corner of the reception area was an over-stuffed flower-printed brocade chair under a large oil painting. Next to it sat a table draped with the same matching fabric. On top of it were stacks of wallpaper samples and catalogs.

"Hello, can I help you?" A cheery voice sang out across the room, drawing his attention to the receptionist.

He smiled, even showing white teeth. "Hello, my name is Mapfumo Matona. I am here to engage your services."

"Please have a seat and someone will see you shortly."

Minutes later, a reed-thin young woman, wearing a bright turquoise suit, breezed out of a corner office and walked briskly toward him.

"Hello, I'm Antoinette Harrison. May I help you?"

He quickly shook her outstretched hand,

eyeing her thoroughly. He had not expected such a breathtaking beauty. "It is a pleasure, Miss Harrison. I am Mapfumo Matona. I am interested in hiring a decorator for a place I'm leasing."

Putting on a sunny smile, she said, "Well, you've certainly come to the right place. My partner and I —"

"You have a partner?" Even the sound of her voice was a delight.

"Yes, her name is Kim Jennings. As a matter of fact, I expect her shortly. Mr. Matona, have you any idea what you want?"

He smiled widely. "Yes, I know exactly what I want."

She led him over to a table laden with sample books filled with wallpaper and fabric swatches. Handing him a form on a clipboard, she instructed, "Please fill out this form for me. It'll give us an idea of what you're looking for and the budget."

Mapfumo admired Antoinette's long, shapely legs as she moved about the office. She was indeed a beautiful woman and built for childbearing, but he had no interest in having an American for a wife. Many years ago, he would have considered it, but Mapfumo refused to think about the past right now.

Kemba was pleased to see her partner with a client. Business was certainly picking up. For that, she was extremely grateful. Smiling, she headed toward Antoinette's office. "Knock, knock." It was their practice to meet and personally greet all new and potential clients.

"Oh, hi, come on in. Mr. Matona, this is my partner, Kim Jennings."

"Hello, Mr. Matona. It's very nice to meet you." She offered him her hand. She admired his bright white teeth against the contrast of his dark complexion. She trembled slightly when she reached his eyes. There was something lurking in the depths of those eyes that bothered her and sent a clamor of warning along her spine. Something far from harmless.

"It is a pleasure to meet you, Mrs. Jennings."

Perhaps it was the way his dark gaze seemed to devour her with an intensity that left her feeling chilled even though the weather was still warm.

For a moment she was thunderstruck. She released his hand. His accent. He was African. Kemba forced her smile to remain in place. *So what,* she admonished herself. *There are hundreds, maybe thousands of Africans in Los Angeles.* She couldn't go around suspecting all of them. She shook her head slightly and dismissed the feeling. It was just her imagination. "It's Ms. Jennings, but please call me Kim. I believe you'll be pleased with our services."

"I believe I will be also. I have found what I've been looking for. For now, I must leave because I have another appointment."

The thin line of his lips as he smiled down at them and the ill-concealed hardness in the dark eyes that held nothing of the softness of his smile made Kemba tremble.

"I'll be out to your house tomorrow around ten in the morning," Antoinette promised.

"I will be expecting you. Thank you for your help."

"Thank you, Mr. Matona."

"Mapfumo."

"Thank you, Mapfumo. I look forward to working with you."

He smiled widely, showing brilliant white teeth, and then was gone.

Antoinette turned to her friend. "He sure has a sexy accent, don't you think?"

Kemba was quiet.

"Kemba? Are you okay?"

She nodded. "I'm fine. He just struck

me as strange, that's all."

"Strange?"

"It's weird but I can't explain it. I didn't feel comfortable around him. You'd better be careful, Antoinette. I don't trust him."

"You worry too much. He just contracted our services to decorate his house. He even put down a fat deposit."

"You'd better call the bank and verify funds before you start jumping up and down for joy," Kemba advised.

"He gave us cash. Now what have you got to say for yourself?"

"Cash?"

"Cash."

"Maybe I'm just overreacting a little."

"I would say so. Why do you dislike him?" Antoinette sat on the arm of her sofa, crossing her long, slender legs.

"I don't dislike him. He just makes me a little uncomfortable. I can't explain why."

"He's African, right?"

"Yes."

"Maybe you should think about asking him about your family. Who knows, he may know something about them."

Kemba shook her head. "Africa is a big continent. And according to my mother, I don't have any family left over there."

"But how could she know something like

209

that for sure? I'm sure you must have some cousins or something. Were your grandparents only children?"

Kemba thought for a moment. "Hmmmm, that's a good question. I don't think so. I do remember hearing my dad talking about a favorite uncle once. And I know he had at least one brother."

"You probably have loads of cousins running all over Africa. Who knows, you may even be related to Mapfumo Matona."

"God, I hope not."

"Why'd you say it like that? He's a very handsome man."

"I can't put my finger on it, but he seems dangerous."

"What? You can't be serious. He looks harmless to me."

"I can't explain it. I don't know what it is. He just bothers me somehow." She leaned back in her chair. "Enough about him. Let's talk about something else. Something pleasant."

Grinning, Antoinette plopped down onto the couch. "Oh yeah, you never did tell me how your barbecue went with your preacher man."

"There's nothing to tell. It was very nice. He even invited me to church for Holy Night."

Antoinette frowned. "What is Holy Night?"

"Like Halloween, but instead of witches, monsters and goblins, you have angels, I guess. I don't know why he invited me, but I'm going to take Mila. I'm sure she'll enjoy it."

"Hmmmm, sounds like you wanted to be invited somewhere else." Antoinette stood up and moved to admire the huge bouquet of flowers in her office. They were from a satisfied customer and had been delivered that morning.

"Ha, don't be silly!" Kemba turned up her nose at the very idea. She attempted to change the subject. "Look at the little grape hyacinth. See how it pulls together all the colors in the arrangement." The diminutive, unifying flower complemented the harmony of the purple anemones, lavender delphiniums and chartreuse snowball viburnums. Normally, it might go unnoticed by a less discriminating eye, but Kemba had a talent for spotting what she considered artistic masterpieces.

Although she absorbed the beauty of the flowers, behind her eyes the image of Eric formed in her mind. Kemba never thought she'd fall in love again after Carl died. Each time she'd thought about dating, she felt as if she were betraying him in some way. She had now come to the realization that even though she'd decided to move on, Carl would always hold a special place in her heart. She glanced up to find Antoinette's intense gaze penetrating into her soul.

"You've got a thing for him, don't you?"

Kemba tried to deny her feelings. "No, not really."

"Hey, it's Antoinette you're talking to, remember?"

"Okay. Yes, I'm attracted to him. Doesn't matter, though. He doesn't see me that way."

"How do you know? I saw the way he kept watching you that night we were at El Torito's."

Shaking her head in disbelief, Kemba said, "I think you're wrong. I think he sees me as some poor lost soul."

"Don't you let that hunk of a man get away, girlfriend."

"He's a minister. Or have you forgotten that tiny fact?"

"He may be a preacher, but he's still human — and he's still a man." Antoinette arched her brow with slight arrogance. "A very sexy man at that."

"Girl, lightning's going to strike you down for sure."

"I didn't say seduce the man. I'm just saying that his being a man of God should not stop you from going after him. I'm sure men of the cloth date, unless they're Catholic or something."

Kemba laughed. "You need to go to church with me. As a matter of fact, come to Eric — Pastor Avery's church with me on Sunday. I think I'll drop in and surprise him."

Antoinette giggled gleefully. "You know, I just might." She nodded. "Hey, I will. I'll go."

"There's hope for you yet." Kemba sat watching in delight, a smile trailing her lips.

"Well, you know what they say. You can find a good man in church."

Kemba shook her head. "I'm not sitting next to you."

"Okay, *okay*. I'll be good. Maybe I'll even learn something."

She nodded knowingly. "Now that I don't doubt."

"You're a true itch, you know."

Kemba laughed. "I love you too. Now I'll leave your office. I've got work to do."

"Sure leave, but you'll be back." Antoinette said this like the Terminator.

Kemba exaggerated a bout of shivering. "Ooh, now I'm really scared."

CHAPTER 15

On a Monday evening Kemba pulled into the driveway of her former home and parked. Eric was already there. Leaning his slender frame against the trunk of his car, he waved. She quickly got out and walked over to him.

"Hi, I'm sorry I'm late. There was an accident on the way here."

"That's fine. I just got here about five minutes ago myself." Eric pushed up off the car. "Are you ready?"

"As ready as I'll ever be," she mumbled.

Together they walked into the house.

"It feels kind of strange being here." A brief shiver rippled through her. Kemba wrapped her arms around her body.

"I had a cleaning service come in," Eric said. "It should be okay."

She nodded. Kemba hadn't been sure she could handle seeing the bloodstains. . . . She didn't want to think about it.

Eric placed an arm around her. "Are you okay?"

A knot rose in her throat. "I'm fine." His nearness kindled feelings of fire. She warmed under the heat of his gaze. "I'll be okay."

As they neared the area where Malcolm was shot, Kemba felt Eric's body sway. It seemed as if he were now leaning on her for support. She snaked her arm around him.

"Eric?"

"I . . ." He shook his head sadly. Clearing his throat, he said, "I'm okay."

He turned, pulling her into his arms. Kemba could feel his uneven breathing on her cheek as he held her close. She had no desire to back out of his embrace, so she settled against him, enjoying the feel of Eric's arms around her.

Reluctantly they pulled apart.

Eric rubbed his hands across his face. "Where are we looking, by the way?"

"I was thinking that we should start in the hidden room." Kemba led Eric into the library. She walked straight to the bookshelf.

Eric watched in amazement as she stuck her hand behind the shelf. The hidden panel slowly swung open, its hinges whining.

"This is straight out of the movies," he said, peeking into the dark stairway.

Pulling a flashlight out of her purse, Kemba asked, "Are you ready?"

"I think so."

Kemba wrinkled her nose at the musty odor. Together they walked down the stairs. Kemba reached out to take Eric's hand. "You have to be careful going down these stairs." At the bottom they entered a cozy little room.

Eric glanced around, checking out the sitting area, the king-size bed, a bathroom and another door. Walking into the room, he stated, "This is incredible, Kemba." He pointed to the door across the room. "Where does that lead?"

"Outside. It's hidden on the other side, basically. You really have to be looking for it to notice."

"You can't even tell from the basement that this room is here. Your father designed this himself?"

"Yes." Kemba opened a drawer, pulling out a towel. She wiped the dust from a huge trunk that sat in front of the bed.

"I think if it's anywhere — it should be in here."

Together they went through the contents.

"Nothing. It's not here." Kemba felt like crying.

"Why is this map so important?"

"Because it's been in my father's family for generations."

"Your father had a map to some hidden treasure, and where exactly this treasure is supposed to be buried?" Eric scratched his head. "I have to tell you this sounds straight out of a movie."

"It's all true. King Dumisani had some of his most loyal men bury this treasure. After that, he had them killed — all except his son. Dumisani kept in his possession one diamond. That one, he gave to his son and also the map to the treasure. Since then, they have been passed down to the eldest son in each generation."

"Do you *really* believe that there is a hidden treasure? I mean, deep down, don't you think this could just be a myth?"

"Yes, I do believe it's true. Why wouldn't I? My father had the stone — why would he lie to me about a map?"

"I'm not saying he lied. I'm just thinking that if this map is being passed down — has anybody verified that this treasure really exists? And if so, why hasn't someone already taken it from its hiding place?"

"Because it had been lost for a while. My father happened upon it by chance right before he left Africa. But from what I remember, I guess they've tried to find it over the years but no one has been able to do so."

"Why not? Isn't that why you have this map?"

Kemba nodded. "I know it sounds strange, but for whatever reason it hasn't been found. My father told me that he knew exactly where it's buried."

Eric looked skeptical.

"When we find the map — maybe it'll make more sense. To both of us. I'm just as confused as you are."

"When you find it, what are you planning to do? Go to Africa?"

"If I have to. Mama and I could use the money."

"If your father and my brother were killed because of that stone, what do you think will happen when you find the map?"

"No one will know that I'm in Africa or my reason for being there."

"Kemba, you could be putting yourself in grave danger. Your mother too."

She was touched by Eric's concern. "I'm going to be careful. Really, I am."

"I just want you to be safe. Greedy people are dangerous people."

She sighed heavily. "Looks like you don't have to worry. I don't have any idea what it looks like or even where it could be."

"Maybe your father destroyed it?"

"No, tradition meant a lot to him. He never would've gone against what had been drilled into him."

"Well, let's call it a night."

"I think that's a good idea." Kemba closed the trunk. "Would you mind if I take this with me? It belongs to my parents."

"You can take anything you want out of this room."

"Thanks."

"I'll carry it out. Do you want to check out the basement? Maybe there's something there."

Kemba shook her head. "No, I doubt if it's anywhere out there. I'm sure my father would have hidden it somewhere in this room."

Eric yawned. "If it's here — it's got to be right under our noses. Maybe we should try again another day?"

Kemba nodded. "I guess you're right." She glanced down at her watch. "I didn't mean to detain you all of this time. I thought we'd come in and find it right away."

"No problem. I'm just sorry you didn't find it. I have to wonder if the map really does exist. It just sounds too incredible."

"My father wouldn't have lied to me, Eric. He wouldn't." Deep inside, Kemba wondered if she really believed that.

Eric walked her to her car. Smiling, Kemba glanced up at him. "Thanks for doing this for me." She opened the trunk of her car. "Mama is going to love having this back."

He placed the trunk inside. "It belongs to your family, Kemba."

Kemba talked Antoinette into attending church with her. She wanted to see Eric in his environment. After the morning services Jillian strode over and said, "Good morning, Kemba."

Kemba returned her greeting and introduced her to Antoinette.

"I'm beginning to see you on a regular basis," Jillian stated. "I think it's wonderful."

Kemba didn't know how to respond. "Eric and I are just friends."

"That's a great foundation for any relationship, you know."

Antoinette elbowed Kemba softly. "You need to keep that in mind."

"How did you enjoy the service?" Jillian inquired.

"I really enjoyed it," Kemba responded.

"He touched on a lot of things I needed to hear."

Antoinette agreed. She lapsed into some of the points Eric made in his sermon.

Kemba contributed to the conversation. "I learned a lot about the Book of Job this morning."

Eric soon joined them. He embraced his cousin before shaking hands with Kemba and Antoinette. "I'm glad you ladies decided to join us this morning."

"Pastor, I enjoyed the service," Antoinette stated. "I was just telling Kim and Jillian how enlightening it was."

"Thank you."

Jillian made up an excuse to leave. Following her lead, Antoinette did the same. Eric and Kemba were left alone, but not for long.

"Pastor, I was just looking for you," a voice behind Kemba stated. Tossing a look across her shoulder, Kemba recognized the woman as the one who was having dinner with Eric a few weeks ago.

She gave Kemba a smile that didn't quite reach her eyes. Holding out her hand, she said, "Hello, I'm Jennifer Whittaker."

Kemba shook her hand, replying, "I'm Kemba Jennings. It's nice to meet you."

"You too," Jennifer intoned. "It's a pleasure having you here at church. I hope you'll visit with us again."

"Thank you. I'm sure I'll be back."

Jennifer's eyes narrowed upon hearing Kemba's comment, but she didn't respond.

Eric spoke up. "You needed to speak to me?"

"Yes, I do."

Kemba moved to leave. "I'll talk to you later. Antoinette's waiting on me."

He nodded. "Thank you for coming."

She glanced at Jennifer before nodding. Kemba took her leave.

CHAPTER 16

On Halloween night Mapfumo sat in his car watching as Eric drove away from his house. To be sure he had made no mistakes, Mapfumo peered up and down the street before venturing any farther. Under the cloak of darkness, he eased into the backyard. Using a thin tool to manipulate the lock, Mapfumo let himself into the house. He wasn't worried about an alarm system because he'd been in the house once before tonight — the good pastor didn't have one.

Once inside, Mapfumo drifted from room to room looking for the diamond. He cursed in frustration as he checked under the beds, chairs, everywhere. There wasn't a safe to be found.

Going through the den once again, he still turned up nothing. "Where is it?" he yelled out. He'd searched everywhere he imagined someone would hide a safe-deposit key. He was sure that after Malcolm was murdered, the diamond would be placed in one.

She has to have it. "Kim Jennings is the key — she has to be." He had thought she would have given it to Eric Avery. Mapfumo frowned. Maybe she never gave it to him at all. She probably kept it for herself. He grinned. "Yes, that is it. She kept it for herself."

He surveyed the room once more, then decided to leave. *I won't find anything here, but I will find the stone.* Mapfumo clenched and unclenched his fist as he walked briskly back to his car. Frustrated, he drove off into the night. Kemba's building was not as easily accessible. She had nosy neighbors, but he would find a way. He vowed not to leave America without his family's legacy.

"Mila, you look adorable. I just love your costume." Kemba picked up her 35mm camera. "I've got to take a picture of you before we go."

"Miss Kemba, do you really like it? Mommy made it, didn't you?" She looked over at the full-figured woman standing next to Kemba.

Tanya grinned. "I sure did. I stayed up all last night trying to finish it too."

"It's really beautiful. You look just like a fairy princess." Kemba knelt down to snap a close-up of Mila. "These are going to come out so nice!"

"Kemba, I really appreciate your taking her to the church. Trick-or-treating is not like it used to be when we were kids. Mila just doesn't understand why I won't let her go door-to-door, like the other kids."

Kemba gave Tanya a hug. "It's no problem. She's such a sweetheart. Are you sure you don't want to come with us?"

Tanya shook her head. "No, I'm so tired. I figured I'd just lie in front of the TV and take a nap. Might do some reading, but I doubt it. I've been too tired to even catch up on my romance novels. And you know how much I love them."

Kemba nodded. "Why don't you let Mila sleep over at my house tonight? That way, you can go on to bed and get some rest. I promise not to let her eat a lot of candy."

Tanya raised an eyebrow. "You sure you don't mind?"

"You know I don't. You're working two jobs and raising Mila. I know you have to be tired."

"Girl, you don't know the half of it. I really appreciate this. I do."

"If you want me to, I'll keep Mila all weekend. I'm going to stay with my mom and I can take her with me. Mama loves Mila to death."

"Ooh, can I, Mommy? Please? I want to go see Granny Sarah."

"Are you sure Sarah's up to it? She's only been out of the hospital a few weeks."

"She'll enjoy the visit. I'll come over in the morning to pick up an overnight bag for Mila."

Tanya leaned down to plant a loud kiss on Mila's chubby cheek. "Have fun at church, sweetie."

Hugging Tanya tightly, Mila replied, "I will, Mommy. I love you."

"I love you too." Tanya reached up and hugged Kemba. "You're such a dear friend. I don't know what I'd do without you."

"You've been good to me, Tanya. And you take real good care of Mama when she's at the hospital."

"I'm just doing my job."

Kemba shook her head. "No, Tanya, you go above and beyond the call of duty."

"You two get on outta here. I'll see you in the morning. And breakfast is on me. Just come on over when you get up."

"We'll see you later." Kemba picked up her purse and camera bag. "Let's go, Mila."

Thirty minutes later, she pulled into First Christian Church's parking lot. She took several deep breaths before getting out of the car.

"Are you all right, Miss Kemba?" Mila looked scared.

Patting the little girl on her shoulder, Kemba nodded, feeling foolish. "I'm all right, sweetheart. I didn't mean to scare you." Hand in hand, they headed toward a huge building next to the church.

Eric greeted them at the entrance of the social hall. "Hello, Kemba. I was about to think you changed your mind."

"No, I — I didn't change my mind. I stopped to talk to Mila's mother. Time kind of slipped by us."

Eric looked down at her companion. "This little princess must be Mila."

"I'm not just a princess. I'm a fairy princess," she announced proudly.

Eric laughed. "I stand corrected." He leaned down and offered his hand. "I am Pastor Avery, but all the children call me Pastor Eric."

"I want to call you Pastor Eric too. I like it."

"Why, thank you. If I'm not mistaken, there's a game going on over there. Would you like to join in?"

"Can I, Miss Kemba?"

"You sure can. You can participate in all the activities if you want. I'll be right over here, where you can find me. Okay?"

"Okay." She went running, a tiny blaze of white, pink and lavender chiffon.

"She looks like a baby doll."

Kemba was entranced. She liked this paternal side of Eric. "I know. She is such a delight to be with."

"I imagine she keeps her parents busy."

"She keeps her mother busy. Her father walked out on them before Mila turned a year old."

"Too much of that happens these days. It's really a shame too."

"It's his loss." Kemba checked out her surroundings. "Everything looks so nice," she commented.

"The committee did a wonderful job."

Kemba had the strangest sensation that someone was watching her. This was not the first time she'd felt like this. The first time was at Malcolm's funeral. She glanced tentatively around. Her eyes found Jennifer Whittaker standing next to an older version of herself. Kemba knew it could be none other than Jennifer's mother. They were glaring at her and Eric, their eyes spewing forth hatred. She trembled slightly.

Eric nudged her lightly. "Kemba, are you okay?"

She looked up to find Eric watching her.

"Yes, I'm fine." Scanning the room for a couple of vacant chairs, Kemba spotted two and pointed them out to him. "Do you mind if we sit down?"

"No, I don't mind." He led the way over. "Here, let me move this stuff and you can sit in this one."

Kemba smiled. She glanced once more to where Jennifer stood. She was still glaring angrily at them. Kemba looked away to find Eric's penetrating gaze on her.

"What is it, Kemba? I know something's bothering you."

"I'm beginning to wonder if it was a good idea for me to come."

"Why would you say that?"

"Have you noticed the way people are staring at us? I think we're the subject of everybody's conversation." Even now she could feel Jennifer's heated glare burning into her back.

"Does that bother you?"

"A little. I kind of feel like I'm on display."

"I'm sorry."

Kemba placed a hand on his arm. "It's not your fault. People are people. They're nosy. You can't change them."

"It's not their business, Kemba. I invited you here tonight as my guest. No one should have a problem with it."

"I think your friend over there has a serious problem with my being here." It was obvious to Kemba that Jennifer was attracted to Eric and she bore a strong dislike for her because of it.

"Who? Jennifer?"

Nodding, Kemba replied, "Yes."

"Jennifer knows that she and I are only friends. I've never led her to believe otherwise."

"That doesn't stop her from being a little territorial, though. She's definitely not happy about my being here."

"I'm sorry. I really want you to be comfortable, Kemba."

"I'm fine. Don't worry about me. Besides, I'm here now, and Mila is having a fabulous time. I'm not leaving."

Eric relaxed visibly. "I'm glad to hear that."

"Er, excuse me, Pastor, but could you come help us in the kitchen for a minute? We're having a bit of a problem with the dishwasher." Ida pushed up her bosom and stood scowling at Kemba behind his back.

"I'll be right there." He turned to Kemba. "I won't be gone long."

"Take your time." Minutes passed and Kemba smiled as she watched Mila play with the other children. She was having a good time.

Joining her again, Eric bent low to sit, stretching out his long legs. "I apologize for the interruption. By the way, how is your mother?"

"She's fine. She told me to ask that you keep her in your prayers."

"She doesn't have to worry about that."

"No, I suppose she doesn't." Kemba gave him a big smile.

"She's really a nice lady, your mother."

"I certainly think so." Kemba shook her head. "I don't know what I'd do without her."

"You two are very close, aren't you?"

"Yes, we are. No two people could be closer. We have no secrets between us."

Eric smiled, radiating a vitality that drew her like a magnet.

Watching him out of the corner of her eyes, Kemba thought she detected something in his expression, but she couldn't be sure. It was gone in a flash.

"Did you mean what you said earlier?"

"About what?"

"Am I going to see more of you?" he asked, his voice a tempting caress as he leaned toward her, the mischievous smile on his face sending an irritative jab of desire through her body.

She smiled. "It's up to you, Eric."

"I'll take that as a yes."

She spotted Mila waving at her. Standing up, she said, "Looks like I'm being summoned. I'm going to play some games with Mila, and I know you need to play host. Just give me a call sometime."

"I didn't invite you here to abandon you. I wanted to spend time getting to know you as well."

Kemba smiled. "Thanks for saying that. I didn't want to presume anything."

"You go on and play with Mila. I'll join the two of you shortly."

"Okay." Kemba was cut off by Jennifer.

"Well, I see you're becoming a regular around here."

"I don't know if I would say that," Kemba responded.

She nodded in Mila's direction. "Is that your daughter?" Jennifer asked. "She's a beautiful little girl."

"No, she isn't, Jennifer. How are you?"

"I'm fine. Tell me, are you thinking about joining our church?"

"I don't know," Kemba answered honestly. "It's something I don't take lightly." She glanced over at Mila. "It's nice talking to you, Jennifer. I promised to play a game with Mila."

"Of course."

Kemba moved around Jennifer.

"I hope you're enjoying yourself."

"I am," Kemba threw back. "Mila and I are having a wonderful time."

In the midst of their game, Kemba glimpsed Eric coming their way. She smiled and waved.

"Looks like you two are winning," he observed.

"It's all Mila's doing. I'm just following her."

After the game the trio went in search of refreshments. Kemba stood silently by, watching Mila and Eric together. *Tonight was perfect.* Feeling Jennifer's gaze on her, she amended her musings. *Almost perfect.*

CHAPTER 17

As soon as Eric walked into the house, the hairs on his neck stood up. Someone had been in his house. He was sure of it. Walking slowly, he gave the room a cursory glance; nothing appeared out of place, though.

He'd felt this way a couple of weeks ago, but after a thorough search, he had found nothing out of place. At the time Eric dismissed it as a case of jittery nerves, but not this time. Whoever it was, they had to be looking for the diamond. They wouldn't find it here. It was safely hidden away in a safe-deposit box at Wells Fargo Bank. Eric continued to move silently through the house, checking here and there. A former marine, he kept a gun safely hidden away.

Satisfied that the intruder was no longer in the house, Eric returned to his bedroom. Tomorrow he would have an alarm system installed and change all the locks. Sliding the closet door open, he reached in and pulled out a metal organizer laden with belts. He searched for one in particular. Eric selected a black one made from lizard skin. He unzipped the hidden compartment and removed the contents. A safe-deposit key. Grinning, he put the key back into the compartment, zipping it shut. Eric then returned the belt among the others. "I guess this is what you were hoping to find. Too bad, 'cause you'll never find this one. Tina and I are the only ones who know where it is."

Checking once more through the house, making sure all windows and doors were secure, Eric prepared for bed.

"Kemba Jennings." Eric said her name again, slowly, letting the sound echo softly through the room. He had met many women, some very attractive, a few intriguing. What was it about this woman that put such an overwhelming desire in his heart to protect her, and why did it mean so much to see her smile? Most incredibly, how could she, within thirty seconds of meeting him, plant herself so deeply into his thoughts and inhabit his dreams? Around Kemba he lost all sense. Around her he wanted in a way he didn't remember ever wanting. She made him feel whole again. She made him feel like a man.

As long as he was being honest with himself, Eric admitted he wanted more.

He wanted all of her. Everything Kemba had, everything she was. He wanted her laughter, her smiles, her sadness, even her anger, everything. She was the one, the woman meant for him. The knowledge burst upon him like the sun breaking free of the horizon at dawn.

Eric picked up the telephone twice, each time returning it to the cradle. He felt like a kid with his first crush. Finally he decided to call. Eric was about to hang up when he heard her pick up.

"Hello."

"Kemba, this is Eric." He wondered if she could hear the loud beating of his heart.

"Hi. How are you?"

Eric relaxed. She actually sounded excited to hear from him. "I'm fine. . . . I hope you don't mind —"

"Actually, I'd been thinking about giving you a call. I really had a nice time tonight. So did Mila."

"I'm really glad to hear that. The reason I called is because I'd like to take you to dinner."

"Dinner. As in a date?"

"Yes, as in a date. I'm asking you out on a date." When he heard nothing but silence on the other end, he prompted her. "Kemba?"

236

"I'm here. Yes, Eric, I'd love to go on a date with you."

"Whew. I'm glad that's over."

She laughed. "Was it that hard?"

"I told you I was out of practice."

"You did just fine, Eric."

"I'm glad you didn't turn me down."

He could feel the warmth of her smile. "If you hadn't asked me, I would have asked you out. I'm glad you saved me from embarrassing myself."

"Hey, I thought you were one of those '90s women?" Eric teased.

"Not really. I'm aggressive in business but not in my relationships."

He heard Mila's voice in the background. "She's spending the night with you?"

"Yes, I thought I'd give her mother a break. She's a registered nurse and she works some dreadful hours."

"I can imagine. Well, since you're having a slumber party, I'll let you go. I'll give you a call sometime tomorrow."

"Call me at my mother's house."

"Okay."

"I look forward to hearing from you, Eric."

"I'm looking forward to spending time with you." Eric clicked off. There was a definite attraction between the two of them.

Kemba stood outside of her office, looking down at a card so intently that Antoinette, passing her, had to speak twice before she heard her. Once more, Eric had dominated her thoughts.

"What's up, sistah girl?"

She followed Antoinette into her office. "I was just thinking about something."

"No kidding," exclaimed Antoinette, with both hands on her hips. "Girl, you look like you were in another world. What's bothering you?" She plopped down in her chair, settling back in a comfortable position.

"I . . . I have a date and I have nothing to wear." Kemba crumpled into a nearby chair.

"What do you *mean*, you have nothing to wear? Girl, your closets are filled to capacity. *All three of them.* Now, me, I'd have to go shopping. I like my sexy, little, barely there dresses."

Kemba bit back her laughter. "Who're you trying to kid? You dress as conservative as I do."

Antoinette crinkled her nose. "I have my little skimpy dresses too. Lots of them."

"Should I wear a suit?"

Pursing her lips into a displeased line, Antoinette declared, "Hell naw. At least not a real conservative one. Wear that cute little navy-blue-and-white two-piece dress."

"You mean the one with the military-style blazer and pleated skirt? That's not a conservative suit to you?"

"Yeah, it is," Antoinette confessed. "But I think it looks real good on you."

Kemba thought about Jennifer and the old-fashioned dresses she'd seen her wear. "You don't think it looks too tight or something?"

"*It's supposed to fit, Kim.* It fits you just right. And it's a very sexy dress."

"I don't know. Maybe I should just wear a pantsuit." She caressed her temples, trying to quiet the cacophony of thoughts.

"The dress will be fine. Trust me," Antoinette assured her.

Kemba hoped so. She wanted to make a good impression on the handsome minister.

Kemba glanced into the mirror. The blue-and-white dress was quite flattering on her. The doorbell sounded once. Nervously she opened the door to a grinning Eric.

239

"Hi, Eric. Come on in."

"Hello, Kemba. You look beautiful. I like your suit. It reminds me of my military days."

She smiled. "Thank you. I wasn't quite sure what to wear."

"I guess I should have told you something comfortable," Eric said, misunderstanding her comment. "But as it turns out, your dress is perfect."

Kemba admired the cut of his black tweed suit. Underneath the double-breasted jacket he wore a crisp white shirt and a bloodred tie. "You look very nice yourself."

"Thank you."

She picked up her navy blue purse and asked, "Where are we going?"

"I thought we might try the new restaurant on La Brea Avenue. The new Jamaican restaurant everyone has been talking about."

"I've been planning to go there, but I can't seem to get Antoinette away from the Mexican restaurants."

Eric laughed as they headed to where he had parked his car. He held the car door open for her. "So, Antoinette loves Mexican food."

"Love is not the word. Every time we

have dinner, we somehow end up at El Torito's. Antoinette would eat there every day if she could."

Eric smiled at that. "I love Mexican food, but I don't think I'd want it every day."

"I'm with you. You'd think I could speak Spanish for all the Mexican food I've consumed, hanging around with Antoinette."

At the restaurant they were led to their table. Kemba's expression was one of surprise when she glanced down to find a long-stemmed red rose on her place setting. She raised her eyes to find Eric watching her, analyzing her reaction.

"Thank you," she whispered, her voice thick with emotion.

"I want to make this an evening you'll never forget."

"I don't think I will." Kemba reached over, placing her manicured fingers over his.

After the waiter took their food order, they sat staring into each other's eyes until Eric broke the spell.

"What were you just thinking about?" Eric asked.

"The night I saw you at El Torito's, I remember being under the impression you were already involved. I never thought in a million years that I'd be having dinner with you."

"Why not? Couldn't you tell that I was interested in you?"

"I kind of thought so, but then —" She stopped short.

"What? What is it?"

"I wasn't sure what was going on with you and Jennifer. When I saw you two at the restaurant . . ."

He shook his head. "There isn't anything between us. She is one of my church members. That's all. She and her mother have adopted me, I guess you could say."

Kemba nodded knowingly. "I'm sure."

Eric laughed. "I am in no way interested in Miss Jennifer Whittaker. Besides, if I married her, I'd gain two wives."

"How do you figure that?"

"She and her mother are a package deal."

Kemba laughed. "You're kidding, right?"

Eric shook his head again. "No, I'm not. If you take one, you have to take the other one too."

"Good luck."

"What's that supposed to mean?"

"With two women fighting for the same cause, you're in a lot of trouble, Pastor."

"Please call me, Eric. And while I do not

plan to offend the Whittakers, I do not plan to fall into their trap either."

"As I said before, good luck." Kemba held her glass to his.

The waiter brought their dinner.

"Everything looks delicious, don't you think, Eric?"

"Yes, it does."

She looked up to find him watching her. "You do know I was talking about the food?"

"I know." Eric chuckled deep in his chest.

Looking up into his handsome face, Kemba could not speak for a few seconds. "You like teasing me, don't you?"

"You're cute when you blush."

"Gee, thanks, Eric." She lowered her lashes. "Now you're embarrassing me."

He looked at her and suddenly laughed, shaking his head.

"It's not that funny." Kemba sat back in her chair, arms folded across her breasts. She finally gave way to her own laughter.

Eric picked up his fork. "I'm glad you decided to join me for dinner. I don't know why, but I really like you. I especially like seeing you laugh."

She returned his smile. "It feels real good to be out. It's been such a long time.

Since I've been out on a date." She reached over and patted Eric's hand. "Thank you for inviting me." She smiled shyly before removing her hand.

As they finished their dinner, they talked about the decorating business. Eric paid the check and they made their way to the car.

"I have flavored coffee at home. I'll make us some if you'd like, Eric."

"Are you sure it's no trouble?"

"It's no trouble."

At her apartment Kemba handed Eric the keys upon his asking for them.

"You are such a gentleman." She held the door open for him to enter. "You go ahead and make yourself comfortable. I'll go make the coffee."

His face creased into a sudden smile. "Sure you don't want me to help?"

She gently pushed him into the living room. "I'll be fine, Eric. Just find a good movie on TV."

"In this day and age?" Eric grimaced. "Wish me luck."

"There are several Christian channels."

"Do you ever watch them?" he questioned.

"I watch them, but not on a regular basis. Are you surprised?"

Shaking his head, Eric answered, "No, I'm not. I suspected as much."

His grin was contagious. "You're just saying that."

He stepped forward, clasping her body tightly to his. Leaning forward, he kissed her. Giving herself freely to the passion of his kiss, Kemba's lips parted under his. She felt the damp roughness of his tongue as he traced the soft inside of her upper lip. She tasted him again as he ran his tongue against the ridge of her teeth.

Her lips were more than pliant beneath his touch. Kemba thought nothing. She felt everything. It was she who pressed for a deeper kiss. Kemba arched against Eric's chest, slipping her arms around his shoulders and running her fingers across the silky waves in his hair.

"Whoa, baby," he whispered softly, raising his head. "I think we'd better stop while we still can."

Kemba took a deep breath and let it out slowly, hoping to clear her mind of the throbbing ache in her loins. "Have you changed your mind about the coffee?"

"I think we better call it a night," they both said in unison, a confused silence holding them captive for a moment as they searched each other's eyes for answers to contradicting feelings pounding in both their hearts.

Eric bent down and kissed her swiftly. "I'd better go, but I'd like to see you again."

Her gaze traveled over his face and searched his eyes. "I'd like that too, Eric. As a matter of fact, why don't you come over Friday night? I'm playing Monopoly with Mila and her mother. We can all play."

"I'll think about it and give you a call, okay?"

Kemba nodded. "Drive safe."

When Eric left the condo, she permitted herself to go weak at the knees. His kiss made her feel like a breathless girl of eighteen. A delightful shiver of wanting ran through her. From the window Kemba fingered her necklace as she watched Eric drive off.

He'd kissed her and she'd liked it. Eric was so gentle and humble. She needed that touch of tenderness in her life right now. She trusted him. There was no better way to explain the complexity of her feelings than that simple truth. She'd depended upon men before for protection and security, but never had she given over the private aspects of herself the way she had to Eric. And he'd known instinctively what to say.

Part of being a minister, she supposed. But somehow she suspected his sensitivity ran deeper than that. It was as if he were very much a part of who she was.

"Can I buy a hotel?" Mila asked.

"You sure can, sweetie." Kemba sipped her Coke. "As long as you have money, you can buy whatever your lil' ol' heart desires."

Tanya threw the dice. She landed on New York Avenue. Grimacing, she asked, "Okay, Pastor. How much is this going to cost me?"

"Hmmmm." Eric held his hand to his mouth. "Doesn't look like you have enough cash to pay me. Looks like you're going to have to sell some of your property."

"I'll tell you what — why don't we leave things right here and finish up tomorrow? I'm so tired I can't think straight."

Kemba looked at Eric. "What do you think? Do you have any plans for tomorrow?"

"Just spending the day with 2.5 beautiful women. We've got to finish this game. I'm winning so far and I'm not going to let you three wimp out on me."

"Ha! We're just tired right now. We've

been playing for the last three hours." Tanya yawned. "As you can see, we need our beauty rest."

"Excuses, excuses . . . ," Eric muttered under his breath.

Kemba and Tanya doubled over in giggles. "We heard that."

Mila pushed away from the table. "Pastor Eric, would you read me a story? I have a book of Bible stories." She grinned. "It's my favorite book. Miss Kemba gave it to me for my birthday when I turned four."

"I'll be more than happy to. That is, if your mother doesn't mind."

Tanya nodded her approval. "Mila, honey, you go take your bath real quicklike. When you're all dressed, put on your robe and slippers and come out here."

"I'll be right back. Don't go nowhere."

"Mila." Tanya looked back at Kemba and rolled her eyes. "I don't know what I'm gonna do with that girl sometimes."

"She's a good child, Tanya."

"Yeah, she really is." Tanya gave a sad smile. "Mila's asking questions about her father now."

Eric spoke up then. "We have a group at the church that offers counseling to children from single-parent homes. I've seen them do a lot of good within the community. If you're interested, I'll give you the number."

Tanya nodded. "I'd like that, Pastor. I really would."

"As a matter of fact, why don't you come visit? Kemba is planning to come on Sunday —"

Kemba snapped her fingers. "That's right, Tanya. I was planning to ask you, but I forgot."

"Mila and I would love to come. I haven't been to First Christian in a long, long time. Do you all still have that gospel choir — the one that won all those state awards?"

"Yes, we do. You know, I thought you looked familiar. You used to come all the time with Mrs. Wrice. Patricia Wrice."

"Yeah. She used to be my stepmother. When she and my dad divorced, she married Harry Wrice. He didn't want her associating with me. Always accused her of trying to see my dad on the side. He thought I was the go-between."

"Is that why you stopped coming to church with her?"

Tanya nodded. "I didn't want to cause any problems for her. She's the only mother I've ever known." Her voice broke.

"I'm sure she'll love seeing you this Sunday. Harry hasn't been to church in a long time. I doubt he'll be there."

"I'd love to see her. I miss her."

Mila rushed into the living room, where the three adults sat. "I'm ready for my story, Pastor Eric." She climbed onto the couch to sit beside him.

Eric glanced over at Kemba and smiled. "Okay, little lady, which one would you like me to read?"

"The one about David and Goliath. It's my favorite."

"I'll help you in the kitchen, Tanya."

"Girl, you don't have to do that. Just come in and keep me company." As they headed into the kitchen, Tanya leaned over and whispered, "He's such a nice man. And a good preacher too."

Kemba grinned. "He's a good person."

Tanya turned around to face Kemba, her hands on her ample hips. "Is that all you've got to say about this man?"

"What else should I say?"

"How about, how much you like him. That he's the best-looking man you've seen in a long time. I don't know, but say something." Tanya tested the running water. Finding it to her liking, she added dish detergent.

"Tanya, I'm crazy about him. I just don't know if I have the right to be."

"Just take one day at a time. Enjoy each other and everything else will fall into place. If it doesn't, then move on." She watched Kemba pick up the yellow-and-white dishcloth. "Oh no you don't. I told you to keep me company — not help me do dishes. I'll have them done in no time."

Half an hour later, the two women were sitting down having coffee when Eric walked in. "Mila's asleep on the sofa. She went halfway into the story."

"Thank you for reading to her." Trying to stifle another yawn, Tanya asked, "Would you like some coffee?"

"No, thank you. I'm fine."

Kemba downed the contents of her cup. "Thanks, Tanya, we really had a nice time, but we'd better be going." They navigated toward the door.

"I'll see you all tomorrow."

"Tomorrow I win the game."

"Right, Eric," Kemba responded. "Let's get out of here. See you tomorrow, Tanya." Grabbing him by the hand, she led him out the front door.

In her condo, Kemba turned on the TV. "I hope you had a good time tonight."

"I did. I had a great time. Thank you for including me."

"No problem."

"There's something I've wanted to do all night long."

"What's that?"

"This." His mouth swooped down to capture hers. As the kiss grew more fervent, Kemba felt its searing heat burn all the way down to her feet. She returned his kisses with equal ardor. Knowing that there would be no way for them to stop if they kept this up, Kemba disengaged herself from Eric's arms and stepped back.

"I guess you'd better go," she whispered.

"To be honest, that's the last thing I want to do right now," Eric said hoarsely.

"Me too," Kemba agreed with a sparkling laugh.

Growling, Eric lowered his mouth to hers.

His kiss made a hopeless muddle of Kemba's thoughts. His gentle touch was remarkably soothing, while the feel of his smooth, muscled body beneath her fingertips provided a rush of excitement. Eric's lips caressed hers sweetly and then his tongue slid into her mouth.

"Please tell me that wanting you isn't wrong, is it?" she whispered against his mouth.

He swallowed hard. "We're attracted to each other — I don't think anything is wrong with that, but we really shouldn't act on our attraction."

She sighed. "You're right, I know."

"It doesn't change the way I feel. I'm a man, Kemba."

There was a spark of some indefinable emotion in his eyes. She retreated a step, then said, "You are a good man."

Eric shook his head. "I want to be a better man."

Kemba surveyed his face; her eyes were sharp and assessing. "No matter how much you want me?"

"Are you okay with that?" he asked.

Kemba nodded her approval. "Actually, I'm impressed."

He inclined his head. "Impressed? Why?"

"I've never met anyone like you before."

Eric laughed. "I have to admit, I've never met anyone quite like you either."

She placed her hands on her hips. "Now, what exactly is that supposed to mean?"

"You don't meet a jewel thief every day."

Kemba grinned. "Hmmmm, I guess I'll let that slide by. For now."

"I guess I'd better be leaving before we get into some" — he kissed her deeply —

"trouble, sweetheart. I'll call you tomorrow about finishing the game, okay?"

"Uh-huh. Oh, call me here at home. I'm not going into the shop tomorrow."

"Taking a day off?"

"Yes, I need it."

Kemba walked Eric to the door. Eric leaned down to kiss her once more. "Sleep tight, honey."

She watched him leave, then headed to her cold, empty bedroom.

CHAPTER 18

Sarah tossed fitfully in her sleep. Over and over in her mind, she relived the terror of one night long ago. Drenched in sweat, she woke up with a start. Sarah painfully eased out of bed to go stand by the huge window in her bedroom. "Why have you come back to haunt me now?" she whispered to the empty room. All these years she'd tried to forget. Twisting her hands, Sarah decided it was because of Malcolm Avery's murder and that diamond. *That cursed diamond.*

Sarah thought back to when she met the love of her life. She had been twenty at the time and a missionary in Africa. Her first week in what was then known as Rhodesia, she met Molefi Rufaro. It had been love at first sight for the two of them. Shortly after their meeting and a brief courtship, Molefi asked her to marry him. Sarah couldn't have been happier; that is, until she had been kidnapped one night and raped. Raped by Molefi's brother.

Although Sarah shunned Molefi after that, he was persistent. He loved her and still wanted to marry her; he told her so over and over again. When she once again believed that they could be happy, she found herself pregnant. The baby she carried had been fathered by Mapfumo Rufaro.

Forced to tell Molefi the truth of what had happened between her and Mapfumo, he once again became her knight in shining armor. He insisted they marry as quickly as possible, and he swore that no one would ever find out the truth. It would go with them to their graves.

"Oh, how I miss you, my love. You were so good to me." Tears streamed down her face, staining her peach-colored nightgown. Sitting on the side of her bed, she pulled out a thick leather-bound book and started writing.

When the sun rose in the early morning, Sarah was still writing. Exhausted, she finally lay back against her fluffy pillows, falling into a peaceful sleep.

"Did you sleep okay last night?" Eric asked Kemba the next evening when she sat down beside him on the sofa. "I thought I was going to have to carry you out of Tanya's apartment."

"No, I didn't." She punched him playfully. "And it was all your fault. That's why you won Monopoly today. I was too tired to concentrate."

"Hey! I could say the same. Every time I closed my eyes, I did nothing but think about you. I had some heavy repenting to do."

Kemba laughed. "Serves you right."

Eric reached into his pocket. "I brought this to you. I found it when I went to pack up Crystal's things for her. I thought you'd want to have it." He handed her a letter.

"What is it?"

"An old letter. It's addressed to your father."

"Really?" Kemba examined the letter. "It's from Bekitemba Rufaro." She looked up at Eric. "Rufaro?"

"Is something wrong?"

"I've never heard of Bekitemba. My father had a brother, but I don't recall his name. Maybe this is from his brother."

"Why don't you ask your mother?"

"You know what, I will. I've always felt I was missing something by not having a family — just my mother and father."

Eric pulled Kemba into his arms. "I've had a wonderful time with you."

"So have I. But, Eric . . ." Kemba hesitated, dreading what she felt needed to be said.

"Yes, what is it?"

"I really like you, and we have fun together, but . . ."

"But what?"

"Well, you're a minister. I don't know if —"

"Does my being a minister offend you?"

"That's not what I —"

He sat up then. "What are you trying to say?"

"I just don't think I'm right for you."

"Why not?"

She thought about this for a moment. "Well, I don't go to church that often. I mean, I have been going more since I met you. Don't know the Bible word for word, and, well, just look at me and the way I dress."

Eric threw back his head laughing.

"What's so funny?" Kemba asked in a huff.

"You think those are the requirements for a minister's wife?"

"Sort of. My point is that your wife should be above reproach. She has to dress a certain way, behave a certain way and probably be very active in your church. People will look at her as a reflection of who you are, Eric. That's why you have to be careful about who you let into your life. Even the women you date will be put under a microscope."

"Therefore, I shouldn't find a wife who's human."

"That's not what I mean, and you know it. I'm a believer, but I don't do all the things I should. I love to read romance novels, go to the movies and even go dancing every now and then. I like having fun."

"So, you think we ministers and our spouses don't have any fun?"

"Eric . . . ," she pleaded. "You know what I'm trying to say."

"Yeah, I think I do."

"I'm just not right for you. I wish I was because I really like you. I like you a lot." She kissed him lightly on the cheek.

"I care for you, Kemba. I haven't felt this way in a long time about anybody."

"I care for you too, Eric. I just don't want to compromise you —"

He could not resist the sweet temptation of her lips so close to his own. Eric kissed her with a hunger that belied his outward calm.

"Eric —"

"Stop worrying," he murmured against her mouth. "Let's just take one day at a time."

"I couldn't bear it if I did something to

make you lose your church."

"You won't, sweetheart. We're meant for each other."

"How can you be so sure?"

"I have it on the highest authority." He raised his eyes heavenward.

"You're sure?"

Eric grinned. "Very. Look, Kemba, there's something you need to understand. Even though I am a minister, I'm also very human. I like to have a good time like the next person. When I romance someone, it's not to spirituals." He kissed her. "Stop worrying."

"Eric, I don't want you to have any problems over me, that's all. I know I'm a good person, but I'm not willing to prove it to your entire church."

"You don't have to do that, Kemba." Taking her by the hand, Eric said, "Let's just take this one day at a time. We'll worry about my church members when the time is necessary, okay?"

Kemba nodded, but deep down, she didn't feel at ease. She was beginning to have real feelings for Eric and wanted to be the woman of his heart.

Kemba entered her mother's town house with her key. She found Sarah lounging in front of the television. Kissing her on her forehead, Kemba said, "Hi, Mama. I thought I'd find you in bed when I got here."

"No, I felt like watching some TV, so I came out here. I get tired of lying in bed, so I thought I'd just lie on the couch. I may sleep out here."

"It's that comfy?"

Sarah grimaced. "No, I'm just tired of my bed."

Kemba sat cross-legged on the floor. "How're you feeling?"

"I'm fine — just a little tired. How about yourself?"

"I'm okay. Mama, who's Bekitemba?"

Sarah sat up then. "What did you say?"

"Bekitemba Rufaro. Eric found a letter to Papa from him. It's dated a few weeks after Papa's death. Did you ever meet him?"

Sarah sat with her hands pressed to her chest. "I met him once. A nice man."

"Maybe he's still alive. I thought I'd take a chance and write him a letter." Kemba rambled on, missing the stricken look on Sarah's face. ". . . I thought all Papa's family was dead." She chanced a glance at Sarah. "Mama? What's wrong?"

"I . . . This is very upsetting."

Kemba was puzzled by her mother's reaction. "I don't understand. . . ."

"Thinking about Bekitemba, Molefi — all of it. I don't want to talk about this."

"But, Mama, why? All I want to know is who is Bekitemba, and is he really my uncle?"

"He is most likely dead by now. What does it matter?"

"What happened in Africa?"

"What do you mean, Kemba?"

"Why are you so upset right now? Did Papa's family hurt you or something?"

"They didn't like me, Kemba. Bekitemba was your uncle. He and Molefi were very close."

"He didn't like you?"

"Oh, no. Bekitemba and I had a good relationship. He has a very kind heart."

"You think he's dead?"

Sarah nodded. "Yes, I do." Sarah looked down at Kemba, her eyes filled with pleading. "Please. I don't want to talk about this anymore."

"That's fine, Mama. I'm sorry I brought it up. I didn't want to upset you."

"Kemba, your father is gone, and so is his family."

"Yes, Mama." She decided to let the matter drop for now, but Kemba knew there was more to this story than Sarah was willing to tell.

They settled back to watch TV. Kemba was still contemplating her mother's reaction over the letter from her uncle. Her mother's voice traveled through her thoughts.

". . . and Doris said her daughter got pregnant on her wedding night. The month-early baby was born weighing in at nine pounds."

"Huh?"

"You're not listening to me," Sarah accused.

"Yes, I am. My mind just drifted to Eric," Kemba fibbed. She didn't want to upset her mother more.

"He's so handsome, dear. A gentleman if ever I met one. You did real good, Kemba."

She laughed. "We're just friends, Mama."

"Humph! I don't believe that for a moment. Have you kissed him?"

"Mama."

"I'm waiting for an answer, young lady," Sarah demanded, her hands folded in her lap. "Well?"

A flash of humor crossed her face. "Yes, I've kissed him."

"I thought as much."

"I really like him, Mama."

"Girl, you're in love with the man! I can see it in your eyes."

"You think you know me so well."

"Child, I do."

Kemba erupted in giggles. But in the back of her mind, she formulated a plan. She was going to write to Bekitemba Rufaro. And if she heard from him, she would then travel to Africa. It was time to find out the truth.

"My sister and I are going shopping on Saturday. Do you want to join us? We could make a day of it."

Kemba did not respond. Her mind was elsewhere.

Nudging her gently, Antoinette asked, "Kim? Did you hear me?" She shook her head. "Something sure has got you in a tizzy. I bet you didn't hear a single word I said."

"Antoinette, what am I going to do?" Kemba's expression was one of mute wretchedness. They were sitting in her office having lunch. "I feel so comfortable with Eric, more every day. These last six months have been wonderful, but I'm not sure —"

"Still afraid of getting in too deep, are we?" Antoinette attacked her sandwich with a vengeance.

"Maybe that's it. I really don't know. Last night we drove to San Pedro. Everything was so still and the sunset was so beautiful. I don't know, maybe it's just me." She gestured helplessly. "Antoinette, can you understand? Am I making any sense at all? I sound like a blabbering idiot."

"You've got it bad," Antoinette said quietly. "You're in love with the good pastor. You're afraid if you allow yourself to love him, the wrath of God will come down on you."

Kemba started to deny it but couldn't. "I — yes, something like that. I'm *so* confused," she moaned.

"Well, I won't begin to tell you what to do — seeing as how my love life's been going. But I can tell he cares for you a lot."

"So, you think I shouldn't care that he's a minister?"

Antoinette shook her head. "I think you shouldn't worry so much. Why not relax and just enjoy the relationship? Take it slow. Who knows, you two may decide you don't really want to be together."

"Let's not talk about Eric anymore. I'm

getting really depressed." Kemba tossed a handful of raisins in her mouth. "By the way, what's going on with you and Michael?"

Antoinette tossed the remnants of her lunch in a nearby wastebasket. *"That SOB is getting married."* She stood up to peer out the door of her office.

"What?"

Antoinette turned to face Kemba. "Uh-huh. He's getting married. I was his last fling before he tied the knot. I should have known he was too good to be true."

"I'm so sorry, Antoinette. I really am."

She shrugged valiantly, but Kemba could see the hurt in Antoinette's eyes. "You were too good for him anyway."

Bracing her hands on her hips, Antoinette made a face. "It doesn't matter. It was great sex, that's all. I wasn't in love with the man. Anyway, that's old news." She reclaimed her seat, pointing at Kemba. "You're not getting off the hook that easy, girlfriend. Right now we should talk about you and Eric. You love him. How can you just ignore that?"

"I can't ignore it — I can't act on it either." She flung out her hands in simple despair.

"But why?" Antoinette took a gulp of lemonade, her mouth puckering from the bitter taste.

Kemba bit her lip to keep from laughing. "He's a minister."

Pushing the drink aside, Antoinette said, "I don't see what that has to do with anything."

"You just don't understand."

"Kim, you're the one who doesn't seem to understand. If Pastor Eric didn't approve of you, I don't think he would be pursuing you."

"I really love him." Her voice broke miserably. "That's what is making this so hard."

"Then why give him up? It doesn't make sense."

"I wish I could make you understand."

Tossing her light brown mane, Antoinette ran her fingers through the tresses. "Naw, I wish you could understand. You're going to mess around and lose the best man you've ever met."

"Antoinette —"

"Kim, get a grip, girlfriend! If the two of you love each other, then it's right. The two of you should be together."

"*Don't you understand?* I want that and he may want it too, but he has to answer to his church. The wrong choice in a wife could ruin him as a minister," Kemba explained.

A soft gasp escaped Antoinette. "You've got to be kidding."

"No, I'm serious. His wife has to be above reproach."

"So what, you haven't done anything."

"I know. I just think —"

"Stop thinking, Kim. Just go with the flow."

"I can't. What I need is to get away for a while," she said firmly.

"Where do you plan on going?"

"I've been thinking about going to Zimbabwe. Eric found a letter that was written to my father. He had a brother, and I want to meet his family. I have some cousins still living there." Kemba forced her lips to part in a curved, stiff smile.

Antoinette hesitated, blinking with bafflement. "Is your uncle still alive?"

"Yes. I wrote him and he wrote me back. I got the letter yesterday. He seemed shocked to hear that my father was dead."

Antoinette held up her hand. "Kim, I'm a little confused here. I thought you told me that your father was an only child. Why did you think that?"

"I did tell you that because that's what my mother told me."

"Didn't she know about your uncle?"

"I tried to ask her about it, but she got so upset, I just dropped it."

"Hmmmm, that sounds strange."

"I agree, but I don't want to upset Mama." Kemba reached over to take one of Antoinette's French fries. "Do me a favor and look out for her for me. And don't tell her I'm in Africa. Just tell her I'm on a buying trip in Europe."

"Sure thing. Keep your pager on, so I can reach you at all times."

"I will. I appreciate this. I really need to find out who I am, and about my family. My dad valued his history and his family. Somehow I have the impression that a huge chunk is missing. I have to find out. Besides, this gives me a chance to think about my relationship with Eric."

"I understand. Family is very important. As far as Eric — I think you already know what to do."

"I should only be gone for about a week and a half. Two weeks at the most."

"No problem. Joyce and I can handle things on this end. But you be careful over there in Africa."

"I will. Who's going to harm me? My family certainly won't."

Mapfumo stood in the doorway of Antoinette's office, watching her. She was an extremely beautiful woman, he acknowledged.

She turned around with a start. "Mr.

Matona! You scared the living daylights out of me."

"I apologize. Your receptionist was not here."

"Oh, it's okay. I just never heard you make a sound. What can I do for you?"

"Well, I wanted to tell you that I'm going to have to leave the country. Return home."

"I'm so sorry to hear that. I hope nothing's wrong."

"My family needs me. I would like to take you out to dinner — my way of thanking you for your time."

"You're very sweet, but you don't have to do that. I'll write you out a check for the rest of your balance —"

"No, keep it," Mapfumo interjected. "You and your partner have earned it."

"Thank you, Mr. Matona."

"Call me Mapfumo, please. I really would like to have dinner with you — before I leave for Africa."

Antoinette tossed her curling tendrils away from her face. "Sure. When did you have in mind?"

"How about tonight?"

"Right now okay?"

"That is fine."

She smiled prettily. "Just let me lock up

and turn on the alarm. Then I'm ready to go." Antoinette quickly keyed in a series of numbers before walking out of the shop. "I need to stop at my house for a minute. I want to freshen up a bit, if you don't mind?"

"I will follow you to your house, and then we can go from there to the restaurant."

Mapfumo pulled out a chair for Antoinette. They had just been shown to their table by the hostess at El Torito's.

Tossing her curling strands away from her face, she smiled prettily. "Why, thank you. I don't meet very many gentlemen these days."

"A beautiful woman such as yourself? I cannot believe that."

Antoinette grinned.

"How long have you and your partner known each other?"

"Oh gosh, we've been friends forever! We know practically everything about each other."

"I see."

"Kim's father was from Africa, you know."

"Really?" If she heard his quick intake of breath, she didn't show it. She continued with her story.

"Yes, they moved to the United States about twenty-eight years ago. Right before Kim was born."

"Where is her father now?"

"He was killed twenty years ago."

Mapfumo held his breath for a moment, showing no reaction. "That is unfortunate. Did they find the person responsible?"

Antoinette shook her head. "Naw, they never did."

"Is Kim married?"

"Naw, why?"

"Her last name is Jennings, isn't it?"

"Her mother remarried and her step-father adopted her."

"I see."

"She has never forgotten her real father, though. She says he used to tell her stories about some treasure that's supposed to be hidden in Africa."

"Really?"

"Yes, according to her, he was a great storyteller."

Mapfumo sat back in his chair. This was becoming quite interesting. "So, she never believed the stories?"

Antoinette downed the last of her wine. "I'm not sure. I think she did. It's some type of family legacy, and her father had the map, I think."

Mapfumo signaled to the waiter to bring more wine as he listened to what Antoinette had to say. Excitement flowed through his body.

"Is there really treasure in Africa?" Antoinette's voice cut through his musings.

He gave a small laugh. "Well, you know we have the diamond mines and gold."

"Yeah, but somebody owns them. I mean, are there really diamonds and gold hidden somewhere in the wilds of Africa?"

He shook his head. "It is only a story." He moved his food around, not really eating.

She shrugged. "I figured as much. I told Kim that before she left. Hey, why aren't you eating? Don't you like Mexican food?"

"It is good." He paused. "Left? Your partner went somewhere?"

"Yes, she's in Africa. She went to find out more about her family."

"Her family?"

"Uh-huh. She found an old letter from an uncle. She wants to meet her father's family."

"I see. How fortunate for her." Mapfumo could have hugged Antoinette. She had just given him what he needed. He considered himself fortunate; his patience had paid off.

"I think it's great," Antoinette was

saying. "Kim values family very much. This trip is extremely important to her."

"As it should be. Family should always come first."

Mapfumo's gaze was drawn to her full breasts. Dreaming of them fired his blood within his veins and caused a tightening in his loins. He forced himself to pay attention to what she was saying.

". . . You're right about family. I just wish my father knew that."

"Perhaps you should tell him so."

She smiled. "You know what? I will. I'll do just that."

They made small talk as they finished their meal. Mapfumo paid the check and they left the restaurant.

Walking her up to the door, Antoinette invited him in. "Thank you so much for a terrific evening, Mapfumo. I really enjoyed myself."

"I am glad to hear that. I admit that I enjoyed myself as well. You are a delightful dinner companion." At last giving vent to the passion that had been building up, Mapfumo moved closer, pulling her into his arms. "You are a very sexy woman, Antoinette."

"Am I? I didn't think you'd noticed me that way."

"One would be blind to have not noticed

such beauty. You will never know the joy that you have given me. Our short time together . . ."

"Do you really have to leave?"

Mapfumo nodded. "I am afraid I must." He covered her mouth with his. The kiss lengthened as Mapfumo drew her tongue into his mouth. His mouth left hers, his tender kisses drawing a path downward along her jaw and throat. Pulling his head up, Antoinette brought his mouth back to hers.

After another long, passionate kiss, Mapfumo pulled away, saying in a hoarse whisper, "I want to make love to you, Antoinette. Can we have this night together?"

She nodded. Antoinette backed out of his arms, slowly unbuttoning her jacket to reveal the lacy bra underneath.

Mapfumo watched, mesmerized, as she did a slow striptease. Antoinette, dressed only in thong panties and bra, took him by the hand and led him upstairs to her bedroom.

Afterward Antoinette lay in his arms. "You're a wonderful lover, Mapfumo. I really hate to see you leave."

"Perhaps I will have you come visit me in Plumtree."

"I'd like that."

His lips stole over hers in possessive

tenderness. "Let us not talk anymore," he murmured against the side of her mouth.

Some time later, Mapfumo stood beside the bed fully clothed and looked down at Antoinette. Bending down, he kissed her lightly on the lips. She smiled as he rubbed a curling strand of soft hair between his fingers, then gently brushed another kiss upon her cheek.

"I must go. I have a lot to do before I leave this country."

Antoinette crawled out of bed. He stood there, admiring her nude body as she strolled across the room and into a huge walk-in closet. She came out wearing a robe. "Thank you for tonight."

"It is I who should be thanking you." He held her hand up to his mouth, bestowing a kiss upon it.

She walked behind him downstairs. When they neared the front door, Mapfumo wrapped her in his arms. "I do not know what is happening to me, but I must have you one more time." He opened her robe. "Take it off."

Antoinette let the robe slip from her shoulders.

Their passions sated once more, Mapfumo embraced her. "I am afraid I really must leave."

Antoinette sighed softly. "You have a safe trip back home."

"I will miss you," Mapfumo said sincerely. Antoinette was about to close the door when he asked, "Antoinette, what was Kim's father's name? She reminds me of someone. Perhaps I knew her father."

"Molefi Rufaro. Her name is Kemba Rufaro Jennings."

He fought to control the cry of joy that threatened to escape. "No, I never knew him," he lied.

"Oh, Mapfumo, what time are you leaving town?"

"I will fly out tomorrow morning." Gazing into her eyes, he added, "I think I will stop by here on my way to the airport."

"I was just about to suggest the same thing."

"Until tomorrow."

Mapfumo quickly drove to the house he had been renting. He made a phone call and started to pack. He had found the one he'd been looking for.

CHAPTER 19

Kemba shivered in the cool air. Pulling a cable knit sweater over her head, she immediately felt warmer. Bekitemba was on his way to the hotel. She was finally going to meet one of her South African relatives. Kemba wished Eric could be here to share this with her.

She couldn't seem to stop thinking about Eric. And now, even though she was thousands of miles away from him, she still felt as though Eric might be near. No matter, she resolved to let this trip to her father's homeland revitalize her senses.

She had scarcely opened the door when Bekitemba's strong arms wrapped themselves around her, almost tighter than was comfortable. When her uncle finally released her, Kemba took a step backward.

"It's so nice to meet you finally." Kemba recovered her smile. She opened the door wider to let the stocky man enter.

"It is good to meet the daughter of Molefi."

Kemba thought she could detect tears

rimming his eyes but couldn't be sure, since he turned away. When he looked back at her, his eyes were clear. He quietly observed her surroundings.

"This is a very nice room."

Kemba glanced around. "Yes, it is nice." She sat across from him on the couch. "I can't believe that I have an uncle."

"Pardon me?"

"Like I told you in the letter, I never knew I had any living relatives still here. My mother somehow assumed that you were dead."

"I do not know what happened. We used to write each other, then the letters stopped. I wrote Molefi and never heard anything more from him. I feared something bad had occurred."

"That must have been when my father died. We moved right after that."

"I was shocked to hear of my brother's death. I did not know until you wrote me."

"I miss him a great deal."

"You really loved Molefi."

A strange expression crossed Bekitemba's face, and Kemba was not sure what to make of it, when she answered, "Yes, he was my father. He was a wonderful father."

"What happened to the Dumisani Diamond?"

"After my father died, Mama couldn't find where my father had hidden the stone or the map. She thought it must have been stolen the night Papa died. Anyway, a few months ago, a man named Malcolm Avery, who was living in our old house, found the diamond. Somehow, the person who murdered my father found out. He shot and killed Malcolm. I know the deaths are connected because the man responsible had an African accent."

"How do you know this to be true? Someone else could have killed Malcolm —"

"Bekitemba, I was there that night. I heard his voice. . . . I heard everything."

"I see."

"I was there to take the diamond. The same reason the killer was there. Only I wasn't going to kill for it. Malcolm's daughter was there and she watched that man gun down her father."

"The little girl —"

"Is fine," she cut in. "She hit him with a statue and ran into the library. That's how I got involved. I took her with me through a hidden passageway in the library and we escaped. If I hadn't been there . . ." Kemba sighed softly. "Who knows what would have happened?"

Bekitemba shook his head. "I am so

sorry. The diamond and the legend of the Dumisani treasure have caused so much pain."

"Do you have any idea who would do such a thing?"

"Yes, I do. He is much like his ancestor, King Nyandoro. He, too, was without a heart, I am told."

"Bekitemba, please tell me who is doing this. We've got to tell the police. He can't continue to get away with this."

"I cannot say anything until I have proof."

"What proof do you . . . Wait a minute!" Kemba eyed her uncle warily. "The killer . . . Is he a close friend of yours?"

"No." He took a deep breath. "I believe the man you are talking about is my brother. A brother who has been long dead to me. He has disgraced this family terribly."

"Your brother?" Kemba could not believe her ears. "No, there has to be a mistake." It was hard for Kemba to imagine the murderer to be a family member.

"If what I believe is true, you are in grave danger here. You must prepare to leave this country immediately."

"What is it, Bekitemba? Please tell me."

"Let me check on something. I will be back in a couple of hours. Be packed and ready. You will stay with me until we can put you on a plane back to America."

"Bekitemba —"

He waved his hand to halt her words. "Daughter of Molefi, please trust me. Now hurry, you must pack quickly. I have a house in Hwange. You will be safe there."

"I'll be ready when you return. But first I'm going to run out and pick up a few souvenirs. I should be safe, since no one knows I'm here."

Bekitemba nodded in agreement. "I will see you in a couple of hours." He left quickly, almost as if his life depended on it. Kemba felt a thread of fear. What was going on? She was in danger from family? It just didn't make sense. However, she wasn't going to take any chances.

Kemba opened the door to her hotel room and entered. As soon as she closed her door, the hair on the back of her neck and her arms stood up. *I am not alone.* She whirled around to find Mapfumo standing silently by the window. Forcing down her panic, Kemba swallowed hard and tried to keep her cool.

"Mapfumo! What are you doing in my room? How did . . ." She stopped in her tracks, alarm signals going off in her head.

"I have been waiting for you, Ms. Jennings."

Kemba hesitated for a moment, then rushed to the phone, but Mapfumo was quicker.

Holding up a hand, he said. "Please wait. I need to talk to you . . . about your father."

"My father?" She turned around slowly, her hands folded across her chest. "What about my father?" Kemba asked.

"I knew Molefi Rufaro. Quite well."

As their eyes met, Kemba felt a shock run through her. "I see." She sat down slowly, not taking her eyes off him. "So you came all the way here to tell me this. Why didn't you say something before?"

Mapfumo merely smiled a cold, ominous smile. "I didn't know who you were until Antoinette mentioned your father being African."

"What does this have to do with you?" Kemba felt a thread of fear deep down, because she had a feeling she already knew what his visit was really about. "Why did you feel a need to break into my room? What is so important?"

"You have something I want."

Stalling for time until she could formulate a plan of escape, Kemba said, "I thought you liked Antoinette. How could you do this to her?" She and Antoinette had had a long phone conversation about him right before her uncle arrived.

Mapfumo was thrown for a minute. "I am your . . . uncle, Kemba. I imagine your father never told you about me or my family."

A soft gasp escaped her. "Uncle? You're not my uncle. My father —"

"Your father was my . . . brother. The eldest son of my father. He was firstborn."

"I don't believe you! Bekitemba never mentioned you."

"You have met Bekitemba?" His eyes grew larger with his surprise.

"Yes."

"I see. I suppose Sarah never mentioned me either. She did not want Molefi with his family."

Kemba's eyes opened wide in her surprise. "You . . . You know my mother?"

"Yes, Sarah and I were very close once. We were in love. Before she met Molefi."

"I . . . I don't believe anything you're saying. My mother wouldn't have . . ." Kemba shook her head in disbelief. "No, you could have easily researched my family."

"I assure you, I am telling you what is true. Your mother has deceived you greatly. As she did me, all those years ago."

"What are you talking about?" Kemba demanded to know.

"You will find out everything when the time is right."

"*What about right now?* And I want to know why you felt the need to break into my hotel room before I call the police."

"I want the Dumisani Diamond back," he said coldly, all pretense at politeness discarded. "It should have gone to me! When Molefi chose Sarah over the family, he should have given it to me. It never should have left Africa."

"I don't have it." Kemba moved away, her jaw tightening.

"I also want the map."

"What map?" she inquired as calmly as she could.

"The map of the Dumisani treasure."

"I don't know what you're talking about. Look, if you leave right now, I promise I won't call the police."

"I am not worried about the police."

Something about his voice had been nagging at her all this time. Suddenly Kemba gasped in shock. "*You.* It was you that night."

"That was an unfortunate night."

"That's all you have to say. *You killed an innocent man. You tried to kill his daughter.*

What am I thinking? You even killed your own brother. *How could you?*"

"I am usually a very patient man, but my patience is running very short." He pulled out a gun. "Please keep your voice down."

"Why are you doing this?" Kemba asked, wanting to put all the pieces together.

"I only want what belongs to me."

"Then why did you have to kill my father and Malcolm? Why couldn't you just talk to them?" She watched the play of emotions on his face.

"Your father refused. As for Malcolm, he tried to be a hero. All of it could have been avoided."

"Really? Somehow I doubt that." She could sense the barely controlled anger that was coiled in his body. "Have you ever wondered why your father gave it to mine, and not you? *Maybe he felt my father deserved it.*"

Drawing back his hand, Mapfumo swung at her with much of his strength, his fury in the slap as it struck her cheek and sent her reeling.

"Shut up," he demanded.

The blow was sudden and strong. Kemba braved the assault, her face aching fiercely, but she continued with her digs. "The truth hurts, huh?"

"I said shut up."

Kemba didn't flinch or back away. Meeting his eyes, she asked, "What are you going to do? Kill me too?"

He raised his hand to slap her again.

"*Mapfumo, don't.*" Another man had crept silently into the room. "She is family."

"What does he care about family?" Kemba snapped. When Mapfumo moved closer, she forced herself not to retreat. Instead, she advanced.

"You'd better hope I don't get a chance to escape. Because if I do, I'm going to make you wish you were dead." As if to emphasize her point, she kneed him in the groin.

"*Aargh!* This, this . . . She kneed me in my . . . *aargh!*" He fell on both knees to the floor. Mapfumo tried to get up. He stumbled and tried again, still groaning in pain, much to Kemba's delight. Finally he was able to stand. He moved toward her, but his partner blocked him.

"No, Mapfumo. Do not harm her."

"You stay with her then. *American women are crazy.*"

She stood, with her hands braced on her hips, smirking. "Oh puh-leeze. You're just too focused on your own greed to keep up with the times. Nowadays women have

287

minds of their own as well as opinions."

"You are just like your mother," Mapfumo shouted at her.

"*Thank you!*" she shouted back at him. "And I might add that you're nothing like my father."

"It wasn't a compliment."

"Neither was mine," Kemba shot back. She turned to the other man. "And who are you? *Another so-called uncle?*"

Surprised, the man nodded. "I am Sondisa."

She grimaced. "I used to wish for a family, but now that I've had the misfortune of meeting the two of you, I've learned to be careful what I wish for."

"I've got to get out of here before I kill her." Mapfumo stormed out of the room. "You stay with her and make sure she doesn't touch that phone. Make sure you grab her luggage."

"Why? I'm not going anywhere with you."

"That is fine with me, Ms. Jennings. All I need is your passport."

"You'd better kill me now, because I'm not giving it to you."

Mapfumo shrugged. "Then I will have no choice but to kill Sarah."

"What . . . No." Kemba advanced on him

before she realized Sondisa was once again standing between them. "You stay away from my mother. She . . . She has diabetes."

"The fact remains that I will not hesitate to do what I must. I want the Dumisani Diamond back where it rightfully belongs. Until then, you will not be allowed to return home."

Defeated, Kemba threw her hands up in despair but couldn't resist one last dig. "Who needs enemies with family like you?"

Mapfumo stalked angrily over to the window and glared out.

Hearing the sound of laughter, she whirled to face her other uncle. "What's so funny?"

Sondisa immediately straightened up. "You are like your mother."

"You knew her too? Oh, this is just too incredible," she muttered. "My father never said anything about having brothers. Now you're all coming out of the woodwork. I just can't believe this."

Sondisa and Mapfumo glanced at one another. Kemba wished she could read their expressions.

"Molefi was eldest of nine children," Sondisa stated.

She blinked twice. How could her parents

have lied to her like this?

Mapfumo glanced down at his watch. "Time is up. What are you going to do?"

"I'll go with you, but if you do anything to my mother . . ." She let the threat hang in the tension-filled air.

The phone rang. Kemba started to answer it, but Mapfumo's strong arm stopped her. "Do not answer it."

"It could be my mother."

"Do not touch it. If you want Sarah to live, do as I say."

She knew Mapfumo would not hesitate to take another life. Kemba rolled her eyes as she reached for her suitcase. "It'll take me a few minutes to pack."

"We will wait."

God help her, she thought in desperation. As she opened her suitcase, stinging tears filled her eyes. There was nothing she could do but go with them.

Eric knocked on Kemba's door. When she had failed to return any of his calls yesterday, he decided to pay her a visit.

"Come on, Kemba. Open the door. Are you in there?"

When he didn't receive a response, he knocked once more. After he concluded she wasn't home, he returned to his car and drove away. Next he tried the shop. It was Antoinette who greeted him when he arrived.

"Hi, Eric, how are you?"

"I'm fine. I'm looking for Kemba."

"She didn't tell you?"

He took note of Antoinette's look of surprise, and a wave of apprehension flowed through his body. "Tell me what?"

"Kemba is out of town right now. She's on a buying trip."

"Oh, where did she go?"

Antoinette looked as if she were debating whether or not to tell him. "She's in Europe."

"I see. Any idea when she'll be back?" He had a feeling that something wasn't quite right, but Eric had no idea what it could be.

"She should be back next Thursday."

"Great. Do you have her phone number?"

"She's been calling in. If I need her, I just call her cellular. You have the number?"

"Yes, I do. Thanks a lot." Eric could not shake the bad feelings he was experiencing. He ran to his car and headed toward Sarah's apartment. He could not explain it, but he knew Kemba was in trouble.

CHAPTER 20

Sarah's eyes widened in surprise to find Eric Avery at her door. "Pastor Avery, come in." She motioned for him to have a seat. "How are you?"

"I'm fine, Mrs. Jennings. I stopped by to see how you're doing. I just found out Kemba's out of the country. I've been trying to reach her."

"She travels to Europe twice a year. This is her third trip, though, this year. I guess the way her business is growing, she'll have to travel more."

"Have you talked to her? I was wondering when she's coming home."

"She called last night. Antoinette said she should be back next week sometime. Now that I think about it, Kemba didn't sound like herself. I'm kind of worried about her."

"I'm worried myself," Eric admitted.

The telephone rang, interrupting them. Sarah reached to answer it. "Excuse me, please," she said to Eric. Speaking into the receiver, she said cheerfully, "Hello."

"Hello, my sweet Sarah." The voice on the other end was cold and exact. "How are you, my dear?"

Sarah slumped down in the armchair next to the telephone table. She took a quick sharp breath. "W-who is this?"

"I am offended. How could you forget —"

"Mapfumo!" Her body stiffened in shock. She glanced over at Eric, blank amazed and obviously very shaken. He moved to sit next to her, a questioning look on his face. "What do you want?"

"I want you to listen to me and no one will get hurt. I want what rightfully belongs to me and my family."

She stared at the phone, wordlessly, for a minute. "I don't have your cursed diamond! I never wanted it in the first place!"

"I'm sorry, but I do not believe you. I don't trust you. *I never have.* Not after you deceived me." There was a bitter edge of cynicism in his voice.

"D-deceived you. What are you talking about?"

"Have you forgotten how you led me to believe you wanted me until you met Molefi; then you left me to look the fool. Now I want restitution. You must bring the Dumisani Diamond and the map to me."

"The map? What map?" Sarah's voice rose an octave.

"The map to my inheritance. My ancestors' treasure. Surely, Molefi told you of it. When he broke my nose, he warned me that the two of you had no secrets. He knew the truth as you told it. He would not listen to me. Your distorted version of what happened between us."

"He told you the truth. We had no secrets. As far as the treasure, it's just a story. Meant only to entertain. There is no hidden treasure."

"Is that what he told you?" Mapfumo gave a brittle laugh. "I assure you it's a true tale. There is treasure from the past hidden right before King Dumisani died."

"How do you know?" Sarah asked bitingly. "I'm sure if you really believed that you would have already dug up all of Africa by now."

"I only want what rightfully should have been mine. My family and I should have it. Not someone who turned his back on us. You and Molefi lived in a mansion, while my family and I live in houses built from burned brick. Molefi turned his back on us for you! He didn't deserve to have the diamond. He was not family."

"I don't know where it is. Now do not call here —"

"I . . . have . . . your . . . daughter," he said, spacing the words evenly.

Sarah gave Eric a sidelong glance of utter disbelief. When Eric mouthed "what," she pointed to Kemba's picture. "W-what are you saying?"

"I have Kemba. She gave me your phone number. Your daughter will remain my *guest* until I have the diamond and the map to the Dumisani treasure."

The sound of his soft-spoken words evoked a maternal rage in her. "Kemba is off on a buying trip. *In Europe.* I spoke to her just last night."

"I assure you, Kemba is in Bulawayo with me."

"Oh God!" Sarah began to shake as fearful images built in her mind. "Why involve Kemba? She knows nothing of this."

"I believe she knows more than you about this. I told Molefi not to marry you. Especially after our night together. Do you remember, Sarah?"

"I could never forget what you did to me." Her fear turned to anger. "You almost destroyed my life. If not for Molefi and his love —"

"We could have been good together. I

loved you then, did you know that?"

"*You call that love?* You are insane."

"Be careful what you say to me," he threatened. "Remember, I have your precious daughter. No harm will come to her if you do exactly as I say. Do not involve the police or you will never see Kemba again."

Sarah bit her lip as she tried to maintain her fragile control. "What do you want me to do?"

"I want you to bring the diamond and the map to me."

"I can't travel to Africa. I — I'm ill."

He was quiet for a moment. "I am very sorry, Sarah. I really am."

"I don't want your pity. Listen, Mapfumo, there is something you must know." Sarah swallowed with difficulty and found her voice. "Kemba . . ." She glanced at Eric. "Kemba is not . . . Molefi's daughter. She's yours."

"*What?*"

"She is your daughter."

There was a long, brittle silence. Sarah breathed in shallow, quick gasps. Her chest felt as if it would burst. She felt Eric's hand cover hers, lending her his strength. The tense lines on her face relaxed. Calmly she said, "I never wanted you to find out."

"You're lying." Mapfumo's voice hardened ruthlessly. "You would lie to save her life."

"I swear on my dying bed. I was a virgin the night you raped me. Molefi and I never made love until after Kemba was born. You raped me in June, and Kemba was born in March." She gulped for air and choked on a sob. "I'm sure even someone like you can count."

Tears overtook her. Eric held her while she wept. Taking the phone from her, he took over. "Mapfumo."

"Huh, what — who is this?"

"My name is Eric Avery. I know you shot and killed my brother, Malcolm."

"Mr. Avery, it was an unfortunate accident. He tried to take the gun from me, but it went off. It was not my intention to harm him in any way."

"Nonetheless, he's still dead. I have your diamond. So I'm the person you want to talk to. I'll bring it to you, but how do I know if you really have Kemba?"

"Kemba did not leave on a business trip as you have been led to believe. She came to Africa instead. You can have her once I have the Dumisani Diamond *and* the map."

"The map? I don't have a map."

"Find it," he ordered. "You have twenty-

four hours. I'll call Sarah with further instructions."

The phone went dead.

"Oh God, Pastor." Her voice broke off and Sarah looked up at Eric with renewed devastation. She leaned into him weakly, a soft spill of tears beginning again. "What am I going to do? What if he's telling the truth?"

She felt his start of surprise and then heard his quiet question. "Why would Kemba keep something like this from you?"

Sarah took a frantic breath. "She knows how I feel about Africa. She probably thought I would be upset." She pulled away from Eric and reached for the phone. "I've got to call Antoinette. She has to know where Kemba is."

The doorbell rang. Eric opened the door. "Antoinette. We were just about to give you a call."

A strange look came over Antoinette's face, and she asked? "What's wrong?"

"Where is Kemba? Is she really in Europe?"

"Mrs. Jennings . . ."

"Please, Antoinette," Eric implored her. "We really need to know where she is."

"She's not in Europe. Kim went to Africa.

She's in a town called —"

Sarah gave a sudden cry as she slumped down on the sofa, her hands covering her face. "Oh Lord, she went to Bulawayo, didn't she?"

"Yes, ma'am. She's staying at the Holiday Inn there." Antoinette looked up at Eric. "What's wrong? Has something happened to Kim?"

"She's been kidnapped."

"Oh, dear Lord! But why?" Antoinette glanced from one to the other. "Who would do something like this?"

"How did he know she was going to be there?"

"Kim has been corresponding with an uncle named Beki-something."

"Bekitemba. She's been writing to Bekitemba?" Sarah wore an expression of astonishment.

"Yes, ma'am. She wanted to find out more about her father's side of the family."

Eric inclined his head toward Sarah. "Do you think he's —"

Sarah shook her head. "No. Bekitemba would not have anything to do with Mapfumo —"

"Who did you say?" Antoinette interrupted. "What was that name again?"

"Mapfumo. Why?"

"We have a client. His name is Mapfumo Matona. He was from Zimbabwe. I went out to dinner with him before he left. . . ." Antoinette paused, then she glanced from Eric to Sarah. "Oh, my God. It's all my fault. I told him. I told him that she was in Africa. I'm so sorry, Mrs. Jennings. He left a couple of days ago." She started to cry. "It's all my fault." Antoinette pressed her hand over her mouth convulsively.

Eric reached out to comfort her. Patting her shoulder gently, he said, "You had no way of knowing, Antoinette. It's going to be all right. I'm going to leave for Africa as soon as we hear back from Mapfumo."

"But what can you do?" Antoinette asked. She gazed at him in despair.

"I have something he wants."

"This is all about some treasure, isn't it? Kemba told me about it, but I didn't think she really believed the story."

Sarah sighed heavily. "It matters little whether or not she believes it — Mapfumo believes it's true and will stop at nothing to get what he wants."

Antoinette looked up at Eric. "Is . . . is he the one who killed your brother?"

"Yes. He killed Malcolm and Kemba's father."

Antoinette hung her head in both her

hands. "This is so hard to digest. He seemed like such a nice man. I can't believe I opened my big mouth."

"There was no way you could have known. Please don't beat yourself up over this." Sarah patted her hand. "We have to have faith that Kemba is going to be all right."

Eric nodded his agreement. "Antoinette, I'm going to need your help. We need to go over to the house in Brentwood. We've got to search from top to bottom to find that map. Mrs. Jennings, do you have any idea where Molefi would have hidden it? Would it be in the hidden room?"

"No, I don't think so. Molefi said it would be safer if hidden in plain sight. I never wanted to know where it was. Kemba brought me the trunk and there's nothing in it but mementos. I'll go through it again."

"In the meantime, we'll head on over there. We haven't much time. Ready, Antoinette?"

"I sure am. I've got a pair of jeans and an old sweatshirt in my car. I'll change into them before we leave."

Eric nodded. While Antoinette ran to her car, he sank down beside Sarah. "I'm going to do everything in my power to bring Kemba home to you. Try not to worry."

"Kemba is going to need you. She's going to find out the horrible truth."

"What horrible truth?"

"That Mapfumo is her father."

"She may not. I won't tell her, Mrs. Jennings."

"She will know that I've lied to her all these years."

"When I bring her home — sit down with her and explain everything to her. Your daughter is a very understanding person. She will not hold this against you."

Antoinette returned. "Just let me change into these and we're on our way."

When she came out a few minutes later, Eric squeezed Sarah's hand, then stood up. "I'm going to find that map. Then I'm going to Africa to bring Kemba home."

CHAPTER 21

Eric and Antoinette walked into the house, both frowning over the musty odor.

She put a dainty hand to her face, covering her mouth and nose. "Phew! You need to air this place out. So, where should we start?"

"Why don't we start in the basement? I think that's where we'll find the map."

"Why do you think that?"

"That's where Malcolm found the diamond. He told me he had been going through some of the old trunks that were left in the basement."

Three hours later, he and Antoinette sat on the stairs, dusty and tired.

Eric flicked off a dust ball. "I think we've checked out that basement from top to bottom. It has to be in here somewhere, but the only thing that I saw relating to treasure was an old copy of *King Solomon's Mines.*"

Antoinette piped up. "Kemba told me once that her father said the story was loosely based on the legend surrounding the family treasure. We were about nine or ten at the time."

"Are you sure?"

"Yes, do you remember where you saw it?"

Eric jumped up. "Yes, it's over there. On the bottom of that bookshelf, I think." He covered the area in three strides. He knelt and scanned the contents of the oak bookcase. There on the bottom, he found a leather-bound copy of the book. He retrieved it and stood up.

Opening the book, Eric shook it gently. Nothing fell out. Sighing loudly, he started to throw it back onto the bookcase, but a thought came to mind.

He ran his fingers over the back cover. "There's something under here." Pulling out a key, he ripped the paper lining and pulled out an old, tattered piece of cloth.

Holding it up to the light and examining it closer, he said, "This must be it. Boy, this is old."

Antoinette peered from behind him. "Well, it definitely looks like a map of some kind. It's a crudely drawn one, but I guess it qualifies as a map."

"This has to be what Mapfumo's talking about. Let's head upstairs. I want to get a better look at it."

Eric eyed the map as he sat down behind a huge oak desk in the library. Silently shuffling through papers, he pushed them aside and thoughtfully studied the diagram before him.

"Antoinette, come look at this and tell me if you can duplicate it."

She leaned over and inspected the drawing. "I can copy that. No problem."

"What I want is for you to make some tiny changes. I don't intend to hand over the original. Not until I have Kemba by my side. We may have to use it to bargain for our lives."

"Is Mapfumo really the horrible person you all say he is? I mean, maybe Mapfumo Matona and Mapfumo Rufaro are two different people."

"I don't think so, Antoinette," Eric said softly. "You're much better off without him."

She nodded. "I have such awful taste in men. I feel like such an idiot."

"Don't be so hard on yourself. You had no way of knowing."

She glanced down at the map once more. "I have just the right type of fabric for this. I can treat it to give it a more aged look. You'll need to take me to the shop."

Eric nodded. "All right. How much time do you need?"

"Everything shouldn't take more than a couple of hours. Is that okay?"

"That's fine."

"Do you think he'll hurt Kemba?"

"I don't know, Antoinette. All we can do at this point is pray."

"When are you leaving?"

"I'm going to leave sometime tomorrow evening. I couldn't get on an earlier flight."

"Be careful, Pastor. And bring Kemba back."

"I intend to do just that."

A solid thudding of shoes on a wooden floor broke the quiet of the evening. Kemba eased silently across the room, moving to stand beside the door. In her hand she held a brightly painted vase.

Sondisa opened the door; then turning his back, he bent to pick up a tray laden with fresh fruit and a pitcher of water. Pressing flat against the wall, Kemba raised her hands high over her head. As soon as her uncle backed into the room, the clay vase came crashing down on Sondisa, soliciting a loud howl of pain as he stumbled to the floor in surprise.

Using her leg, Kemba shoved him aside, leaving him to lie crumpled in the doorway. As she neared the front door to freedom, Kemba spared a hasty glance over her shoulder. Sondisa was getting up. Seeing him struggle to his feet, she felt every nerve and muscle in her body come to life. Adrenaline pumped through her veins, causing her heart to beat wildly. She eased out of the house, ready to burst into her swiftest pace.

She heard a noise as Sondisa burst out the door. He spun himself around, sprinted around the corner and raced after his niece. She could hear him cursing as he chased her down the dusty road. Spying a house just a few yards away, she increased her speed. Hopefully, someone would help her. Kemba slowed her pace enough to turn the corner, running smack into Mapfumo. Kicking him as hard as she could, she tried to escape his clutches.

Mapfumo grabbed her by the ankle, causing her to fall. By that time Sondisa had caught up with them. She felt her upper arm being clasped in a firm grip. Paralyzing dread swept over her.

"Let me go. I'll scream."

Mapfumo was not one to easily oblige her demand for release. His grip was like a steel vise encircling her flesh and she struggled harder.

He laughed. "Go ahead. Scream all you

like. There is no one to help you. All the houses you see belong to me."

Kemba fought harder. "I said, let me go."

He tightened his grip and shook her to maintain a forced control. "Listen to me, Kemba. You will return to America when we have the Dumisani Diamond and the map. I give you my word."

"Your words don't mean crap to me." She fought back tears of panic as she realized the jeopardy she was in. She was completely at their mercy.

"No one will be happier to see you leave than me," Mapfumo said. He was panting hard.

She stumbled as she was pulled along behind them without a second thought.

"Then take me back home now. I will give you the diamond," she called out breathlessly.

"It has all been arranged. The diamond is to be delivered to me. As we speak, it should be on its way," he said with a grunt as he relentlessly pulled her along.

"If you harm my mother, *I'll kill you myself.*"

Mapfumo stopped and smiled coldly. "If I wanted to harm Sarah, there would be nothing you could do to stop me." He moved forward menacingly. Sondisa pulled Kemba behind him. "She will not escape again."

"You had better see that she does not." Mapfumo gripped a nearby chair, then flung it against the wall.

Turning to Kemba, Sondisa pleaded with her. "Please do as you are told. This will all be over soon."

She glanced up at him, anger flowing through her veins. "Why do you let him bully you around? Can't you think for yourself? What are you afraid of?"

Sondisa appeared little affected by Kemba's outburst. "I am afraid of nothing. Mapfumo is my brother. He saved my life. Now do as he says, please. Go back into your room."

Shrugging in resignation, Kemba retreated back into the bedroom. Sondisa nodded slightly before closing and bolting the door. Her knees caught the back of an old weathered bench, and she dropped abruptly. She bit her lip to keep from crying. From the other side of the door, she heard Mapfumo's voice.

"If you try to escape again, I will have to tie you up. I would not like to treat you that way. After all, *you are a guest in my home.*"

His chilling words washed over Kemba and created the threat he intended.

"Go to hell!" Kemba cried out in anger and loathing.

Mapfumo dialed, then waited for Sarah to pick up. When he heard her voice, he spoke. "Sarah, I hope you slept well."

"You know I didn't sleep at all! What have you done to my daughter?"

"*Our daughter,* you mean, do you not? How could you not tell me about my child? You would have Molefi take everything from me?"

"Is Kemba all right?" Sarah's voice trembled.

"Yes, she is fine."

"Please, Mapfumo, please let me talk to her. I just need to hear for myself that she's okay."

"I am sorry. I cannot do that. You will have to take my word for it. Have you found the map?"

"Yes, Pastor Avery found it. He will soon be on his way to Africa. Mapfumo —"

"Sarah," he interrupted. "We could have been good together."

"I didn't love you."

"I do not believe that. Had you told me about the child, I would have married you."

"I didn't want you to marry me, or anything. You raped me —"

Mapfumo had heard enough. Each word she flung at him pierced his heart. All the feelings he had for Sarah, the love and adoration, his desire to make her his wife, everything had been a waste. She had never cared for him at all. "Do not say this," Mapfumo ordered, lashing out in anger. "It is not true."

"I beg you to please leave Kemba out of this —"

He cut her off by asking, "Do you think I would harm my own daughter?"

"You killed your own flesh and blood — your brother. Why would a daughter you've never known be any different?"

"I will not harm her," he said quietly.

"I — I'm sick, Mapfumo. Please do not harm my daughter."

"I swear. Sarah, if I could make you well, I would. . . ."

"Just bring no harm to Pastor Avery or my daughter. It's all I ask."

"After I have the diamond and the map back in my hands, you will never hear from me or see me again. I give you my word." Mapfumo hung up the phone, an evil grin plastered on his face. Sarah would pay for rejecting him. He would hurt her where she was most vulnerable.

CHAPTER 22

"I'm sorry, Sarah, but at this point we have to seriously consider a kidney transplant."

"I thought as much." She stood up slowly and went to stare out the window. "Will a new kidney make me better? At my age and my health?"

"Sarah . . ."

She turned to face her doctor. "Will it help?" she asked firmly.

He sighed. "I don't know. The drugs you will have to take to prevent immune rejection of the new kidney may put you at a greater risk of infection. I'm sorry."

She brushed away a tear. "There's nothing for you to be sorry about, Doctor. You did all you could for me. I appreciate all you've done. It's now time for me to get my house in order. No matter what happens."

"Is Kemba here with you?"

"No, she's on a business trip. She should be back soon."

"If you like, we can tell her together —"

Sarah shook her head. "Oh no, Dr.

Wilson. I don't want you to say nothing to her. Kemba . . . ," she faltered. "My baby can't handle news like this. I don't want her to know." Tears streamed down her face. She turned to face the window again, admiring the scenery. "I've lived a good life, you know. There have been some ups and some downs, but I was grateful for it all." She nodded. "Yes, I was grateful for it all."

"Sarah, I don't think you should deal with this alone —"

"But I won't, Dr. Wilson," she interjected. "You see, I have Jesus standing with me. He's going to see me through. I believe that."

"Are you saying you don't want to have the kidney transplant?"

"Oh no, that's not what I'm saying. I want the new kidney. I'm just preparing myself for whatever happens."

Sarah returned to her chair and picked up her purse. "I guess I should get going. I've got a lot to do, as you can well imagine." Finding a Kleenex, she wiped her face and touched up her makeup.

She walked out of his office with her head held high.

Sarah had no idea how she made it home. But as soon as she made it to her bedroom, she crumpled down on her bed in a heap. She cried until the tears refused to come.

She crawled off the bed and headed to the bathroom, where she proceeded to wash her face.

When she came out again, Sarah stood in front of her full-length mirror and stared. As if she'd had a glimpse into her future, she murmured sadly, "I'm never going to see my baby walk down the aisle. I'll never get to meet my grandchildren. . . . *It's just not fair.*"

Sarah felt the white-hot anger course through her veins. She suddenly felt empowered by it. Picking up a nearby vase, she threw it straight at the mirror, shattering it into thousands of little pieces. Next she picked up her favorite perfume bottle and was about to throw it, when someone knocked on her bedroom door. She stood immobilized, frozen by fear, unable to speak.

"Mrs. Jennings? Are you okay? It's me, Eric Avery. The front door was open. I was worried."

Relief swept through her. "Pastor Avery, hold on just a minute." She reached into her closet and quickly put on a thick terry cloth robe. Sarah opened the door. "I just rushed in from the doctor. I guess I forgot to close the door."

Eric surveyed the room. Shards of glass lay on the dark brown carpet, reminding him of sparkling gems. "Mrs. Jennings, are you okay?"

"I'm f-fine. . . ." She burst into tears.

"What happened? Is something wrong with Kemba?"

She shook her head. "I went to the doctor. I have . . . I have to have a kidney transplant." She sank down slowly on the bed. "I have a feeling that I'm not long for this life, Pastor. I can't tell you how I know, but I do. I know that even having this transplant — it won't save me."

Eric knelt down in front of her, cupping her small hands in his large ones. He bowed his head and began to pray. "Father, you promised that there would be faith and strength and hope to meet life's problems. Father, give that strength to my sister whose . . ."

Sarah could feel her rage dissipating slowly as his words comforted her. She felt ashamed of being angry with God. So angry she had thrown a tantrum.

"It's okay to be angry, Mrs. Jennings. Our Father understands," he said softly as if he knew what she'd been thinking. "He is with you and will never forsake you. Perhaps even more so, in this time of need."

"Thank you, Pastor. I'm glad you came by when you did. I was about to destroy this whole house. It's not that I'm . . . I can't say that — I'm angry. Very angry."

He sat on the bed beside her and started to write on a piece of paper. "I want you to give this lady a call. I think you two can comfort each other."

"She . . . She's going through the same thing?"

Eric nodded. "She's a longtime member of my church."

"Pastor, you are such a kind man. A caring man." She looked down at her hands. "I need to know something."

"I love your daughter. I want to marry her, Mrs. Jennings."

"I'm so glad to hear that, Pastor. You know through this — she's going to need you more than ever."

"Where Kemba is concerned, I'm not going anywhere. I leave this afternoon for Africa and I'm bringing her home."

"Pastor, do me a favor. Don't tell Kemba about . . . about this, please."

"I won't if you don't want me to. Besides, I think something like this should come from you."

"Thank you, Pastor. I just don't think she'll be able to deal with much more. Especially since she now knows that I've lied to her all her life." She shook her head sadly. "I don't know that she'll ever forgive me."

Eric gently patted her hand. "Kemba will understand once you tell her your reasons."

"I never wanted her to find out. Mapfumo is evil!"

"Kemba's a lot stronger than either you or she realizes," Eric assured her.

"I hope you're right, Pastor."

"Kemba and I will be home as soon as we can get back here." He rubbed his hands over his face. "I hate leaving you at a time like this."

"No, I want you to go get Kemba for me. Just bring her home to me. B-bring my baby h-home."

Eric heard the break in her voice and knew she was on the verge of tears. He kissed her cheek. "I will." He stood up. "I'd better get going, Mrs. Jennings. I need to stop off at the church before I head to the airport."

Sarah nodded. "Be safe."

She stood up slowly, using Eric's arm for support. He slowed his pace as she walked him to the door. "I'll be praying for you both," she said.

"We'll be back real soon."

"I have faith," she announced. When Eric drove away, Sarah crumpled on the sofa in tears. "Please let them be safe, Lord."

After drying her tears, Sarah made her way back to her bedroom. She pulled a leather-bound journal out of a drawer. Crawling into the middle of her bed, Sarah wrote furiously.

Bekitemba opened his door to find a slender woman standing there. He nodded as she walked in.

"Mapfumo has the girl."

Bekitemba sighed. "I feared as much. But how did he know she was here?"

"He went to America. Somehow he found her."

"But she came here on her own, Nomsa. It does not make sense."

"Then he must have followed her back to Africa. Sondisa will not say much, but I fear for her life. If he does not get the stone and the map . . ."

"He will kill a third time."

"A third time? What are you talking about, Bekitemba? He has only killed one man —"

"He killed Molefi."

"*No.*"

318

"I'm afraid so. He killed him over twenty years ago."

"All this time . . ." She shook her head, unable to continue.

"I know how much you loved him, but he loved another."

"I have always loved Molefi. She was not right for him. Look what has happened. He did not live." Nomsa put her hands to her face, sobbing.

"He died at the hands of Mapfumo — not Sarah. This should not come as such a shock, Nomsa. We have suspected for years now that he was dead."

"I know, but to know that Mapfumo . . ." She looked up at Bekitemba. "Sondisa has known this all these years. He never said a word."

"He knows of your love for Molefi. Sondisa loves you as you love his brother, Nomsa. He and Mapfumo are much alike."

"I have to leave. I am to meet her man at the train in Bulawayo."

"He's bringing the stone and the map?"

"Yes. I pray Mapfumo will release them as promised."

"I do not believe that he will. Nomsa, this is what I want you to do. . . ." He leaned down and gave her his instructions.

Eric stepped off the crowded bus just outside of Bulawayo. He stopped to study the piece of paper where he'd written Mapfumo's instructions. Just ahead of him, a woman walked by carrying a heavy basket on her head, with a young child strapped to her back.

Surveying the surrounding area, he admired the brightly colored geometric patterns that adorned the exterior walls of some of the houses. The whitewashed shops and beer halls in Bulawayo, along with the crowded buses, testified to a social life in a city. People walked slowly, watching him. One bold woman grinned a wide, toothless grin. Eric nodded and waved, walking faster. As he walked, several tractors and old trucks passed him by.

A dark-skinned woman approached him cautiously, wearing a brightly colored print dress and matching jacket. On her head she had tied a bright red kerchief, fastened with a gold-toned pin. "You are Eric Avery?" she asked timidly.

He nodded. "Yes, who are you?"

"I am Nomsa. I was sent here to meet you. Please follow me."

"Where are you taking me?"

"I am taking you to Mapfumo. You still

wish to meet with him, don't you?"

"Yes, I do. Where is Kemba? I need to know if she's all right. If anything has happened to her —"

"She is fine. Mapfumo will not harm her. Here is my car."

Eric stood beside the dusty automobile. "Why isn't she here with you?"

Nomsa shrugged. "I do not know. Mapfumo will tell you everything you need to know."

Eric sat in the car, looking around. "Why didn't he meet me himself? Why did he send a woman?"

"You will have to ask him yourself. I do not know anything else. I was only instructed to bring you to him."

He glanced around once more. Looking down at her, he said, "Well, I guess we'd better get a move on it."

CHAPTER 23

Kemba lay on the bed staring at the ceiling. She missed her mother and wanted to go home. She missed Eric too. Right now she would give just about anything to put her arms around him one more time. Hearing voices, she tiptoed closer to the door and pressed her ear to the crack. She could hear what Mapfumo and Sondisa were discussing clearly.

"That was Nomsa. He has arrived. We should leave now. Nomsa will come here to watch the girl," Sondisa was saying.

"So, Mr. Avery has arrived." Mapfumo turned to his brother. "Soon, my loyal brother, we will have what is rightfully ours. We will not only have the Dumisani Diamond, but the treasure as well. It is a good day for celebrating."

"Do you think he can be trusted?"

"Yes, we have Kemba. He will not want harm to come to her."

She trembled at the sound of his voice. She knew he would kill her without so much as a second thought. And Eric. Her thoughts were confirmed by his next statement.

"Sondisa, bring the gun. We may need it."

"Mapfumo —"

"And bring Lee. I think maybe we should teach Mr. Avery a valuable lesson. He wants to play hero. We shall let him."

"I do not think —"

She could hear the uncertainty in Sondisa's voice, but he would not go against Mapfumo. He was afraid.

"Sondisa, I am doing what I have to — it is for the family. I thought you believed as I do. Molefi turned his back on us. He went to America, lived in a mansion — look at us. We do not live in mansions, drive fancy cars. . . . Royal blood also flows in our veins."

"You are correct, as always."

"I am looking out for the Rufaro family. Something Molefi and Bekitemba did not do. They forgot about us!"

She heard Sondisa leave the room; then Mapfumo left.

Kemba placed a trembling hand to her heart. *Oh God, what are they planning to do to Eric?* she wondered. Biting her lip, she prayed for divine intervention. "Please don't let them hurt Eric."

"Where are we going exactly?" Eric

wanted to know. They were no longer in Bulawayo.

"I am taking you to Plumtree."

"Plumtree?"

She spared a glance in his direction. "It is where we live."

Nomsa was quiet during the drive. It was obvious to Eric that she didn't wish to talk, so he left her alone. Instead, he chose to admire the landscape along the dirt road. Soon they pulled into a vacant area, beside another car. "Here you are. Mapfumo is in that car — he will take you to Kemba."

"Thank you," Eric said as he stepped out of her car.

She pulled out quickly, leaving him with three men. One looked familiar. Eric walked closer.

"I take it you're Mapfumo," he said to the tallest one. "I've seen you before."

"You have a good memory."

"Not exactly. I don't remember where I've . . ." He searched his memory. "Wait a minute. You were at Malcolm's funeral. You killed my brother and you had the nerve —"

Mapfumo interrupted by asking, "Where is the diamond?"

"Here." Eric pulled it out of his pocket. When Mapfumo reached for it, he stepped back. "Where is Kemba?"

"She is safe. Now, where is the map?"

"I want to see Kemba. When she and I are safely at the airport, I'll hand over the map."

Mapfumo took a menacing step closer. "You are in no position to bargain. Now hand over the diamond."

Eric threw the diamond up in the air. It landed a few feet away. Mapfumo, muttering curses, ran over to search for it.

The two men ran over to hold Eric. Mapfumo then stomped over and slammed a fist in Eric's face. "You son of a b—"

Without warning, Eric bent his head low, let out a loud growl and rushed Mapfumo, pulling the other two men with him.

Mapfumo staggered, the look in his dark eyes dazed. Eric lifted a leg, kicking Mapfumo in the groin. Falling to the ground, Mapfumo yelled, "Do not let him get away. Whatever you have to do, do it, but do not kill him."

Eric fought valiantly, first knocking one man to the ground, then the other. He didn't see Mapfumo sneak up behind him, the butt of his gun raised.

Eric felt pain explode in his head as darkness settled over him. At the same time he felt the thud of someone kicking him in his side. Before unconsciousness consumed him, his thoughts were of Kemba and her safety.

Kemba turned around to face the door when she heard the unmistakable sound of the lock turn. She was surprised to see a small woman enter. Her hair was jet black, braided and woven in a bun on the top of her head.

"Your man is here. Mapfumo and Sondisa are with him right now."

Kemba turned completely to face the soft-spoken woman. "Who are you?" She moved closer, in order to hear her soft-spoken words.

The petite woman retreated back a step. "I am Nomsa. Sondisa's wife."

"I see. I guess that makes you my aunt," she commented dryly.

Nomsa raised an eyebrow. "You sound as if you are not pleased."

"Would you be under these circum-stances?" Kemba gestured around the bare room. "I'm under lock and key. Held against my will by my own flesh and blood."

"I am sorry for that. It should not be this way. You are in this situation because of your mother and father. Mapfumo and

Sondisa believe your father turned his back on the family."

"But why am I being held prisoner? I never turned my back on family. I *didn't even know* I had family out here — much less uncles. This is all about greed. Mapfumo cares nothing about family. He just wants the diamond and the map."

"It is not just about the Dumisani Diamond or the treasure. Molefi turned his back on us for *her*. He destroyed the Rufaro family."

Kemba folded her arms across her chest. "I don't believe that for a minute. And by her, I take it you're referring to my mother."

Nomsa grunted. "She used voodoo to take him from his family."

Kemba crossed the room in angry strides, causing Nomsa to back up. "You are a liar. My mother would never do such a thing! He fell in love with her from the moment he first laid eyes on her."

"How would you know such a thing? Did *she* tell you this?"

Kemba placed her hands on her hips and glared at Nomsa. "No, *she* didn't have to tell me. *My father told me.* He and my mother were very much in love up until the day he was murdered."

"He never should have traveled to America. He probably still would be alive if he had stayed here —"

"And what?" Kemba questioned. "*How did you know he was dead?* Even Bekitemba didn't know of my father's death, so how could you? Better yet, how long have you known?"

Nomsa chose to ignore her questions, saying instead, "Molefi and I were in love. He would have married me if your mother had not come along," she spat.

"Oh puh-leeze!" Kemba folded her arms across her chest. "If he loved you so much, he would've married you! He loved my mother."

"You are arrogant like her." Nomsa curled her lips in disgust.

"*Her!* What is it, Nomsa? You can't say her name. It's Sarah. *Sarah.*"

"*You are just like her.*"

"And you're a fool. How can you let Sondisa and Mapfumo manipulate you like this? Are you that bitter over my father?" She was lashing out in anger.

"I will not listen to you." Nomsa stalked out angrily, slamming the door behind her. "You do not understand anything."

CHAPTER 24

"Here is your man," Mapfumo announced as he shoved an unconscious Eric into the room with Kemba.

"Eric?" She rushed over to the area where he lay crumpled on the floor. She dropped to her knees beside him and cupped his face in her hands.

Kemba frowned at the bruises beginning to form on Eric's face. One eye was swollen shut. "Why didn't you stay in Los Angeles?"

Mapfumo laughed harshly. "I don't think he can answer that right now. He put up a good fight, but he cannot protect you."

"*Why did you have to beat him?*" she screamed. Looking down at Eric, she swallowed the sudden lump in her throat.

Mapfumo merely shrugged, then left the room.

She stroked his face lightly. She traced one finger along his lower lip. Firm. Smooth. His lips were . . .

Kemba jerked her hand away, chastising

329

herself for getting carried away in her fantasies.

Kemba felt around his body for broken bones. She breathed a sigh of relief when she felt none. "Thank God there are no broken bones," she whispered. "I could kill you for this, Mapfumo."

She got up and walked briskly over to the door. Knocking loudly, she called out for Mapfumo. "Why did you have to do this? Are you that big a coward? Why don't you act like a real man? You said you wanted the Dumisani Diamond and the treasure." She went through Eric's pockets. She had a feeling that Mapfumo had done the same. "You have it. Now let us go," Kemba demanded.

Kemba stepped back when she heard someone unlocking the door. When it opened, she stood staring into the angry gaze of Mapfumo.

"I can't believe you had the guts to come back!" Kemba stated. "Are you not a man of your word?"

"I could kill you just like that." He snapped his fingers for emphasis. "You are not afraid?"

"What I am is very hurt, Mapfumo. You are supposed to be my family — my uncle. I don't understand how you can be so cold. Or how I can even be related to you. You've *murdered* people."

"I did what I had to do, Kemba. You do not know everything."

"I know what a horrible person you are."

"You know only what you have been told. I could tell you things that —"

"That would only be lies," Kemba interjected. "I'm not interested. All I want is for Eric and me to get on a plane home. Will you let us go?"

"I have no intentions of keeping you any longer than I have to. I ask that you remain my guests for a few more days. Please bear with me."

"Why are you keeping us? My mother is sick, and she needs me."

"I want to ensure that the map is real. Once I have the Dumisani treasure, you and your man will be allowed to return home."

"Of course the map is real! Not everyone thinks like you, Mapfumo." Kemba's voice rose an octave.

"I wonder how the good pastor puts up with you — you drive a man to murder with that mouth of yours."

"Please let us leave and you'll never have to hear my mouth again," Kemba pleaded.

"Your man is beginning to stir. Perhaps

you should check on him." He turned to leave.

"I never thought I could hate anyone, but I hate you."

She watched with satisfaction as his back stiffened before he closed the door behind himself.

Slowly being pulled from a deep sleep by the sound of a woman's voice calling out to him, Eric forced his eyes open. The first thing he noticed was that every inch of his body seemed to ache as he tentatively moved around.

A small noise drew his attention and his gaze settled on Kemba's slender form. There were tears in her eyes. *"Oooh,"* Eric moaned. He raised a hand to his aching head. Trying to sit up, he groaned as agony spread throughout his body. He took several deep breaths. Wincing, Eric tried to clear the fog in his brain. He was soaked in perspiration from his efforts.

Kemba gathered him in her arms. *"Eric. Oh God . . ."*

"Kemba —"

She interrupted him by demanding, "Stay put, Eric. You've been hurt."

"They jumped me from behind."

"I could kill him."

"Don't say that, Kemba." Eric tried once again to sit up. Kemba loosened her grip. He tried looking at her through his one good eye. "Are you okay?"

"I'm fine, Eric. Do you always put others before yourself?"

"What are you talking about?" He felt around his head gingerly. "Ouch!" He rubbed the back of his head.

"You're the one who was beaten unconscious, yet you're more concerned about my safety."

"I care a great deal about you. And I promised your mother that I would bring you safely home. I intend to keep my word."

"I wish you hadn't come."

"I had to. I couldn't let Mapfumo hurt you."

Kemba swallowed the sudden lump in her throat. "I'm sorry." She started to rise, but Eric stopped her.

"I missed you too."

Kemba smiled. She saw him fumbling with the buttons on his shirt. Her hands brushed his hands aside. "I can tell you're in pain. Let me do it."

"I wanted to get out of this shirt. It's ruined."

"I'll help you."

Eric watched her face as she removed his shirt. He told himself to keep everything simple, not bring sex into it, but right now with her this close, with her body touching his, he couldn't. Clearing his throat, he said, "We need to get out of here."

"I know, but you're hurt."

"I'll be fine; that is, if we can escape. If we're still here when they get back, we're dead meat!" He stared into her dark eyes. "I'm really glad to see you."

"What?" Kemba gave a small laugh. "Why are you staring at me like that? What is it?"

"I was really worried about you. And scared out of my wits for your safety."

"I missed you and Mama. Antoinette too. I was scared for you too. I knew they were going to do something to you. I overheard them."

He pulled her down to him.

Kemba tried to pull away. "You're hurt Eric."

"Don't. Don't push me away." He kissed her gently.

They were interrupted by Nomsa. She addressed them both.

"I am sorry about what happened." She looked at Eric. "I did not know that you would come to harm when I brought you to Mapfumo. He promised that no one would be hurt."

Eric looked at Kemba, then at Nomsa, his gaze questioning. "And you believed him? You do know that he killed Molefi?" She nodded. "He also killed my brother. Nomsa, he is a murderer!"

"Where are my *darling* uncles, by the way?" Kemba asked.

"They are away. They won't be back for you until tomorrow."

Eric tried to stand up. "Nomsa, will you help us get out of here? You know he's dangerous. Look what he did to me." Eric pointed toward his bruises.

"That is why I am here." She held out a leather pouch. "I have packed some cheese, fruit and crackers. There is also bottled water. You cannot go the airport because it is not safe. You must head to the mountains near the Zambezi River. It is there you will meet Bekitemba."

"Bekitemba? What is going on, Nomsa?"

"It is Bekitemba I am loyal to. I owe him my life."

"I see," Kemba said quietly. "I didn't know."

"If you help us, won't they know you did it?" Eric inquired. "I don't want to risk your life, Nomsa."

"I cannot let them kill you as they did Molefi and your brother."

Kemba didn't miss Nomsa's tear-bright eyes at the mention of her father's name. "You really loved my father."

She appeared to give it serious consideration. "Yes, my heart belonged to Molefi. It will be that way until I take my final breath. We must hurry. I will get some rope. You will have to tie me up." She walked out of the room, only to return a few minutes later with a thick coil of rope. "You should know that there is a man outside. He has a gun."

Eric nodded. "Thanks. I'll handle him."

She pointed into the dining room. "There, on the table, is a map and a set of car keys. The keys are to Sondisa's car. You can leave it abandoned somewhere. Here is some money."

Kemba took the money. "Thank you. Nomsa, I need to know something. Why are you doing this for me? You don't exactly care much for my mother. That much you've made very clear. You can't care much for me —"

"You are family. You are Molefi's daughter. I honor the only man I have ever loved by helping you. Besides, I am weary. I do not wish to see more blood shed over greed." She sighed heavily. "Because of Mapfumo, Sondisa and I have been banished from our families." A large tear slipped down her cheek.

Kemba felt sorry for her. "What are you going to do?"

Nomsa smiled briefly. "I will be fine. Bekitemba has promised to keep me safe and return me to my family. Do not worry about me. We must hurry. Here is where you should wait for Bekitemba. Stay there and he will find you."

"Why there?"

"Because those mountains are sacred. King Nyandora's remains are sealed in a hillside tomb somewhere up there. It is also believed that King Dumisani is also buried up there. Mapfumo fears them. It is the only thing he fears."

After they tied Nomsa up, Eric eased up to a nearby window. He peered out. Climbing out, he touched down without a whisper in his rubber-soled shoes. He looked left, then to the right.

Spying a man relieving himself in a wooded area, Eric sneaked up behind the man. Clamping his mouth shut to block out the pain in his side, Eric chopped once on the side of the guard's neck, knocking him unconscious. He lowered him in the bushes, taking the man's gun with him.

Feeling all was safe for the moment, he helped Kemba climb out. They ran across the open yard like clouds skimming the midday sun.

"Eric, why did you take the gun?"

"In case we need to defend ourselves. Come on, let's get out of here."

He and Kemba started running toward the car as fast as their legs would take them. Eric stopped and inhaled a deep breath.

"Are you all right?" she asked.

He nodded.

Kemba held up the keys. "You check out the map while I drive, okay?"

He hunched over, his arms resting on his knees. "You sure you want to drive?"

As soon as they were in the car, Kemba turned to him, saying, "You need to rest, Eric. Your body took a beating."

"Let's just get out of here! I'll rest later."

After leaving Sondisa's car in Bulawayo, Eric and Kemba caught the train to Hwange. Kemba released the long breath she had been holding when she heard the wheezing of the train as it gathered strength. The straining chugs bellowed loudly, keeping with the strong rhythm of the rails.

All around them, passengers chattered with each other. Kemba sat silent, fingering her necklace.

"Are you okay?" Eric asked in an intense whisper.

"I'm fine. Just glad to be away from Mapfumo." She chewed on her bottom lip.

Eric nudged her gently, his fingers stroking her arm sensuously. "What is it? You seemed in deep thought."

She had a quick and disturbing thought. "Do you think he'll go after Mama? I don't want to lose her."

"I don't think so. As far as he's concerned, he's gotten everything he wanted."

"But he wouldn't let us go. I hope you're right." Kemba laid her head on his shoulder and closed her eyes.

Thirty minutes later, Kemba woke up. She straightened up and rubbed her eyes. "I guess I was tired."

Eric nodded. "Yeah, I guess you were. You dozed off right in the middle of my conversation."

"I'm sorry."

"Don't be." He laughed. "I'm only kidding you."

"*You.*" She punched him lightly on the arm.

One hour later, they pulled into

Hwange. From there, she and Eric rented a car and drove toward the Zambezi River. Getting out of the car, they scanned the area.

"I guess we're supposed to follow that track right there," Kemba said, pointing.

Grabbing the bag containing their fruit and water, he said, "Let's head up."

Climbing the hills formed of granite and gneiss, Kemba glanced back at Eric, and anxiety leaped to her chest. It was obvious he was in pain. "Eric, are you feeling okay?"

"I'm fine. J-just keep going. I'll be fine."

Kemba didn't believe him. Her heart pounded with fright when she saw him wobble precariously, his eyes rolling and looking unfocused, as though he were losing consciousness. She stopped to sit on a smooth rock. "Why don't we rest a bit?"

"We can't. Not right now," he insisted.

Kemba stood up. "Lean on me, Eric," she ordered, reaching around his waist.

He leaned heavily on the surprisingly strong woman, his arm draped around her narrow shoulders as she slowly led him up, higher into the hills.

"I can walk by myself," he insisted, his masculine pride refusing to admit his dependence on Kemba. "I'll be fine."

Beads of sweat broke out on his forehead. Suddenly he began to weave back and forth, grabbing hold of a tree for support.

She studied him as she led him beneath a tree. "We can rest here for a while."

"I said I was fine."

"You may be fine, but not me. I'm tired. I need a break, Eric," she lied. She knew he was in pain.

Eric valiantly tried to stand up, but finally gave up. He collapsed under the huge tree. She cradled his head in her lap. "Why don't you close your eyes and rest for a while?"

He didn't respond because he had already fallen asleep.

Twenty minutes later, his head restlessly tossed, and when his eyes opened, they fixed on her in confusion, then with a spark of recognition. She smiled down at him.

"How are you feeling?"

He sat up slowly, grimacing in pain. "I'm fine."

"We're going to rest for a while longer. You need your strength."

Eric nodded. His features clenched up, but when she worriedly said his name, he managed a mild smile. "I'll be fine, sweetheart."

"I'm so sorry, Eric. This is all my fault,"

she told him apologetically.

"It's not your fault and please stop apologizing." His arm made a cautious circle about her as she settled in against him. By the time her head nudged in beneath his chin, he had fallen asleep once more.

"Eric?"

"Yes, sweetheart?" he mumbled sleepily.

"I've missed you terribly."

His soft laughter made a pleasant vibration. She rose and fell with his lengthy sigh of weariness, and it was shamefully easy to feel right at home within his embrace.

Kemba woke up and checked her watch. They had been asleep for one hour. "Eric?" She shook his shoulder until he woke up with a rumbling moan. "Eric, we'd better get moving. Bekitemba is probably somewhere around here looking for us."

"Okay," he muttered thickly. They slowly made their way into the mouth of a cave.

"We can probably camp out here," Kemba suggested.

Eric observed his surroundings. "Are you sure these caves are safe?"

She looked around. "I don't have a clue, but I don't think Bekitemba would have us hide up here if they weren't."

Eric clicked on a miniature flashlight as

they entered a dark cave. "Hey? Come look at this!"

"What is it?"

"See for yourself." He gave her the flashlight. "Look at the walls."

He pointed to the primitive drawings on the walls. Colorful pictures of animals and people painted in shades of yellow, red and brown.

Kemba moved closer, obviously in awe. She gently traced the drawings with her finger. "These are well preserved."

"Any idea who did this?"

"Probably the San—"

"The who?" Eric interrupted.

"The bushmen. They lived here in these caves over two thousand years ago."

"Look over here," Eric pointed. "Here's a drawing of a king."

"Let me see that." Kemba moved closer. "It's King Dumisani. On the day of his installation."

"How do you know that?"

"Because my father talked about it all the time. He used to tell me about that day often. His father used to tell it to him."

Eric shook his head. "There's so much history here. I'm embarrassed that I don't know much about African history. Outside of slaves coming to America and Nelson Mandela."

"You shouldn't be embarrassed. My father was born and raised in this country. When he left, it was still known as Rhodesia. Papa was adamant that I learn about this part of my ancestry." Kemba paused. "He just forgot to tell me about his own immediate family. And I can't understand why."

"You've met Mapfumo and Sondisa. Would you brag about brothers like that?"

Kemba thought about this for a moment. "I guess you have a point."

Eric gathered dried grass, twigs and wood to build a fire. In minutes he had a small one going.

Kemba shivered slightly and Eric pulled her closer to him. She had no place to put her arm except around him. They sat together within the security of the surrounding walls, alert and listening for the slightest sound.

Eric opened the bag and pulled out the fruit Nomsa had given them. He handed Kemba an orange. "Nomsa isn't so bad. I'm glad she had a change of heart."

"Me too." She slowly peeled the orange, sucking the tangy juice off her fingers. "It seems that they are all hung up on the past, though. Nomsa is bitter because my dad married my mother. It seems everyone thought they would be the ones getting married."

"Really?"

Kemba nodded as she chewed on a piece of fruit. "As for Mapfumo — he's just plain crazy."

CHAPTER 25

"This has to be a fake." Boiling with anger, Mapfumo threw down the map. They had taken it from Eric's jacket before throwing his unconscious body in the room with Kemba.

"Then they still have the real one."

He trembled out of pure rage. "Of course they have the real one. We have wasted a whole day on foolishness. I am going to kill that —"

"Mapfumo. You said no more killing."

"I know what I said. But that was before they tried to make fools of me — of us." He moved to stand closer to Sondisa. "Look what the whites did to our king. They stole his country from him. Look how Molefi turned his back on us. He stole from this family. Our legacy."

Sondisa bowed his head. "You are right, Mapfumo."

"We have to do whatever is necessary to take back what is ours."

Sondisa nodded. "What do we do now?"

"We head home. There is nothing here

but wildlife. I have seen enough."

Mapfumo curled his fist and pursed his lips throughout the train ride to Plumtree. He fantasized about killing Eric Avery as a pleading Kemba watched. *My daughter.* She was his daughter. Mapfumo did not find that thought comforting. Waves of bitterness spread throughout his body. Even his child had been stolen from him by Molefi. They would all pay.

As soon as they arrived home, Mapfumo knew something was wrong. He surveyed the area. "Something is not right."

"I don't see my car," Sondisa said. "Nomsa would not have left."

Mapfumo jumped out and ran into the house. "Lee, what has happened here?"

"The man — he hit me from behind and took my gun. I found Nomsa tied up."

"I see." He pulled the tiny woman up. "How did they get out, Nomsa?"

"I heard the girl scream and I went to see what was wrong. She said her man needed help. They grabbed me and tied me up. Lee found me and removed the ropes. We have searched everywhere for them."

"How did they get the rope?"

"She went searching all over the house while he held me."

"Are you all right, Nomsa?" Sondisa asked as he entered the house.

"I am fine."

"She is lying." Mapfumo raised his hand and slapped her. Nomsa fell to the floor, striking her head.

Sondisa rushed to her side. "Nomsa!"

"*Leave her.* We have to find Kemba and Eric Avery."

"I cannot leave her like this," Sondisa said firmly. "She is my wife. I will not leave her."

Mapfumo slammed his fist on the wooden table.

Sondisa did not return until hours later. Mapfumo looked up when he entered the room.

"How is she?"

"She will live." Sondisa moved to stand face-to-face with Mapfumo. "Do not ever strike my wife again."

"Or what?"

"Or I will have to kill you, brother."

Mapfumo grabbed Sondisa by the throat. "You dare to threaten me? I will squash you like a bug. After all that I have done for you. You wear expensive clothes — you fly to London to shop . . . and you dare to confront me about a *vatorwa*."

"Nomsa is not a stranger. She is family,"

Sondisa said through gritted teeth. "I will not let you kill her too."

"You are like Molefi — blinded by the love of an outsider." Mapfumo muttered a string of curses.

"Nomsa is not —"

A man rushed in, managing to pull the two men apart. "Mapfumo, I found Sondisa's car. It was abandoned near the train station in Bulawayo. It is most likely that they are long gone."

Mapfumo glared at both the man and Sondisa. He turned and stormed out of the house.

Kemba kissed Eric gently on the forehead. "Eric, I still can't believe you're really here."

He smiled down at her. "I am, sweetheart."

"I'm glad you're here with me, but a part of me wishes you weren't. I don't want anything to happen to you. I couldn't bear it. Did you let the police —"

Eric shook his head. "They don't know what's going on."

"But why?"

"Your mother didn't want to take a chance with your life."

Kemba nodded. "I guess I can understand that. They don't just want the diamond;

they also want the map. I tried to tell him that I didn't have a clue where the map could be. He didn't want to hear me. I think old uncle dear has lost his ever-loving mind."

"*I have the map.* I found it."

"*What?*" Her mouth dropped open. "Are you serious?"

He nodded. "Antoinette and I went back over to the house."

"But where did you find it?"

"On the old bookshelf in that hidden room. In *King Solomon's Mines.* It was hidden in the lining of the book."

" 'The treasure can be found where the story is told,' " Kemba mused aloud.

Eric gave her a sidelong glance. "Huh?"

"It's nothing — just something my dad wanted me to remember. It's never made sense to me. I guess he was trying to tell me where I'd find the map. I looked for it when we were at the house but when I couldn't find it, I just assumed that Papa had made up that part of the story. Mama wanted me to believe that it was just a legend."

Eric reached inside his jacket. "It's gone," he announced. "I had a feeling they would search my clothes."

"They took the map." Kemba gave a

heavy sigh. "Maybe now they'll leave us alone. The have the diamond and the map."

"All is not lost, Kemba," Eric announced.

"What do you mean?"

"I gave them a fake map." Eric removed his belt. "Here is the real one." He pulled the small, tattered map out of a secret compartment in his belt.

Kemba turned the piece of cloth over and over in her hands, examining it. "I can't believe it! There really is a hidden treasure." She glanced up at Eric. "I'm glad you didn't give it to him. But won't he be able to tell the difference?"

"I don't think so. I tried to duplicate it exactly. Antoinette used her artistic abilities to help me."

"I'm sure they would've noticed it immediately if they had been suspicious."

"I didn't want to just hand everything over to them. In case we needed to bargain with our lives. Good idea, huh?"

There was no response.

"Kemba?"

Eric turned around to face her. He opened his mouth to speak, to ask what was wrong, but the panic in her eyes stopped him. He scanned the crevices, searching for the source of the terror in her eyes. Eric found nothing.

"What?" he mouthed.

Kemba wanted to scream, but some inner sense of survival warned her not to open her mouth. Without moving her head, Kemba cast her eyes to the side, then back to him. Eric followed her gaze and his heart practically stopped beating. There was a ten-foot-long black mamba snake crawling out of a rock crevice.

"Don't panic," he said, keeping his voice low and quiet. "Don't move. Just try to remember to remain calm. Okay?"

Her heart leaped turbulently in her chest as the full seriousness of the situation finally communicated itself to her brain. She could die. Kemba's head barely moved when she nodded. Her breath started coming faster and faster and the panic increased in her eyes.

"Honey, don't look down at the snake. Look at me," he encouraged without moving, except for the hand he slid toward his gun. "Keep looking at me, sweetheart."

A muscle in Kemba's cheek twitched and her mouth grew dry. Sweat and tears ran down her face. She beseeched Eric with her eyes to save her. The snake looked like it was coming straight for her.

"Do you trust me, sweetheart?"

She nodded ever so slowly.

"I need for you to trust me now," Eric pleaded. "I'm going to shoot him. I won't let him bite you. I promise I won't." He gave her a quick look for reassurance, then focused again on the snake. "Okay, sweetheart, I want you to close your eyes. Come on, baby, do it now," he ordered urgently.

He glanced at Kemba again and found her squeezing her eyes shut.

Coming in rapid gasps, her own breathing suddenly seemed to be roaring loudly.

Eric knew she was about to become unglued any second. He would have to hurry if he wanted to save her. The snake was poised, his head flattened and ready to strike.

Eric murmured a quick prayer, raised the gun and aimed. True and straight, the gun fired, blowing the head off the snake, leaving the body thrashing wildly.

With her eyes still shut, Kemba stiffened. Unable to contain her panic any longer, she screamed hysterically. Eric rushed to her, kicking the snake remains as far away from them as possible. He closed his eyes and offered up a prayer of thanks. Pulling her into his arms, he held her close to him. "I've got you, sweetheart. You're safe now. I've killed him."

Kemba clung to him, shaking so hard, her teeth chattered. "I — I was s-so scared. I t-thought I was going to die."

He clasped her tighter to his chest. "I've never been so scared, sweetheart. Oh, baby, I don't want to lose you."

Her arms tightened around his neck. Burying her face against his shoulder, she cried with all her might. Eric held her and let her cry it all out. Gradually she calmed down.

Kissing her forehead, he asked, "Feeling better?"

"I-I'm okay. I just want to get out of here."

"Kemba! Kemba, are you up here?" a voice called from outside.

Raising his head, Eric asked, "Who —"

"It's Bekitemba. He's here." Kemba wiped her tears and ran to the mouth of the cave. "We're in here, Bekitemba."

Eric stood back and watched Kemba and an older man embrace. Grabbing him by the hand, she led him over to Eric. "Bekitemba, this is my friend Eric Avery."

"Hello, Mr. Avery. It is very nice to meet you." He glanced around the cave and saw the remains of the snake. Concern etched on his face, he asked, "Are you both okay?"

"I'm a lot better now. I just want to get out of here as fast as I can."

"I was so worried about you. I called and called the hotel. When I didn't hear from you, I grew worried."

Kemba glanced back at the dead snake. "Please let's get out of here."

Bekitemba nodded. "Come, we will go to my house. Mapfumo will not look for you there. At least not for a few days."

"Thank God you told me about this place, Bekitemba. But I wish you would've told me about the snakes too. Ugh!"

She walked fast and far, practically running, more out of fear than out of necessity. "I'll meet you both down the mountain. *I can't stand snakes.* Seeing that one up close and personal is more than I can take. *I'm outta here.*"

Eric and Bekitemba shared a look of pure amusement.

"I guess this is not a good time to mention to her that this country is full of snakes."

Eric shook his head. "No, sir, I don't think so. In fact, I wouldn't mention it at all. That one back there scared us both."

"You were afraid for both of your lives, yet you killed the snake without hesitation."

"I did what I had to do. I'm not going to leave Africa without Kemba alive and well.

I promised her mother that I would keep her safe. I intend to keep my word."

"You are an honorable man, Eric. My niece is fortunate to have found such a man. Molefi would be pleased."

They made their way down the mountain. Kemba was way ahead of them.

Still shaken over the snake incident, Kemba tried to read once they arrived at Bekitemba's home, but found she couldn't concentrate. Giving up, she wandered outside for a breath of fresh air. After thoroughly surveying the ground for creatures of a crawling nature, Kemba ventured farther. On the side of the house, she took note of the strips of meat hanging from a wire. She'd noticed them earlier when they arrived but wasn't sure of what they were. Curiosity getting the better of her, she navigated back toward the meat.

As she neared the dangling strips, Kemba heard the unmistakable sounds of someone approaching. She turned, expecting to find Eric. It was her uncle.

"Bekitemba, what is this?" She pointed to the drying meat.

"It is called biltong. And it is very good."

Kemba decided that whether or not it tasted good was still open to debate. She wasn't sure she wanted to even sample it.

"Come, I am about to prepare some. Would you like to watch?"

Not wanting to insult her uncle, she nodded and said, "Sure, I'd love to watch." They walked back indoors. Kemba found Eric seated in a corner, reading a Bible and making notes. She came to an abrupt halt but decided not to disturb him. Following Bekitemba into his kitchen, she stood silently by as her uncle prepared a work area.

Bekitemba cut beef into long strips. Next he packed the meat into an earthenware container, sprinkling each layer with a salt, pepper and brown sugar mixture as he went along. When he was done, he sprinkled the whole lot with vinegar.

"Now we will leave it like this overnight."

"What happens next, Bekitemba? Do you just hang it up like the others?"

"Tomorrow I will dip each strip in a mixture of hot vinegar and water. It will help to remove the excess surface salt. Then we hang it up to dry."

"How long do you have to leave it hanging?"

"If it is a sunny day, I leave it for one day, then move it to a shaded area where it will continue to hang for another seven to ten days." Bekitemba moved to the sink to wash his hands. "Over there." He motioned with his head and said, "In that container. Try some."

Kemba opened the airtight container to retrieve a strip covered in plastic wrap. After removing the wrap, she checked out the brown outer layer and summoned her courage to sink her teeth into a piece. The inside was soft, moist and red in color. She closed her eyes and savored the flavor. "Mmmmm, this is *so* good." She opened her eyes and bit off another piece. "Can I take one to Eric?"

"Take what to me?" Eric stood in the doorway. "What are you doing?"

She walked over to stand in front of him. "You should try this. It's good." Kemba handed him a wrapped strip. "It's called biltong."

Eric sampled the meat. "I like it." He glanced over at Bekitemba, who stood with a proud grin on his face. "Did you make this?"

"Yes, I did," he answered.

"It's very good, Bekitemba. Can we take some with us?" Kemba asked.

Bekitemba grinned. "You are so much like your mother. She loved it too."

"Did she really?" When Bekitemba nodded, Eric continued. "Maybe we should take some back to her. Will it last?"

"We will put it in an airtight container. It will be all right."

"What do you think, Kemba?"

"About what?"

"About taking some of this . . . What is it called again?"

"Biltong," Bekitemba supplied.

"Some biltong back to Sarah. Do you think she'll like some?"

Kemba nodded her agreement. "I think she might enjoy it. Yes, let's take her some back." Sticking her hand in Eric's, she asked, "You're still reading the Bible?"

Eric smiled. "I am. You want to give it a try?"

"Are you serious? I wouldn't have a clue as to what I was reading. I told you my experiences with studying the Bible. I don't understand it. That's very frustrating to me."

"Come on, we'll do it together." She was caught by the elbow and escorted into the other room.

They sat side by side on the sofa, reading and discussing various Scriptures.

Bekitemba watched them for a while, then went outside to tend to his farming.

Later, Eric asked, "Now, that wasn't so bad, was it?"

Kemba leaned against the taut smoothness of his shoulder. "No, it wasn't. You really know a lot about the Bible, don't you?"

"I'm still learning."

"Eric, can I ask you a question?"

"Sure, whatever you want."

"Do you . . . you know . . ." She paused, lowering her eyes. "Do you ever think about me sexually?"

"It creeps into my mind at times, but I try to stay focused." Eric smiled. "I am a flesh-and-blood kind of guy. I have needs too. I simply have to deny myself."

"Is it hard —" As the words came out of her mouth, Kemba covered her face with her hands and started giggling. "I —"

Eric joined in the laughter. "Bad choice of words, eh?"

She nodded, her hands still covering her face.

He pulled her hands down. "I'm extremely attracted to you, Kemba. I take cold showers, pray a whole lot and meditate, but when I see you, my body still reacts."

"I wasn't asking *that*." Kemba looked embarrassed.

He touched her cheek in a sensual gesture. Dipping his head slightly, he whispered huskily, "I know, but you wanted to know *that* also."

"Yes, I did." She burst into laughter again. "I'm so terrible."

Eric shook his head. "No, you're not. You're honest and I like that."

"I want you too. I know that I shouldn't, but . . ." She opened the Bible. "Why don't we read some more?"

CHAPTER 26

Antoinette handed Sarah a white blouse. "Mrs. Jennings, Kemba will be all right. Eric is over there with her in Africa. The good pastor is not going to let anything happen to her."

"I know, but I can't tell my heart not to worry. She's my daughter. My only child."

"Eric loves her. I believe that," Antoinette reassured her. "He would do anything to keep her safe."

"I know, I can see it in his eyes. I just hope they'll be careful."

"They'll be fine. Who knows, they'll probably come back married."

"They'd better not," Sarah said with a huff. "They had better not deprive me of seeing my only child married."

Sarah and Antoinette giggled.

"Honey, thank you for coming shopping with me today. Some days I really don't know if I'm coming or going."

"I had a ball, Mrs. Jennings." Antoinette took hold of the garments that Sarah was holding. "Here, let me take those for you.

Kemba is going to love this dress. She's been eyeing it for weeks now."

"She's going to fuss because I spent so much money on her." Sarah sighed softly. "You can't take it with you, though."

"Mrs. Jennings, you're not going anywhere. Not for a long time."

Sarah gave Antoinette a sad smile.

Eric left a sleeping Kemba on the sofa. He was finding it more and more difficult to keep his hands off her. Lately, when he closed his eyes, he envisioned them married, making love, and her pregnant with his children. Unable to stop himself, he groaned aloud. How was he going to make it back to the States without making love to her?

He was planning to ask her to marry him before they left Africa, but the right time had not presented itself. Eric stood in the doorway, watching her sleep. She was snoring softly. He smiled and resisted the urge to fantasize about waking her up with kisses all over her chestnut-tinted body. In his mind he could hear her soft moans of protest and pleasure.

He shook himself mentally. *I've got to maintain control. I can't let my emotions get out of hand,* he admonished himself. Eric turned around when he heard Bekitemba come up.

"You are in love with Kemba." Again he stated a fact.

Eric nodded. "I love her."

"I am pleased. You are a good man. A man of God."

"Bekitemba, we have to leave," Eric stated. "I think we should head to Harare. We can board a plane there and fly back to America."

"I think this is a good idea. Mapfumo and his men are most likely looking all over Bulawayo for the two of you. You cannot go back there."

"I'd like to use your phone to make the plane reservations."

"Go right ahead."

Kemba sat up. She looked at them both sleepily and smiled. "What are you two up to?"

"I was just about to make our plane reservations. Hopefully, we'll be able to leave tomorrow," Eric said.

Bekitemba and Kemba talked while Eric was on the phone.

Eric hung up and announced, "We can leave tomorrow night."

Kemba nodded. "I'm glad. I'm ready to go home. This has been some adventure."

She settled back into the fullness of the sofa. "To be honest, I kind of hate leaving without finding the treasure." Her eyes were full of pleading. "Since we have the real map, can't we stay another day? Mapfumo won't know where to look for us."

Eric shook his head. "We're going home, Kemba. It's not safe here."

"But why can't we look for the treasure?" she questioned. "It rightfully belongs to me."

"I, for one, would like to live a long life. That's why."

"Eric, please?"

"We're going home. I promised your mother that I'd bring you back safe and I intend to keep that promise."

"Eric is right, daughter of Molefi. You must leave this country. It is not safe for you to remain here any longer than necessary."

"I understand what you're both saying, but all I'm asking is for one day. We can leave after that."

"Kemba, honey, we need to be on that plane tomorrow night. Your mother is worried sick over you."

"I'm going to call her in a few minutes," Kemba stated. "I know she's worried and probably angry that I didn't tell her what I was planning to do."

"Your mother will understand, I'm sure. What she won't understand is your refusal to leave Africa without finding the treasure. Honey, we've overstayed our welcome." Eric knew she was disappointed but he couldn't let that knowledge weaken his resolve. Sarah needed Kemba. She needed her alive.

Mapfumo slammed his hand on the table. "Where the hell did they go?"

Sondisa shrugged. "I do not know. Nomsa is saying nothing."

He turned to look at his brother. "Where is Nomsa? Why is she not here with you?"

"She left me. She says she is going to her father's house. She said she is never coming back."

"You don't need her, Sondisa. We have *this*." Mapfumo held up the emerald-shaped diamond. "We will be rich. Women will flock to us. We will have to beat them off with a stick."

Lee knocked before entering the house. "Mapfumo, I have news."

"Well, what is it, Lee?" Mapfumo asked impatiently.

"I have been watching the Holiday Inn for the man and the woman. They have not returned there."

"Do you think she will contact Bekitemba?" Sondisa asked.

"He is the only person she knows." Mapfumo gave a grudging nod. "Yes, I believe she would. As a matter of fact, I believe we have found them." He pulled out his wallet and handed several bills to Lee. "Thank you for your help."

The skinny man grinned, then was gone. Mapfumo turned to Sondisa. "Call and make train reservations to Hwange. We will leave within the hour."

CHAPTER 27

"Where are we going?" Kemba asked as she followed Eric and Bekitemba out of the house. "Why can't we stay here?"

"I have arranged for you to have a rental car. I think it would be better if you and Eric stay in Harare until the time for you to head for the airport. Mapfumo will probably come here to look for you."

Forty-five minutes later, Kemba and Eric waved good-bye to Bekitemba as they drove away from the rental-car agency. When they neared Victoria Falls National Park, Kemba begged Eric to stop. "I've heard so much about Victoria Falls; can we please stop for just a few minutes?"

"Just a minute or so, Kemba. I don't know if you understand that you and I could be in danger here."

"Yes, I understand, Eric. I'm only asking for a couple of minutes, that's all."

Against his better judgment, Eric agreed to park the car and they got out.

"It's beautiful here," Kemba murmured softly as she eyed the beautiful pools of green water protected on both sides by enormous black canyon walls, one belonging to Zimbabwe, the other Zambia.

She and Eric strolled near the cliffs, through the rain forests. Along the path they enjoyed the panoramic view of the Knife Edge Bridge.

Eric pointed below. "I hope you don't want to venture down there."

Kemba glanced down and shook her head. "It's called the Boiling Pot, I think. I saw a sign back there somewhere." She placed a hand on Eric's arm. "We can leave now. I just wanted to photograph this beautiful image in my mind. Thank you."

Glancing around, Eric uttered, "Let's get out of here."

As they headed to the car, they watched cows walking with women carrying bundles of wood on their heads. Kemba wanted to snap pictures of them but Eric grabbed her hand.

"Don't, Kemba. Leave them to their privacy."

Along the drive they could see fires beginning to burn and the stars coming out in the sky.

"It's really very pretty out here. Just look up in the sky. . . ." Kemba looked up to find Eric's eyes on her. "What is it?"

"Kemba?" His knuckles rubbed along her cheek and jaw. His look was so tender, her soul dissolved beneath it.

Her brow puckered in bewilderment. "What's wrong? You look so serious."

"I love you, Kemba. I think I've loved you from the first moment I saw you."

"I love you too," she confessed. "I've been trying to fight it, but I can't."

Eric smiled. "I'm glad to hear that."

"I'm still not totally sure if I'm the right kind of woman for you."

"Are you sure that I'm the right kind of man for you?"

Kemba didn't hesitate with her response. "You're perfect, Eric."

"And you're perfect for me. I want you to know that," he reassured her. "You are the only woman for me, Kemba."

"So where do we go from here?"

"To Harare for starters. Let's head back to the car."

"Wait." Kemba pulled his head down to hers and planted a kiss on his lips.

Bekitemba opened his door to find Mapfumo standing there. A muscle flicked angrily in his jaw. "What are you doing here?"

Mapfumo smiled coldly. "Bekitemba, it

is good to see you too."

His eyes searched swiftly around the room. Bekitemba knew why he was there but asked anyway. "Why did you come here, Mapfumo?"

Mapfumo strolled past his brother, not bothering to wait for an invitation. "You do not bother to come visit me. Why is that?"

"Why are you here? Is there something you want?"

"Actually, I'm looking for two people. A man and a woman. Have you seen them? I believe you met the woman. She is Molefi's daughter." His lips twisted into a cynical smile.

"No, I have not seen them. Tell me, why are you looking for these two people?"

"They have stolen from me."

"Are you sure it is not the other way around?"

"Are you calling me a thief?" Mapfumo's voice hardened ruthlessly.

"You did not answer me."

"Bekitemba, we are brothers. Do not turn your back on family, the same way Molefi did. Look, he has not written in over twenty years. Since he has been gone."

"Perhaps he is dead and cannot write."

He glared at Mapfumo with burning, reproachful eyes.

"Why do you say that?"

"That is the only reason I can think of that would keep him from writing."

Fury almost choked Mapfumo. "It is because of that woman! Sarah has turned him against us. His family."

"You are still angry that she chose our brother over you. It is long past for you to accept that Sarah and Molefi loved one another. I know what happened all those years ago. Between you and Sarah."

"I do not know what you are talking about."

"Molefi confided in me the day before he married Sarah," Bekitemba stated. "Even then you couldn't change the way our brother felt for this woman. His love for her was too great."

"The woman means nothing to me."

He shook his head. "I do not believe you. I know you, brother."

"And I know you." He moved closer to Bekitemba. "Where are they?"

"I have no idea, Mapfumo."

"Would you tell me if you had?"

"No, I would not."

Mapfumo moved toward the door. "I will leave you then, Bekitemba."

"Do not come back to my house. You are not welcome here." He waited until Mapfumo had driven down the road before picking up the phone.

When Eric and Kemba arrived at the hotel, a slender, dark-skinned woman with long, flowing braids pulled them over to the side. She introduced herself as Ayisha and handed Eric a piece of paper. "Bekitemba wants you to follow his instructions carefully."

Eric read the message twice.

"What's wrong, Eric?" Kemba asked.

"Mapfumo went to see Bekitemba," he announced.

"He was looking for the two of you," Ayisha explained. "By the way, I am engaged to your cousin Kazandu. He is Bekitemba's son."

Kemba smiled. "It's very nice to meet you. I haven't met Kazandu yet. I had hoped to see him before I leave."

"He was looking forward to meeting you as well, but he will not be home until this weekend."

Taking the note from Eric, Kemba read it.

"You must stay in your rooms," Ayisha advised. "Do not leave until it is time for

373

you to head for the airport. I have arranged for food to be delivered to your rooms. My cousin will deliver all of your meals. Her name is Sarreta."

"Thank you, Ayisha," Eric said. He glanced over at Kemba. "Well, we'd better get up to our rooms."

"Let's go." Kemba reached over to hug Ayisha. "Thanks so much for helping us." Kemba stayed close to Eric as they approached the large, ornately carved counter of the hotel. While Ayisha proceeded with the check-in, Kemba glanced nervously around the lobby.

Growing more apprehensive by the minute, she slowed her step to position herself behind Eric, as if standing in his confident shadow would give her the courage she needed somehow.

They headed to the elevator with keys in hand.

After checking out Kemba's room, Eric stated, "I'm going to shower and change. The meals will be delivered to your room."

Kemba smiled. "I'll see you in a few minutes then."

Eric went to the adjoining room next door.

She had already taken a shower and changed clothes by the time Eric knocked lightly on the door.

When she opened it, he stood smiling. "You look good."

"Thank you. It feels so good to be in a hotel. Usually, I hate staying in them, but I sure am glad to be in this one." She watched him cross the room. He stopped at the window, lifted the curtain and stared out. Her breath caught in her throat as she eyed him from head to toe.

Kemba moved to join him at the window.

Eric pulled her closer, his hands moved possessively up and down her back, pressing her lightly to his hard arousal. "You are so beautiful," he whispered hoarsely. His kisses were intoxicating, making Kemba crave his touch, his sweet words of seduction.

Even though she trembled from her fear that this was wrong, she knew this was what she wanted. Desire exploded in her body and she arched toward the loving hands that caressed her breasts.

Looking deep into each other's eyes, they silently affirmed their love for one another. There would be no turning back now. There was only the present — this moment. There would be time tomorrow to think of life without him.

"Sweet, sweet Kemba," he whispered, running his tongue along the outline of her parted mouth. "I love you beyond reason."

She wanted to tell him that he shouldn't say such things, but the words froze in her throat. "Eric . . . oh, Eric." She levered back slightly so he could look directly into her eyes. Her fingertips spread over the lean angles of his face, easing back until they meshed in the tight curls of his hair. Then she tugged him forward to meet her kiss. Her lips were soft and expressive, moving over his with a lingering wealth of emotion.

A soft knock on the door caused them to part reluctantly.

"I guess that's Sarreta with our dinner."

Eric nodded. "You stay here and I'll check to be sure." He walked across the room in quick, silent strides.

Kemba watched as his shoulders relaxed visibly. It was Sarreta.

A few minutes later, they were seated at the small table in the room, eating dinner.

"Eric, I've been thinking . . . ," Kemba began slowly. "Maybe we can look for the treasure tomorrow. We could get an early start in the morning, and if we don't find anything, at least I can leave Africa knowing that I tried."

"Bekitemba said for us to stay in our rooms, Kemba."

"I feel like a sitting duck."

"There are quite a few hotels here in Harare. I don't think it'll be easy finding us," Eric assured Kemba. Reaching for his glass, he took a sip of water.

Kemba played with her food.

"Your mother misses you. I can't forget the fear on her face when she discovered that Mapfumo had you. You should go home."

"Mama and I talk every day. She knows that I'm fine." Kemba eyed Eric. "When you saw Mama — how was she doing?"

"She was understandably upset."

Kemba chewed on her bottom lip. "I guess you're right, Eric. Maybe we should just stay in the hotel until it's time to head to the airport." She pushed her meat around.

"I know it bothers you, honey. And I'm sorry."

She nodded sadly. "I just feel like I'm letting my father down."

CHAPTER 28

Kemba watched Eric as he headed to his room.

She knew he was right about not going after the treasure, but Kemba couldn't make peace with knowing that she'd made a promise to her father. Mapfumo had the diamond in his possession and she could not sit by and let him take the last of her legacy. She just couldn't do it.

A desolate feeling overwhelmed her — if only Eric could put himself in her shoes.

She swallowed painfully and whispered, "I'm sorry, Eric, but I have to do this. I can't leave Zimbabwe without the treasure. I owe it to my father." Kemba headed to the door and tiptoed out of her room.

She released a long breath when she made it to the elevators. Now she just hoped to make it downstairs. Kemba patted her pocket to assure herself that the map was there. Eric had given it to her earlier for safekeeping.

Kemba was scared.

She didn't want to do this alone — she

needed Eric. Only he would never agree.

Downstairs she sat in the lobby for a while, trying to decide what was the right thing to do. Did it mean walking away from Eric in order to keep her word to her father? Kemba didn't want to choose.

Eric paced back and forth in his room.

Over and over in his head, he replayed his conversation with Kemba — she was determined to obey her father's wishes. Although he understood how much family meant to her, Eric couldn't understand her disregard for her own safety. But the fact of the matter was that he didn't believe there was really a treasure to be found. He believed that if the story was true, the treasure would have been found years ago.

Eric got a sick feeling in his gut. Walking briskly, he knocked on the door of Kemba's room. There was no answer.

He knocked again.

No answer.

Eric rushed to the elevator and went in search of Kemba.

In the back of his troubled mind, a small spark ignited, fanning a terrible thought. She was going to try to find the treasure.

Spotting her, Eric paused to catch his breath, his heart pounding out a beat of fear and anticipation so intense he still breathed with difficulty.

He watched her curl her lips together, her tensed shoulders. Her hands were folded across her chest, her knuckles pale.

Just as she reached the car, he caught up with her. "Kemba," he said, "you shouldn't be out here."

She jumped at the sound of her name. "Eric! You scared me." Looking around, she whispered, "Neither should you." He sighed before stepping back in resignation. "You were going to find the treasure, weren't you?"

"I'm so sorry, Eric." Her gaze wavered. "I know you don't understand, but I really need to do this. Now you can either help me or leave me alone."

"Kemba, you could be killed over this mythical hidden treasure! Don't you know that? Your father and my brother have both died because of the Dumisani Diamond. What —"

"Eric, you can't change my mind," she interrupted. "I made a promise to my father and I intend to keep it. Now you can come with me and we'll find it, or you can leave without me. If you come with me, we can find it together and most likely still make our plane reservations."

"I don't believe you, Kemba," Eric stated honestly. "If you don't find it, I don't believe you'll just get on the plane and forget about it."

"There is nothing you can say. I wish I could make you understand."

Eric felt the fight drain out of him. He placed his hands over his face, then sighed heavily. "I really think we should head back inside and to our rooms." He turned and started to walk away.

Kemba caught up with him. "Eric, please don't be mad."

"Kemba, I'm tired. . . ."

"Will you agree to help me? We can look for it, and if we don't find it, I'll fly home with you. I promise."

Eric eyed her for a moment before saying, "Fine. I'll help you look, but if we don't find it, I'm taking you home even if I have to carry you." He wanted to tell her about Sarah's condition, but she had sworn him to secrecy. She wanted to be the one to tell Kemba.

She wrapped her arms around him and hugged him tightly. "Thank you so much, Eric."

"I hope I don't regret this."

"You won't." She stood on tiptoe to place a kiss on his cheek.

Against his better judgment, Eric said, "I think we should wait until daylight to leave. We won't find much in the dark. Besides, I need a couple of hours' sleep." He kissed her. "Let's head back to our rooms."

Kemba readily agreed. "I really appreciate this, Eric. You'll never know how much."

"I think I do."

They walked hand in hand toward the elevators.

Upstairs Kemba said good night before planting a kiss on his lips. "I'll see you in the morning."

Eric nodded.

Pleased with the way the evening had turned out, Kemba undressed and readied for bed. She climbed in and reached for the phone. She wanted to talk to her mother and Antoinette.

After calling, Kemba settled back in bed and watched television. She was too anxious to sleep at the moment.

CHAPTER 29

Mapfumo and Sondisa ventured into the Holiday Inn. This was the fifth hotel they'd visited. They walked up to the front desk.

"Hello, may I help you?" The beautiful woman with bright, laughing eyes greeted them.

Mapfumo quickly scanned her name tag. Plastering a handsome smile on his face, he said, "Hello, Ayisha. I am here to see if my niece is checked into this hotel. She left me a message; the name of the hotel was cut off, though." He shook his head. "Answering machines . . ."

She nodded her understanding. "I know what you mean, sir." She tapped into her computer. "What is her name?"

"Kemba Rufaro Jennings."

Mapfumo could hear the rapid clicking of the keyboard as she typed. He and Sondisa had checked several other hotels but turned up nothing. He was tired and irritable.

"No, I'm sorry. No one is checked in by that name."

Anger swept through him. "I see. I am sorry to have bothered you." He turned to leave.

"Have a nice day," she sang out.

A fuming Mapfumo headed out the door with Sondisa following in his wake.

Ayisha watched them for a minute before picking up the phone.

"That was Ayisha," Eric announced, lowering the handset. "Mapfumo and Sondisa just left here. I think we'd better leave now."

"I'm ready." Kemba picked up the small overnight bag. "I'm grateful to Bekitemba for getting us some clothes. I don't know what we'd do without him. Actually, I think we need to get him to help us find this treasure. He knows this country better than we do."

Eric agreed. "I think that's a wise decision. But I'm wondering whether or not Mapfumo will go back to see Bekitemba."

"I don't think he will. I'm sure he's figured out by now that my uncle is not going to tell him anything. He won't go back there."

When Bekitemba arrived home, he found Eric and Kemba waiting for him.

"Ayisha told us that Mapfumo and

Sondisa were looking for us. We didn't know where else to go, so we came back here. I hope you don't mind." Kemba handed him the map. "We need your help in finding the treasure."

"I am glad to see that you are okay. I was worried when Ayisha said you left before she could find out where you would go," Bekitemba said.

"She was busy, so we didn't want to disturb her." Kemba checked her watch. "I'd better call and check on Mama. I'm sure she's worried about us."

"You can call her from here."

"Thanks, Bekitemba."

She dialed quickly. "Hi, Mama. How are you?" She closed her eyes. "We're fine. We left the hotel today." She paused. "We're leaving Africa tonight."

They talked for a few minutes more, then Kemba handed Bekitemba the phone. "She wants to talk to you."

"How is she?" Eric asked.

"She's okay. At least that's what she's telling me."

"You don't believe her?"

"I just get the feeling that there's more going on with her. How did she seem before you left?"

"She was worried sick about you."

"Maybe that's it." Kemba wasn't entirely convinced, though. Her mother didn't quite sound like her usual self.

When Bekitemba hung up the phone, Kemba questioned, "Why is Mapfumo such a terrible person? How can he be related to you or to my father?"

"When he was younger, he had a dream one night. A sickness came along with it. He became deathly ill."

Kemba and Eric exchanged puzzled looks. "What has that to do with anything? Did he lose his mind or something?" she asked Bekitemba.

"We believe that the spirits of strangers who die in this country without ritual burial wander about until they find a possible medium. They then reveal themselves to that person in a dream. Mapfumo had such a dream. The potential medium can refuse to accept this spirit but must have a diviner exorcise it."

"What happens if they accept the spirit?" Eric asked.

"Then the medium is thought to acquire the dead man's characteristics, whether good or bad."

"So you think Mapfumo is possessed?" Kemba wanted to know. Her hand reached out to find Eric's.

Bekitemba nodded. "It is my belief."

"Why didn't you and the rest of the family do something about it?"

"We tried. Mapfumo has to refuse the spirit; otherwise —"

"I see. What about Sondisa? Is he possessed too?"

"No. Sondisa sees Mapfumo as a savior."

"A savior?" Kemba and Eric exchanged looks.

"But why?" she asked.

"Sondisa ran away to Harare when he was just sixteen. He lived on the street for a while, then began sleeping in the city center. During that time he started sniffing glue. When I found him, he was lying in the street, nearly beaten to death. I brought him home with me."

"What happened? How did he end up with Mapfumo?" Eric asked.

"He decided he was too good to help me herd cattle, plow or tend to the gardening. With the aid of Mapfumo, he even stole my eighteen cows to give to Nomsa's father as a bride gift."

"Couldn't he have been killed for something like that?"

Bekitemba nodded. "By old law, yes. But he is my brother. I did not want to harm him. Nomsa came to see me and begged for his life. She even offered to give them back."

"But you didn't take them, did you?"

"No. Nomsa is a lovely young woman."

"So what happened then? With Sondisa?"

"He chose to follow Mapfumo's way of life. Expensive clothes, cars . . ."

"How does Mapfumo support his lifestyle? Where does the money come from?" Kemba asked.

"By dealing drugs, and other unspeakable acts."

Kemba played with her necklace. "Oh. Is that why they have been detribalized?"

Bekitemba nodded.

"Have you tried to talk some sense into Sondisa?" Eric asked.

"He will not listen to me or to Nomsa."

"Sondisa is afraid of Mapfumo," Kemba stated. "I could tell."

"What about you?" Eric wanted to know. "Are you afraid of Mapfumo too?"

"He is a dangerous man, and he is my brother."

"Why not just turn him in to the police?" Eric inquired. "Let them take care of him."

"We have no proof of his crimes," Bekitemba replied.

Kemba swallowed hard, trying not to

reveal her anger. "But he admitted them to me. I can testify against him."

"He will deny it," Bekitemba replied. "Mapfumo is a very powerful man here at home."

Kemba was quiet.

"I am sorry, Kemba." Bekitemba's tone was sincere.

"Just not enough to avenge my father's death," she said matter-of-factly.

Bekitemba's eyes opened in surprise. "You expect me to kill Mapfumo?"

Shaking her head vehemently, she said, "No, that's not what I meant." Kemba found Eric staring at her. "What is it?" she asked him.

"What did you mean, sweetheart?"

"I don't know. I still think we should tell the police. They can investigate —"

Bekitemba held up a hand to interrupt Kemba. "I do not think that is such a good idea."

"And why not?"

"We have family and friends that are police. They are loyal only to Mapfumo. They believe as he does, that Molefi turned his back on the family."

Kemba and Eric both gulped and leaned forward in unison, his eyes round with surprise, hers with worry.

"I'm afraid Mapfumo will try to kill me before he lets me leave this country."

"I do not believe he will do that. You are family."

"Bekitemba, he is crazy. He killed my father, and that was his brother."

"He will not harm you. He knows you're his daugh—" Bekitemba stopped abruptly when he caught sight of Eric shaking his head. . . .

"*His daughter?* Why would he think that?"

"I meant . . ." Bekitemba hung his head. "I am sorry."

She peered closer. "You meant what you said. Now, why would you say that?"

Eric placed a comforting arm around her shoulder. "Kemba, honey. Let's drop it."

Pushing his arm away, she said, "*Let's not.* I want to know what the hell he's talking about."

"Honey, your mother really should talk to you about this."

"My *mother*. She's a part of this? *Oh God.* How could she be a part of these lies?" Filled with indignation, Kemba yelled, "*Molefi Rufaro is my father!*" But as much as she believed it, she couldn't help but acknowledge what her uncle had said. Kemba didn't want to consider the possibility.

Eric pleaded with her. "Kemba, calm down."

She couldn't shake the feeling in the pit of her stomach. "No! I want to know the truth." Kemba pushed for more answers. "What do you know, Bekitemba?"

"Kemba," Eric continued to plead. "Leave it alone. . . ."

"Tell me, Bekitemba," she pleaded. "Please tell me what's going on. No matter what — I have to know the truth."

"It is not my place. I should not have spoken so freely."

"Well, you did. Now finish," Kemba demanded angrily.

Eric held up his hands in resignation. "Go ahead, Bekitemba. She's not going to forget about it."

"I am sorry, Kemba. Do not be mad at Sarah. It was not her fault. Molefi loved you. I know that."

"What are you talking about?"

"When Sarah came to Zimbabwe, it was Mapfumo who met her first. He was very attracted to her. It was he who told Molefi about her. He was bragging, but then Molefi saw her for himself. They fell in love. Mapfumo was angry. Very angry."

"Did my mother love Mapfumo, or did she lead him on in any way?"

"No. Sarah never led him on. But it did not matter to Mapfumo. He wanted her and that is all that mattered to him. When she rejected him, he promised revenge. He . . . He raped her one night."

"*Oh God.*" She suddenly felt sick. Tears filled her eyes and rolled down her cheeks. Kemba felt Eric's arms around her.

"I'm sorry, Kemba," he murmured softly.

She wiped her face with the back of her hands. "Are you telling me that he's . . . that that horrible murderer is *my father?*" Her dark eyes glistened with tears she barely managed to hold back.

Bekitemba nodded.

Her shock yielded quickly to fury. "You're wrong. It's a lie. My mother would have told me. She would have."

"Honey, he's telling you the truth."

She spoke softly, turning away from him as she did. "You don't know that. He's lying. He has to be." Kemba couldn't bear the thought that Bekitemba might be telling the truth.

"I know you want to believe that, but he's telling you the truth. Your mother told me herself."

"When did she do that?" Kemba swallowed the tears forming a lump in her throat.

"Right before I came here. I was there when Mapfumo called her."

"She told you that day?" Her mouth hung wide open, her eyes wide with shock.

"She told Mapfumo. I overheard. After she got off the phone, she confided in me," Eric said, his dark eyes shifting uneasily from her hurt expression.

"How could she lie to me?"

Eric and Bekitemba exchanged looks but said nothing.

"I will never forgive her."

"Kemba, don't say that. You have to —"

Kemba cut him off by saying, "I don't have to do anything."

"Mrs. Jennings was only trying to protect you from being hurt. Can't you understand that?"

"She didn't have to lie to me. She could have been honest with me. Mama lied about a lot of things, for no reason at all." Fingering her necklace, Kemba sighed. "Why couldn't they have been honest with me. . . . What else is she keeping from me?"

"Maybe I should leave the two of you alone." Bekitemba stood up to leave the room.

"You don't have to leave. We need to discuss what to do with the real map."

393

"There's nothing to discuss — I'm keeping it," Kemba stated.

"Why do you want it? Do you want the Dumisani treasure?"

"How can you ask me that, Eric? Do you still think me greedy? Out to obtain wealth the easy way?"

"I never thought of you that way. I just think your uncle's right. We should give it to Mapfumo. Once he finds his treasure, he'll be out of our lives for good."

Kemba shook her head dejectedly. "He'll never be out of my life. He's my father." Placing a hand to her stomach, she uttered, "The thought just makes me sick to my stomach."

Eric grabbed her by the shoulders. "Mapfumo may have contributed to your birth, but Molefi was your father. And don't you ever forget it!"

"I wish I'd never met him. Never knew the truth." Kemba wiped a tear from her face. "You're right; he can have this map. I don't want it. I don't believe there's any hidden treasure anyway. I think it's just a story."

"I find it a little hard to believe myself. I think someone would have found it long before now."

Kemba turned to her uncle. "I'm sorry

for yelling at you. None of this is your doing."

"I understand."

"Can you call Mapfumo? Tell him we want to meet with him. I'm going to give him this map. Maybe he'll leave us alone from now on."

"Can we trust him?" Eric wondered aloud.

"I'm his daughter. He won't harm me."

Bekitemba picked up the phone. "Mapfumo, we want to set up a meeting." He was quiet, as if listening to instructions. Finally he said, "We will meet you there in one hour." He hung up the phone. "Are you sure you want to do this?"

Kemba nodded. "Yes. The sooner I hand it over, the sooner I can get on with my life."

CHAPTER 30

Three hours later, they stood staring out at Victoria Falls. "I really like this park. It's beautiful," Kemba said.

Eric checked his watch. "I wish they'd hurry up. I want to get you on that plane tonight. It doesn't look like they're coming. I think it's time we leave."

"They should be arriving shortly. Ahhhh" — Bekitemba gestured with his head — "here they come now."

Eric and Kemba turned around. They saw Mapfumo and Sondisa coming toward them. Behind them were two other men following closely.

"Who are those men, Bekitemba?" Kemba whispered nervously. "I thought it would just be the two of them."

"Do not worry. Everything is under control," Bekitemba whispered back.

Mapfumo stood before Kemba. "We meet again."

"So it seems," she said dryly.

"I assume you intend to give me the real map and not some elaborate fake. You have wasted enough of my time."

"It's real."

Bekitemba handed the map over to Mapfumo, then stepped back. "You have what you've come for, now release them. They have a plane to catch."

Mapfumo pulled out a gun. "I am afraid they are not going anywhere just yet."

"What are you talking about?" Eric demanded. "We've given you everything."

Smiling coldly, Mapfumo shook his head. "You three will be joining us on a treasure hunt."

"*What?*" Eric and Kemba said in unison.

"I don't believe this," she uttered in anger.

"*Shhh,* sweetheart. Don't make things worse."

"The man is crazy."

Mapfuma looked at her in amusement. "I assure you that I am every bit as sane as you, Kemba."

"You . . ." Kemba caught the sharp look Eric sent her way and her words died. Shaking her head sadly, she stated, "You're not even worth it."

Mapfumo motioned with his gun. "Mr. Avery, you will guide us."

"*No!*" she shouted. "Leave Eric out of this, Mapfumo. This is between you and me." Kemba wasn't sure whether he would hurt her, but she had to believe that Mapfumo would never hurt his own child.

"Kemba, you are not in charge. The sooner you cooperate, the sooner you and Mr. Avery can be on your way."

"It's okay, sweetheart. I'll do it."

Bekitemba spoke up. "Let me have the map. I am more familiar with this area. I will guide you."

Sondisa nodded his head. "Bekitemba is right. He should guide us."

Mapfumo seemed to give this some thought. Finally he agreed. "Do not try to be a hero, brother."

Bekitemba scanned the map. "I think it is leading us down the Batoka Gorge."

"You cannot be serious. You have made a mistake. It is a trick."

Eric looked at it. "No, Mapfumo, I think he's right. We have to find a little waterfall. It looks like the cave is right behind it."

"And I suppose we have to hire a boat."

"Eric, remember the steps at the fall," Kemba interrupted. "What was it called?"

"The Boiling Pot," Mapfumo answered.

"That's it. It's over there." Bekitemba pointed farther down.

Mapfumo eyed Kemba, then Eric. "What about it?"

Kemba spoke up. "There are steps leading down to the Batoka Gorge. It's a real steep climb. . . ."

"Come on. We are wasting time." Mapfumo grabbed her by the arm. "You will lead."

They climbed down the well-worn steps. From this vantage point, Kemba had a spectacular view of the Zambezi River thundering over the cliff, crashing and swirling over rapids, but could not enjoy it. Every time she stopped, Mapfumo shoved his gun in her back.

"Will you stop sticking that gun in my shoulder blades? I'm not going to do anything."

"Keep going."

Soaked to the bone and cold, the group stopped where the Zambezi River compresses into the deep crevice that turned into the Batoka Gorge. They walked until they found a small cave hidden from view.

"I think we should go inside the cave," Eric suggested.

Once inside, they looked around. "There is no waterfall here," Mapfumo said. "I have no time for games."

"Nobody is playing a game with you," Kemba snapped.

Eric put a hand up to his ear. "Listen."

Mapfumo stopped. "I don't hear any-thing."

"I hear something." He walked farther into the cave.

"Eric?" Kemba called out. When she didn't get a response, she called out again.

Mapfumo raised his gun. "My patience has worn out. If he is not back in two seconds, I —"

"Put away the gun, Mapfumo," Eric interjected. "I've found the waterfall."

Kemba breathed a deep sigh of relief upon seeing him. "Eric, wait up," she said, running to walk beside him. "Why didn't you answer me when I called? I was afraid something had happened to you."

"I didn't hear you. I'm fine." He squeezed her hand.

They followed Eric farther into the cave. There, in a far recess, was a shimmering waterfall.

One by one, they walked through the water into the waterfall. There was another cave on the other side.

"Is that it?" Sondisa asked.

Mapfumo's face lit up in a smile. "It must be."

Turning to the group, he said, "Stay here. Only Sondisa and I will go inside." To his men, he ordered, "Watch them.

Do not let them leave."

Kemba glanced up at Eric. He pulled her into his arms and whispered, "It'll soon be over, sweetheart. They have the Dumisani treasure."

Mapfumo stormed out of the cave with a murderous look on his face. "You tried to make a fool out of me. Where is it?"

Kemba and Eric exchanged confused looks.

"What are you talking about?" she asked.

"Where is the Dumisani treasure?"

Kemba looked at Eric dumbfounded. "*This is the cave. Look at the map.* Do you think we like standing here soaking wet like this?" She was filled with anger.

"It is not there."

"What do you mean *it's* not there? Can't you follow directions?"

Eric placed a hand on her shoulder. "Kemba, don't antagonize him." To Mapfumo, he asked, "What's going on?"

"I'm really sick of you." She glanced over at Sondisa and a man she'd never seen before. "And of your flunkies. I'm going home. We gave you the map. Eric gave you the diamond. The treasure is somewhere in that cave, according to the map. *That's it.*"

"You gave me the map after you and your lover cleaned out the treasure."

Her mouth dropped open. "You've lost your mind! We don't have any treasure."

"There is nothing in there but old monkey skins, some pottery, a cape of ostrich feathers, and a shield. You removed the diamonds and the gold. They were hidden in biscuit tins."

Something clicked in her mind. "Don't you see? King Dumisani buried what he considered to be treasure. The cape of ostrich feathers — he wore it the day he was installed as king. He buried it probably because he knew he would be the last of the royal bloodline."

"What are you talking about?" Mapfumo snapped.

"His legacy," Kemba explained. "King Dumisani buried the staff he ruled with, the cape that covered the father of future generations and the shield that protected a country. Those are the things he treasured most. The very things he felt his descendants would treasure also." She shook her head. "I think somewhere along the line, the story became exaggerated more and more as it was told. To add flavor, so to speak."

"Such as the tale you are telling us now," Mapfumo responded snidely.

Eric shook his head. "You have the Dumisani Diamond. Isn't that enough? Haven't enough people lost their lives over this?"

"We want the rest of the treasure. I am quickly losing patience."

"We don't have it." Kemba yelled.

Eric took off his jacket and tossed it on the ground. "Here, check this too."

When they turned up empty-handed, Kemba smirked. "I hope you're satisfied."

Mapfumo pulled out his gun. "I will ask one last time. Where is the treasure?"

"You would kill your daughter?" Eric asked. "Are you that heartless?"

"She means nothing to me. Sarah deceived me once — why would I believe she is telling me the truth now?"

Never had Kemba believed such an inhuman creature could exist. She suppressed her need to be violently ill.

Eric wore his disgust on his face. "How could you say something like that?"

"I do not intend to shoot Kemba. It is you I intend to kill, unless I get my treasure."

"Please don't do this, Mapfumo . . . ," Kemba pleaded. "We don't have it. I'm telling you the truth."

Mapfumo raised his arm, the gun aimed at Eric's heart.

"Nooo!" Without thinking, Kemba shoved Eric to the ground just as she heard a loud crack in the air. She was vaguely aware of something hitting her arm. All she could think about was saving Eric.

Eric fell to the ground, pulling his gun from his jacket. He aimed to shoot. Kemba fell on him, throwing off his aim as he fired. Out of the corner of his eye, he saw Sondisa fall and the other two men struggling with Mapfumo.

Bekitemba pulled him to his feet. "Eric, do not shoot the others — they are on our side."

Eric slowly lowered his gun. Reaching to help her get up, he said, "Kemba, sweetheart, it's all right. You can get up now."

"I've been . . . shot."

Eric fell to his knees at her side. Catching sight of the blood, he quickly pulled a handkerchief from his bag to use as a tourniquet to stop the bleeding. He cradled her head against his chest. "It's going to be all right, sweetheart," he murmured over and over to her.

Kemba was gasping for hurtful breaths of air. The pressure of her fingers lessened on Eric's hand as darkness consumed her.

"We need to get her and Sondisa to a hospital. I will climb back up and get help.

My men will take Mapfumo with them."

Eric rose to his feet, with Kemba still cradled in his arms. "Hurry up, Bekitemba. I'm not going to let her die."

Eric waited anxiously outside of Kemba's hospital room. As soon as the doctor walked out, Eric pounced on him. "How is she, Doctor?"

"We were able to remove the bullet from her arm. She will be fine. She has been asking for you."

"Can I see her?"

"Yes, please go right in."

He eased into the hospital room. Kemba smiled weakly. Brushing his lips across her forehead, he whispered, "How are you feeling, sweetheart?"

"I'm fine. The doctor said I could leave tomorrow." She tried to get comfortable, but a shock of pain prevented further movement.

As they stared at one another, they heard voices murmuring outside her door.

Kemba asked, "Mapfumo, what happened to him?"

"He's in jail. He may have to return to the United States to stand trial for the murders of Malcolm and your father."

She licked her dry lips. "That's great."

She could see something in his eyes. "What is it, Eric?"

"Sondisa is paralyzed."

"I'm sorry for that. It's too bad he decided to follow behind Mapfumo." She stroked the side of his face and said, "Thank you for saving my life."

"I think it's actually the other way around. You took a bullet that was meant for me. Why did you do it? Why did you jump in front of me like that?"

"I love you, Eric. I didn't want anything to happen to you. Especially since the only reason you were here was because of me and my wanting to honor my father's last wishes."

"I love you, Kemba. The thought of life without you is too painful even to imagine. It's all I've been thinking about since you were shot. I want to spend my life with you."

"What are you saying to me, Eric?"

"Will you marry me?"

"Yes," Kemba replied without hesitation.

"What did you say?"

"I said yes. I want to marry you, Eric."

CHAPTER 31

Kemba clumsily let herself in to Sarah's town house. She found her mother in the kitchen. "Hello, Mama."

Sarah whirled around. "Kemba! Oh, I'm so glad to see you, baby. When I heard you had been shot, I was out of my mind with worry —"

"How could you lie to me, Mama?" Kemba interrupted.

"Kemba, what in the world are you talking about?"

She brushed away angry tears. "About my *father*. How could you tell me lies about my whole life? You're always going around spouting Scriptures and lecturing me about church. Yet you've told me lie after lie."

Sarah leaned wearily against the kitchen counter, twisting her hands. "I did what I thought was best. Molefi may not have been your biological father, but he was good to you. He loved you like his very own child. No father could have loved his own daughter more. I never told you because I didn't want you to know that your birth was the result of rape."

Kemba shook her head. "It was wrong, Mama. My life has been nothing but lies. I grew up not knowing I had relatives in Africa. Relatives very much alive."

"Your life was not a lie, Kemba. I didn't want Mapfumo to know about you. I was afraid. Please sit down. Let me explain."

"I don't want to hear anything you have to say. I'm hurt and I'm very angry. Right now I just can't talk to you, Mama." Kemba turned to leave. "I'm going to the office." Trembling with fury, she added, "I shouldn't have come here."

"Kemba, baby, please don't do this to me. Please . . ."

"I have to go. I'll check on you later."

"*Kemba*. Please don't leave. We should talk about this."

"We should've talked about this a long time ago, Mama. Right now I just want to be as far away from you as possible. I don't want to say something I can't take back later. I'm furious with you, Mama."

Sarah was hurt. Kemba could see it in her eyes, but she was too angry to let this slide. "I — I need to go. I'll talk to you later." She rushed out before her mother could see her tears.

Kemba found herself parked in front of Eric's house. She sat for a moment before getting out of the car. Without preamble, she walked up to the door and knocked.

When Eric opened the front door, she said, "I'm sorry for just showing up without calling first. I just needed to see you."

He kissed her in greeting and led her into the house. They walked hand in hand over to the sofa, where he helped her sit down.

"How did your mama like the biltong?" he asked.

"I didn't even give it to her, Eric. As soon as I saw her, I confronted her about the lies. From there, things just really got heated. She tried to explain but I just didn't want to hear any of it — not right now."

"How could you do that to her? She's been through a lot —"

"*And I haven't?*" Kemba interjected. "I was shot and almost killed by my own father."

Eric raised a hand to halt her. "Honey, I'm not saying that. What I am trying to say is that your mother only did what she did to protect you. You have no idea what she's gone through all these years keeping something like this to herself." He placed his arms around her. "She loves you so much, Kemba."

"I know." She wiped a tear from her face. "I love her too. Eric, she could have told me the truth — it wouldn't have changed a thing between us. It wouldn't have."

"Then go back over to see her. Tell her that. Sweetheart, give your mother a chance to tell her side of the story. Just listen to her."

Kemba nodded. "You're right. I know you're right. I was so angry when I went over there earlier. I need to see her and apologize." She stood up. "I was going to go to the office when I left here, but I think I'll just head back to Mama's house. I don't want this to drag on for days."

"I think that's a good idea." Eric stood and walked her over to the door. "Call me if you want to talk afterward, okay?"

She leaned into him. "Thank you, Eric. I don't know what I'd do without you."

"Remember, just listen and try to put yourself in her shoes," he whispered before kissing her good-bye.

"I am so angry with her, Eric. I don't know if I'll ever get past it anytime soon."

"It's normal to feel that way, but the

anger will die, honey. It will die a little more each day. Then one day, it will be gone — there will be nothing left."

Eric watched Kemba drive away. He sent up a prayer for the restoration of Sarah and Kemba's relationship. Smiling, he mused that there was nothing like a wedding to bring a family together.

Hopefully, Kemba would stay with her mother long enough for Sarah to tell her about the kidney transplant. He didn't know how Kemba was going to handle the news — she'd been through so much lately.

He couldn't help but wonder if she would be angry with him for keeping Sarah's secret.

Sarah was in her bedroom when she heard Kemba call out, "Mama?"

"I'm in here, dear." She hoped to make her daughter understand why she'd been so secretive. For the past couple of hours, she'd tried to reach Kemba, but her calls weren't returned.

"Hi, Mama. Bekitemba sent you some biltong. I forgot to give it to you when I came over before." Kemba set the jar on her mother's dresser.

"I'm so glad you came back. I've been trying to call you."

"I went to Eric's house when I left here.

I never made it to the office."

Kemba sank down on the bed beside Sarah. She could tell her mother had been crying. "I'm sorry. It's just . . ."

"No, baby. I should apologize to you. My intentions were g-good." Sarah's voice broke. "Mapfumo —"

"You don't have to tell me if you don't want to. I imagine it's hard to talk about."

Sarah shook her head. "No, it's time I told you everything. When I went to Africa as a missionary, Mapfumo was the first man I met. I thought he was a very handsome man, but it was the eyes. His eyes scared me. He reminded me of a man possessed. . . ."

Kemba listened without interrupting. Every now and then, Sarah would break down in tears. Kemba reached over, placing her mother's hand in hers.

When Sarah was done, they sat holding each other, crying out their pain.

"Mama, I'm so sorry. Life just hasn't been fair to you."

Sarah held Kemba's face in her hands. "No, baby, now don't you go thinking like that. Life has been life. I've lived to see you grow into a beautiful woman. I've had the love of two wonderful men. I've —"

"You've had to deal with diabetes, then

dialysis," Kemba added quietly.

Sarah nodded. "Yes, I have. Child, it's not something I could run from. You have to make the best out of the life you're given. Don't take the important things for granted. 'Cause I'll tell you this — you certainly don't get a second chance."

"I suppose now you're going to tell me to live life to the fullest."

Sarah smiled. "I don't have to — you just said it."

"But, Mama, aren't you angry?"

"Angry about what?"

"Losing two husbands, your home and the diamond? Fighting almost daily for your health? None of this makes you mad?"

"I'm glad the diamond is gone. It's with the Rufaro family, where it belongs. And I don't miss that big old house. In my condition, who would keep it up — it's enough for me to try to keep this place clean."

"I guess I didn't think about that. All I've dreamed about was buying that house back for you. Papa wanted me to raise my children there, and also their children. From generation to generation."

"I know, baby. But I kept trying to tell you I didn't want it. It was your dream. And your father's."

"I thought it would make you happy, Mama."

"You make me happy, Kemba. I'm so proud of you, baby. Do you know you're the first one in my family to go to college? You're the first woman in our family to have her own business —"

"You and Papa had the restaurant."

"But that was your father's business. If he had lived, I believe that restaurant would have been real popular. It was just beginning to show a profit right before he died."

"Why didn't you keep it?"

Sarah waved her hand. "Child, I didn't know nothing 'bout running no restaurant. I sold it to the first person who said he wanted it. I didn't even know that I could have sold it for a lot more money. See, I wasn't smart like you."

"Mama, you're very smart. You sat there with me and helped me with my studies. You practically did all of my research for my reports."

"I liked helping you. I learned from you."

"Mama, I love you so much. And I'm truly sorry for all the harsh things I said. I never should have disrespected you like that."

"I lied to you."

"You're still my mother. Besides, I've been guilty of telling a few lies myself."

"Like what, dear?" Sarah leaned closer.

Kemba laughed, wagging her finger. "Oh, no, you don't. I'm not falling for that one. It's in the past. Let's just leave them there."

"Hey, I've come clean with you — now it's your turn."

"But you're the mommy."

Sarah laughed.

Later, the two women shared a meal.

Kemba would have normally helped her mother clean the kitchen afterward, but with the cast on her arm, there wasn't much she could do.

"Honey, there's something I need to tell you."

Kemba glanced over at her mother. "What is it?"

"I went to see the doctor while you were gone. They had to do some more tests."

Kemba glanced down at her hand. "You're going to have to have a kidney transplant," she stated.

Sarah nodded.

"So, they put you on the list?"

"Yes."

"I'm going to see if I'm a match. If so, you can have one of my kidneys."

"Kemba, you don't have to do this. You've just gone through something very traumatic."

"I'm fine, Mama. The bullet just grazed my arm mostly. But I have to do something for you. You're my mother and you gave me life." Kemba embraced her mother. "It's going to be okay. I'll get tested first thing in the morning."

Shaking her head, Sarah said, "No. I want you to think about this, Kemba. This is a big decision and I don't want something to happen to you."

"All I'm doing right now is getting tested. Let's just find out if I'm a match, okay? Then we'll worry about what happens next."

Sarah nodded. "I love you, baby."

"Mama, I love you too. Now, I don't want you to worry so. Like I said earlier, everything will be fine." Smiling, Kemba stated, "I have some news of my own. . . ."

Grinning, Sarah responded, "I bet I know what it is. You and the good pastor are getting married."

Kemba nodded.

Her mother eyed her. "You don't seem too happy."

"I am. I love Eric so much, Mama. I can't see my life without him. I'm just not

416

sure I can live up to being his wife — the first lady of a church."

"You can do it, baby. No reason why you can't."

"I don't know what it all means, Mama. As a minister, Eric has to be under a microscope. I will be put under the same scrutiny. I'm not sure I want to put myself in that position."

"But you love Eric?"

"Madly."

"Then you'll do whatever you have to do," Sarah stated. "Eric is a pastor but it is only a part of him. You will have the other part of him — the part that he will only give to his wife."

"But his church members . . . ," Kemba began. "They seem overly interested in his personal life, I think."

"I think it's normal they would be curious about the woman in their pastor's life. I would be," Sarah admitted. "Ministers are put on pedestals, unfortunately. That's why it's so hard on people when they fall. We forget that they're human."

"There are women in the church who have been groomed to be the wife of a minister. I'm nothing like them."

"Eric loves you for you, Kemba. Never forget that."

"I just don't want to do anything to hurt his career." This was Kemba's biggest fear where Eric was concerned.

Later that evening, Kemba settled back on her bed and gave Eric a call. They made plans to meet the next day at the park. They were going bike riding.

Kemba got up early the next morning to take care of all her housecleaning and her laundry. She wanted to enjoy the rest of the day with Eric.

A few hours later, Kemba met him at the park. Eric greeted her with a kiss.

"How did it go with your mother?" he inquired.

"Fine. We made up, but I'm still bothered by it," Kemba admitted. "I don't know if I'll ever be able to forgive her."

"You will. Right now it's still too close to you. And having gone through what you did in Africa couldn't have helped much either."

"Mama needs a kidney transplant," Kemba announced. "I'm going to be tested."

"I'll be tested too."

She looked over at him. "You are such a good man, Eric. I am so lucky to have you in my life."

"You and your mother mean a lot to me,

honey. I want you to know that."

"I do," Kemba confirmed. "That's why I feel so lucky. You know *lucky* is not the right word. I'm blessed."

Eric nodded in approval.

"Jillian called me. The family will be getting together Thursday for Thanksgiving dinner. I think it'll be the perfect place to make our announcement, don't you think?"

Kemba laughed. "I can't think of a better place."

"I'd like to announce it on Sunday, in church."

She didn't respond. Kemba wasn't sure how she felt about that.

"They're my members."

"I know."

"I have to tell them, Kemba. Not only are they my church members — they're like family too."

Kemba nodded in understanding. "It's fine. I'll be there." She knew of at least two people who would not be happy about her upcoming wedding. Jennifer and her mother.

CHAPTER 32

Eric drove Kemba and her mother out to Riverside on the following Thursday to celebrate Thanksgiving.

After everyone had gathered to eat, Eric announced his engagement to Kemba. Family and friends congratulating them soon surrounded the couple. He glanced over at his fiancée and smiled. She looked a little uneasy for a moment, he thought.

It was normal for a woman to be scared, Eric reasoned. Even a little nervous. Marriage was a big step. He stole another look at her and he found her smiling — she looked happy, much to his relief.

Eric left Kemba with his aunt and a few of his female cousins while he went to speak with Ray.

"I'm so happy you agreed to marry Eric," Carrie announced. "He's a good man."

Grinning, Kemba replied, "I think so too. He is one of the sweetest men I know and I feel very blessed to have him in my life."

"I have to admit that I didn't think this was coming for a while," Ivy interjected. "I thought you two would take a little time to really get to know one another."

Regis laughed. "Laine and I only knew each other for five days before we got married, so I don't think the amount of time you spend together really matters. It's whether or not what you really feel for each other is love."

"I love Eric," Kemba confessed. "I love him with my whole heart and I can't see my life without him. I really can't."

"I'm thrilled for you both," Ivy conceded. "It's been my prayer for Eric. I've always wanted him to find a good wife." She reached over and embraced Kemba. "Congratulations, dear heart."

The women drifted off, one by one, eventually leaving Amanda alone with Kemba. She echoed the same sentiment.

"Thank you, Mrs. Ransom. I'm very happy."

"Are you?" Amanda questioned. "I can see something in your eyes."

"I had a fight with my mother," Kemba confessed. "I found out that she'd lied to me about something big. Something really big and I'm having a hard time forgiving her. I know she meant well, but . . ."

Amanda nodded in understanding. "Kemba, parents are human too. You know that, don't you? When you give birth to a child — it's only natural to want to protect that child from all harm. We have no way of knowing how that will affect the child. We do the very best we can. Sometimes we make mistakes out of love."

"Deep down, I know all this." Kemba pressed a hand to her chest. "I know how much my mother loves me. But this . . ." Her eyes watered. "Mrs. Ransom, my mother and I are close. Very close. We're friends too. There was no reason for her to keep my true parentage away from me. I am the result of a rape," Kemba announced tearfully. "The same man who murdered my fath—" She stopped abruptly. "He murdered the man I knew as my father and he murdered Malcolm."

"I'm so sorry, dear."

"I hate him. I hate what he did to me. He destroyed everything I ever believed about my family and me. That murderer took that away from me."

"Only if you allow him to do so," Amanda murmured softly. "Kemba, this man can only do what you give him power to do. It's up to you."

"I'm so angry right now."

"You haven't had time to deal with everything that's happened. It's understandable." Amanda took Kemba's hand in hers. "I can see how much you love your mother. I know you'll find it in your heart to forgive her."

Kemba nodded. "I will . . . in time. I feel especially bad, though, because she's going through so much right now. She just found out that she's going to need a kidney transplant."

"Have they found a donor?"

"I've been tested to see if I can be a potential donor. A kidney from a relative will be a better match and there is less chance of her body rejecting it." Kemba tossed a look across her shoulder. "Eric's been tested too."

"That doesn't surprise me. He is a very caring man and he will give his last to help anybody. I know how much he cares for your mother. Eric adores her."

Watching Eric and her mother from across the room, Kemba replied, "She feels the same way about him." Turning her attention back to Amanda, she added, "Thank you for listening to me."

"It's what I do best."

"How much recovery time is involved in donating a kidney?" Jillian asked.

"About two months," Kemba answered. "I just hope that I'm a match. Mama won't have to wait much after the evaluation and there's less chance of rejection. She also won't have to take so much medicine."

"You will need some help after the surgery," Elle stated. "You and your mother both. Do you have someone?"

"My partner, Antoinette, but she's also got to keep the shop running." Kemba leaned forward in her chair. "I guess I hadn't thought about it much — we're still waiting to hear if I'll be a match. Eric's been tested too."

"Dear heart, I'll be more than happy to help you out in any way that I can." Ivy rose to her feet. "I think I can safely say that the entire Ransom clan will be here for you and your mother — you're family."

Everyone nodded in agreement, bringing tears to Kemba's eyes.

Her mother reached over and took her hand. "These are good people," she whispered.

Kemba nodded in agreement. Eric dropped down beside her. She smiled at him. "Your family is so sweet."

She listened as they made plans to cook meals, clean house and do whatever was necessary to make Sarah comfortable during her recovery period. They vowed to do the same for her if needed.

Everyone was so positive and encouraging, some of Kemba's fear about her mother's future vanished.

A week later, Kemba received a call from Sarah's doctor.

She screamed with glee when she hung up. Eric rushed to her side, asking, "What's wrong?"

"I'm a match."

"Really?"

Kemba nodded. "Thank you, Jesus! Mama won't have to wait any longer for a kidney."

Eric hugged her. "I'm so happy for you, honey. I'm happy for you and your mother both."

"This transplantation has to work, Eric. Mama has tried dialysis and now she needs a new kidney — if this doesn't work . . ." Kemba's voice died as she silently contemplated the worst.

"You can't think that way. Your mother is in the loving arms of God. He will watch over her through this whole ordeal. Remember that you're not going for a skip in the park. You are undergoing serious surgery as well."

"I know. I have to admit that I'm more than a little scared, but I have to do this. I can't lose my mother."

"When is the surgery scheduled?"

"We'll find out later this week. We have to see the doctor on Friday."

Eric and Kemba spent the rest of the evening making plans for their wedding.

When he left for the evening, she gathered up her notes and headed to the bedroom. Kemba readied for bed. She had a long day tomorrow and wanted to wake up early.

The next couple of weeks passed quickly as Sarah and Kemba prepared for the kidney transplant. It had been decided that they would both recover in Sarah's house with Antoinette staying with them. Ivy and Jillian had volunteered to stay with them whenever Antoinette ventured out to the office. Carrie, Regis and Elle planned to prepare meals.

Kemba was impressed with how well organized the Ransoms appeared. They had basically gotten together with Eric and come up with what amounted to the perfect plan.

The day of the transplantation arrived. Kemba prayed that God would see her and her mother safely through the surgeries.

Kemba was vaguely aware of Eric standing beside her when she woke up.

Still groggy from the anesthesia, she asked, "How is my m-mother?"

"She's in intensive care but the prognosis is good." He bent over and kissed her forehead. "Don't worry."

She could barely keep her eyes open. "I'm sorry. Sleepy . . ."

"I understand," he murmured. "Go on to sleep, honey. Get your rest."

Eric sat for a few minutes until Kemba had fallen asleep. He got up and tiptoed out of the room. Antoinette was standing outside the door talking to a nurse. He interrupted them long enough to say, "I'm going to check on Mrs. Jennings. I'll be back shortly."

She nodded. "I'll stay right here."

A nurse was in the room with Sarah, changing the IV bag.

"How is she?" he asked at last. "S-she's going to be all right, isn't she?"

"She's resting comfortably right now. Dr. Wilson will be here shortly." The nurse made her notes on Sarah's chart before strolling out of the room.

Eric moved closer to the bed. "Mrs. Jennings, this is Eric. I'm right here with you," he whispered softly. "Kemba wants you to know that she loves you. She is sleeping right now, but she's doing fine.

She came through just fine."

He continued talking to her as if she were awake. Eric had no doubt that Sarah could hear his words.

The nurse eased into the room to remind Eric that Sarah needed her rest. Visitors were only allowed a few minutes to see family in the intensive-care unit. He bent down and planted a kiss on her forehead before leaving.

Eric spent the rest of the evening in Kemba's room. Every hour or so, he would venture to the ICU to check on Sarah. He was exhausted but had no plans of leaving the hospital until he knew that both Kemba and her mother were out of danger.

CHAPTER 33

Sarah encountered complications from her surgery that prolonged her stay in intensive care.

As soon as Kemba was able to get out of her hospital bed, she had Eric take her to see her mother.

"I can't lose her, Eric. I can't," she whispered as she sat by her mother's bed.

He placed his hands on her shoulders. "I understand."

"Can't you pray for her?"

"I have, sweetheart. I pray for your mother all the time."

"So do I," Kemba admitted. "She's got to be okay."

Sarah's eyes fluttered open. They traveled the room before settling on Kemba.

"Mama, you're awake."

Her mother groaned.

"Don't try to talk. I know you're in pain. Do you want me to call a nurse?"

Sarah nodded.

Eric headed to the door. "I'll get her."

"How a-are y-you feeling?"

"I'm fine, Mama. A little sore, but for the most part, I'm doing okay."

"Hurt . . ."

"I know. I'm so sorry. Hopefully, you'll start to feel better in a few weeks, though."

"Hope so."

"The doctor says that sometimes the new kidney can be rejected but that it's easily treated. He says the kidney is functioning well now."

Sarah gave a slight nod.

"The nurse should be here shortly."

Again Sarah nodded.

"You're going to be fine, Mama." Kemba wanted to reassure her mother. She could see the fear on Sarah's face. The doctor had informed them that not all transplants were successful. Only time would tell how long the transplanted kidney would work — it all depended on individual circumstances such as age, blood sensitivity and quality of life.

Eric wheeled Kemba back to her room, where she found Antoinette waiting for her.

"I need to head to the church for a meeting," he announced as he helped her back into the hospital bed. "I'll be back later tonight."

Kemba nodded. "Antoinette can keep

me company while you're gone."

"Yeah, I'll stay with her. I brought a deck of UNO cards with me."

"Have fun." Eric kissed her and was gone.

Antoinette sat down on the edge of the bed. "He's a good man, Kim. And he cares a heck of a lot for you. Girl, that man loves you to death."

"He's the best thing to happen to me in a long time. I can't wait to marry that man."

"I'm glad you finally came to your senses."

Puzzled, Kemba asked, "What are you talking about?"

"You didn't even want to go out with the man once you found out he was a preacher."

Although she would never admit it, Kemba was still bothered by that fact. It wasn't that she had anything against Eric's occupation — she just wasn't so sure she could measure up to what a preacher's wife should be.

Kemba glanced up from her reading, expecting to see Eric.

"Pastor Avery told me you were in the hospital. I was out here visiting some of our sick church members and so I thought I'd check on you. How are you feeling?"

Eyeing Jennifer warily, Kemba took a moment to respond. "I'm fine."

"You had surgery?"

"I donated a kidney to my mother."

"What a loving gesture. I'm sure your mother must be touched beyond words. I know I would be."

Kemba remained silent.

Jennifer ventured over by the window. "These flowers really brighten up a room, don't they? I love flowers."

"They are beautiful."

"Everyone at church is excited about your upcoming wedding to Pastor." Jennifer pasted a smile on her face. "All of the committees are fighting to have you."

"Committees?"

"Yes. The Women's Day Committee really wants you on board. Then the Scholarship Committee thinks you should be with them. My mother was planning on asking you to teach at Sunday school."

Kemba could feel her panic growing. She wasn't ready for any of this. She and Eric weren't even married and the church was already trying to put demands on her time.

Jennifer continued to talk. "It's a great

honor, you know. Being the first lady of a church —"

She interrupted. "Jennifer, I'm sorry. I'm not feeling well."

"I should be going anyway. I just wanted to come by and say hello. After all, you are almost a part of our family — church family, that is. We're looking forward to getting to know you. We all love Pastor, so I know we're going to love you as well."

When Jennifer left the room, Kemba burst into tears. "I can't do this. I can't marry Eric."

Eric took one look at Kemba's face and feared the worst.

"Mama's fine."

"Then what's wrong? Why do you look so sad?"

"I've been doing some thinking, Eric." Kemba prayed for strength to continue. "I think we may have been rushing things."

"What are you talking about?"

"I don't think we should rush into a marriage. In fact . . ." Kemba took a deep breath. "I think we should call off the wedding."

"Why?"

"I love you, Eric. I want you to know that."

"Why?" he repeated. "Why don't you

want to marry me? What's changed your mind?"

"I just need some time to think things over. Being your wife calls for a huge commitment."

"I'm not sure I'm understanding what you mean by that."

"I believe that being married to a minister —"

"We're back on that again," he interjected. "Kemba, I'm sorry if my job makes you so uncomfortable. God has placed a call in my heart and I can't just dismiss it. But that call does not make me a man who is incapable of love and loving. I can still be romantic, sexy and fun — however, that's something you will never really find out. If you want to end our engagement — fine. It's over."

Having said that, Eric stormed out of her room. He was furious with Kemba. But not only that, he was hurting. He'd just lost the only woman he truly loved.

When he calmed down some, Eric had an idea of what Kemba had been trying to tell him. She would be held to the same standards as he was, and it was a huge commitment. The only difference was that Kemba had yet to see herself the way he did. She would be an asset to the church and a wonderful partner to him. He prayed that God would show her the truth before it was too late.

Sarah was released from the hospital two weeks later. Kemba had been released the day after she and Eric broke up. He'd shown up as usual and had taken her home to Sarah's house. Only he didn't stay long. He'd left her in the care of Antoinette.

While her mother was resting, Kemba sat on the sofa going through an old photo album. She smiled at a picture of her mother and father. "I miss you so much, Papa." She sighed sadly. "I wish you could've met Eric. You really would have liked him." A tear slid down her cheek. "I miss him too."

She put away the photo album and rifled through the cardboard box she'd had Antoinette place on the chair beside her. Her mother was a pack rat and held on to everything. Kemba decided she would go through and clear out some of the old papers.

Opening the box, she proceeded to take out the contents — mementos from her mother's time in Africa and other belongings. She pulled out an unopened pack of stationery and an old leather-bound book. Kemba frowned. "What is this?" It looked to be a journal of some kind. In the back of her mind, she recalled seeing her mother write in similar types of books over the years.

Opening the gold-edged pages, she felt her eyes widen in surprise. Some of these entries were way older than Kemba. Her mother had written of the day she knew she had fallen in love with Molefi. She also wrote of her heartbreak. The day Mapfumo raped her.

Kemba allowed her tears to run free as she read of the day Sarah discovered she was pregnant. She wrote of her love and undying devotion to the child she carried — Mapfumo's child.

She read on. Her mother wrote about the day she told Molefi that she could not marry him, of his persistence and finally joy — the day they were married.

An hour later, Kemba was still reading. Inside the box were several other journals and this one was her fourth. In this one her mother wrote about her feelings of fear, anger and acceptance upon learning she had diabetes.

"You never told me any of this, Mama. Why didn't you come to me when you were scared or angry?" she whispered.

Trying to avoid thinking about Eric, Kemba went through her own mail afterward. A letter from Bekitemba was among the letters.

As she read the letter, tears filled her eyes. He wanted to know when she and Eric would be getting married.

"How am I going to write to you that we're not?" Kemba muttered to herself. She read further. Mapfumo had been killed, trying to escape. Deep down, she was saddened by the news. After all, he was her father.

Kemba shook her head. "No, Molefi was my father."

Wiping away her tears, Kemba folded the letter and laid it on the coffee table. Putting her hands to her face, she allowed herself to give in to a crying spell.

A while later, she was all cried out. Kemba admitted she felt somewhat better. Empty but better.

She heard Mila's high-pitched laughter. Kemba jumped up to answer the door. Tanya and her daughter were coming by to check on her and Sarah. "Hello, you two. Come on in."

"Hi, Miss Kemba. I've missed you." Mila wrapped her arms around Kemba's thighs.

"Be careful, Mila. Miss Kemba is still healing, sweetie," Tanya warned. "How are you, Kemba?"

"I'm okay. I just had myself a good cry and now I feel better."

Tanya reached over to hug Kemba. "I wish I could make the hurt go away."

"I'll be okay, Tanya. I will."

"It does get a little easier with time."

Tanya looked as if she wanted to say more but thought better of it.

"Where's Granny Sarah?"

"She's in her room, sleeping. She should be waking up soon. When she does, I'll let you go in and say hello."

Kemba was grateful for the company. It took her mind off Eric for the moment.

CHAPTER 34

"Kemba, I don't want you overdoing it."

Folding a blanket, Kemba responded, "I'm fine, Mama. You're the one that needs to take it easy. Don't worry about me."

"Why are you trying to stay so busy? You won't forget him, you know."

Kemba raised her eyes to meet her mother's gaze. "What are you talking about?" She laid the blanket on top of the trunk that sat at the foot of her mother's bed.

"Eric."

"I'm not trying to forget him. I just want to take it one day at a time."

"What happened between the two of you?" Sarah asked.

She strolled over to a window and peeked outside. "It was my fault, Mama. When I was in the hospital, one of the women from his church stopped by to see me. She started talking about all the different committees I'm expected to join once Eric and I get married. I don't know what it means to be the wife of a minister. I just panicked, I guess."

"Kemba, you're marrying the man — not the job."

"It's more than a job. It's Eric's calling and it requires a lot of commitment. I just wanted some time to think things through."

"You love Eric, don't you?"

Kemba turned away from the window. "Mama, you know I do. I love him more than anything. I love him enough to know that I wouldn't do anything to harm or embarrass him."

"Why are you thinking so negatively? How do you think a minister's wife is supposed to act?"

Kemba moved toward the bed and sat down on the edge. "She is an extension of her husband."

"All wives are extensions of their husbands, Kemba."

"She runs the church with him. Eric should marry a woman who is as knowledgeable as he is."

"Are you talking about the Bible?"

Kemba nodded.

"You can learn. That's what Bible study is for. Even ministers can learn a few things about the Bible. Honey, you were raised in the church. You know God. . . . What are you so afraid of? Do you think you're going to have to give up something?"

"Not really. I just . . . Mama, I'm not perfect. I will never be perfect. And I don't want to be accountable to an entire church."

"Honey, Eric is not perfect. No one can be. We are all human."

"I know that." Kemba played with her fingers. "I guess I just want Eric to be proud of me. I didn't want him ever to regret marrying me."

"He wouldn't. Eric loves you and it's in you that he found his soul mate. You shouldn't dismiss him so easily."

"It's too late, Mama. I've already lost him."

"Maybe not. I wouldn't count the good pastor out just yet," Sarah replied cryptically.

Two hours later, there was a knock on the door. When Kemba answered it, she was surprised to find Eric standing there.

"How are you feeling?" he asked as soon as he entered the house.

"I'm fine," Kemba responded.

"I wanted to come by and check on your mother."

"She'll appreciate that." Kemba chewed her bottom lip. She tried not to show her disappointment that he didn't come to see her. "I'll let her know that you're here."

She left the living room and navigated to her mother's room. Sarah looked like she'd just woken from a nap.

"Eric's here," Kemba announced. "Did you know he was coming by?"

"He called me earlier to ask if it was okay."

"Mama, why didn't you tell me?"

"He was coming by to see me. It had nothing to do with you."

Kemba released a long sigh. "You're right. Eric doesn't seem to want to have much to do with me — much less talk to me."

"What did you expect?"

"I don't really know," Kemba confessed. "I just thought he would have a little more to say to me. The man hasn't spoken to me in weeks."

"Maybe he's waiting on you to make the first move," Sarah suggested. "Maybe you should be the one to start a conversation."

"I'll bring him back here if you're ready."

"Help me to the bathroom. I'd like to freshen up some."

Kemba considered her mother's suggestion as she assisted Sarah. Maybe her mother had a point.

Eric wasn't quite as prepared to see Kemba as he'd originally thought. His feelings were still very raw and seeing her only made his heartache worse.

Kemba interrupted his musings with her entrance.

"Mama wanted to freshen up a bit before she saw you."

He smiled and followed her to Sarah's bedroom.

"Pastor Avery, thank you so much for coming to see me."

"Don't you think it's time you called me Eric?" He planted a kiss on Sarah's cheek.

Kemba pulled a chair beside the bed. "You can sit here."

Eric thanked her and sat down. Kemba seemed so nervous around him and he wondered why. It was she who had called off the engagement. He hadn't even had a chance to purchase a ring. Eric supposed he should have been thankful.

"I'll be in the living room if you need me," Kemba stated. "Enjoy your visit."

"Eric, would you like something to drink?" Sarah asked.

"No thanks. I'm fine."

Kemba eased out of the bedroom. Her eyes filled with tears and her heart with longing. She missed Eric so much and this distance that now stood between them was tearing her apart.

Eric was enjoying his conversation with Sarah. He genuinely loved her. She reminded him of his aunt Amanda and his mother. Just because he and Kemba were having problems, Eric saw no reason to abandon his growing relationship with her mother.

When he ventured out of the bedroom an hour later, Eric found Kemba lying on the sofa with her eyes closed. He observed her for a moment. She looked so beautiful. . . .

Kemba opened her eyes.

"How long have you been standing there?" she asked as she sat up.

"Not long. You looked so . . . so peaceful. I didn't want to wake you."

"I wasn't asleep. Just resting my eyes."

Eric moved around the sofa and took a seat on the love seat. "How are you feeling, Kemba? Does your arm bother you much?"

"It's fine. The bullet didn't do much damage — it just grazed my skin mostly, so there really isn't that much of a scar. I don't have any problems moving it or anything."

"I'm glad to hear that."

Kemba shifted in her seat. "The only scars left are the ones you can't see."

Eric nodded in understanding. "How's your mother doing?"

"She has good days and bad. It's still too early to really tell anything." Kemba glanced over at Eric. "Just don't stop praying for her."

"I won't."

"Eric, I talked to Bekitemba. He told me that Mapfumo was killed while trying to escape prison."

"How do you feel about that?"

"I don't really know."

"You have to find a way to forgive him."

"I have. I realized that I had to forgive everyone involved. Including myself." Kemba met his gaze. "Eric, I'm so sorry for the way that I treated you. I didn't handle things well at all."

"It's okay."

"It's not okay," Kemba shot back. "I should have been totally honest with you. Eric, I was scared."

"Of what?"

"I was afraid that I wouldn't be able to

live up to the standards of your church members. Jennifer came to see me while I was in the hospital."

He was clearly surprised. "Why didn't you tell me?"

"I don't know. I didn't want to start a bunch of conflicts. She wasn't mean to me or anything. Just kind of pointed out what life would be like married to you. It put me in a panic."

"I see."

"Eric, I put you on a pedestal. I think a lot of ministers are put on pedestals. Compared to you — I'm . . . Well, I just didn't feel I could measure up," Kemba confessed. "I didn't feel worthy."

"Do you still feel that way?"

Kemba shook her head no. "I can only be who I am. I have come to realize that I don't want a life without you, Eric. I love you and I miss you."

He got up and crossed the floor to join her on the sofa. "I love you too, Kemba. I don't want you to change anything about you — I love you just the way you are. You are kind, loving and smart. You are my partner. These are just a few of the qualities I want in a mate."

"Do I have to join all these different committees at the church?"

"Only the ones that interest you, Kemba. And only in time. No one expects you to jump in right off the bat. It's going to take time."

Eric placed an arm around her. "So what does this mean?"

"It means that I want to marry you — if you'll still have me, Eric. I want to be your wife and I won't ever let you down."

"I was never worried." He covered her mouth with his own.

Kemba stroked the side of Eric's cheek. "I knew the night I met you that our relationship would be something special. God has blessed me with a valuable treasure. He has given me you and I will cherish you forever."

Dear Readers:

As always, I have to say thank you so much for your support and your love of the Ransom family. *Treasures of the Heart* was actually inspired by the last king of Matabeleland (now in Zimbabwe).

According to the *Columbia Encyclopedia,* Sixth Edition, after succeeding his father in 1870, Lobengula tried to turn aside the approaches of European colonizers. In 1888, however, under pressure from Cecil Rhodes, he ceded his mineral rights in exchange for a small payment, and Rhodes used those concessions to form the British South Africa Company in 1889. When British gold miners began appearing, Lobengula rallied his people and in 1893 attacked the British. It is rumored that before he died, he sent his most trusted *induna* to bury his treasure.

This story was indeed a joy to write because of my great love for history, and I sincerely hope that you have enjoyed it as well. Our African American heritage is a treasure to be cherished, and I implore each of you not only to delve into your rich and diverse history but also to pass it on. Teach your children about their ancestors, blending the past, present and the future.

Stories passed down from generation to generation often become a combination of truth and exaggerations each time they are told, thus giving birth to legends.

Jacquelin Thomas

ABOUT THE AUTHOR

JACQUELIN THOMAS is the award-winning, best-selling author of several books, including *Stolen Hearts*, *Singsation*, *The Prodigal Husband* and *A Change Is Gonna Come*. *Treasures of the Heart* is her fifteenth romance novel. She is currently at work on her next project.